KILLER WEED

Texas Lady Lawyer vs Raiden Prince

a novel by

MANNING WOLFE

Starpath Books, LLC
Austin, TX
www.starpathbooks.com

Library of Congress Cataloging-in Publication Data: Paperback:
ISBN-13: 978-1-944225-56-8
Ebook: ISBN-13: 978-1-944225-57-5
LCN: 2024942323
Manufactured in the United States of America
10 9 8 7 6 5 4 3 2 1

*With special thanks to Marsha and Greg Rodgers, Terri Emery,
Mary Ellen Garza, and Bill Rodgers for their ongoing support.*

You never know how strong you are until being strong is your only choice.

— BOB MARLEY

1

R aiden Prince prowled the field on foot, a solitary figure moving purposefully in the dark through the field of tall, green, leafy stalks. The summer night wrapped around him like a shroud, making his eyes appear as black as pools of Texas crude oil and concealing his clandestine mission. In the velvet light, only the shape of the vegetation was visible, but the outline of the three-pronged leaves was unmistakable. He threw gasoline from a red gas can onto the field of hemp, backing up as he worked, so as not to soak his jeans or work boots with the flammable liquid. He returned the red can to the bed of his pickup, retrieved another gas can, and moved to the opposite side of the field. There, he emptied the flammable liquid onto a greenhouse made of a steel frame and plastic sheeting, filled with high-grade medical marijuana plants, some labeled Peanut Butter Breath and others Blue Dream.

The silence of the night was broken only by the rhythmic chirping of dog-day cicadas and Prince's off-key rendition of "Red Headed Stranger." He did his best Willie Nelson imitation in his practiced backwoods Texas accent. He mimicked the elastic voices, that he'd heard most Texans use, by eliding certain syllables. All the vowels were stretched out in the middle of each word, and the ends of them clipped, especially ones ending in *ing*. The music was just to set the mood for the evening's tasks. He preferred rap.

After he'd soaked the greenhouse, Prince backed up toward the two-lane county road as he threw the last of the gasoline. He then moved out of the field, onto the caliche roadbed, where he walked back to his old, rusty pickup truck and placed the second gas can in the bed beside the first.

Brad and Thad Lane, each on an ATV with custom paint jobs and extra-large wheels, cut across the pasture from their picturesque home on the hill above the expansive farm owned by the Lane family. They often rode late at night when they could sneak out without waking their mother, Gladys. She was a heavy sleeper, as the pure of heart often are, but she was still a protective mother and didn't like the twins roaming the acreage in the dark.

Brad, the larger of the two, now shirtless, and already tan, played defensive end on the local high school football team. Thad, three minutes younger, wearing a white wife-beater undershirt, played tight end and was the more talented of the two. He was often compared to Travis Kelce because he was fast and often carried the ball in for the team's touchdowns under Friday night lights, a Texas passion.

Riding around the family farm was not an issue for the seventeen-year-olds, even at night. They knew every inch of the family property, as they'd been using it as their personal playground since they could walk. They had certain hiding places for their special crops. Not marijuana, there was plenty of that.

Their secret was growing small patches of maize or clover near their bird blinds so they could enjoy a good season of dove hunting in the fall. It was called baiting, and was illegal, but this was their land and they didn't follow many rules once they entered the gate to the property they called home.

The twins cut low into a narrow creek bed caused by hundreds of years of rain runoff, then peaked again at the top of a low mound overlooking the growing fields. From their vantage point atop the rise, Brad spied a solitary figure below, near the county road, his movements casting eerie shadows against the moonlit landscape.

Brad's brow furrowed in confusion as he pointed out the intruder to his brother. "Who is that?"

Thad's eyes narrowed as he squinted into the darkness, his instincts going on high alert. "Don't think I know him. What the hell is he doing?"

They watched the intruder move farther onto the county road, then recede, taking a squarish object that appeared to be a gas can with him. The man placed the can in the back of a pickup and returned to the edge of the field. He pulled a lighter from his pocket and just as he was about to thumb the wheel, the twins came tearing down the rise, bearing down on the intruder on their ATVs, while shouting obscenities.

"What the hell do you think you're doing?"

"This is private property, Asshole."

At that moment, Prince thumbed the wheel, sparking the flint, and tossed the flaming Zippo, lighting up the edge of the field. The fire caught and expanded, flaring toward the twins. They zigged and zagged, skirting the field and avoiding the flames by driving through a wet creek at the edge of the heat. Marijuana smoke puffed out of the burning field and then the greenhouse, the plants expelling gases that smelled sweet and exotic.

Prince moved back toward his pickup, placing his right hand in his pocket and grabbing his keys to expedite his exit. He moved quickly, but the twins were quicker. Thad bounded his ATV up out of the creek bed and headed straight for Prince. Thad knocked Prince down with the front bumper, and Brad came charging up behind Thad. Prince pulled himself up, dropping his truck keys in the onslaught, and picked up a large limb that had fallen from a nearby oak. He swung it and caught Brad across the chest with the heavy weapon before Brad could come to a complete halt, knocking him from the ATV. The machine continued into the roadbed and across to the neighboring fence, where it was caught by barbed wire and abruptly died.

Thad did a wheelie in the road, turned back, stopped his ATV, and jumped off to help his brother. While he was bending over Brad, Prince came up behind him and slammed the same offending tree limb into the back of Thad's head, knocking him out cold. Prince went down again as his right leg gave way from the injury caused by Thad's ATV. Prince got up, limped nearer to the twins, and hit them again, although they were both already unconscious.

"Stay down."

Prince sat down on a nearby rock outcropping to catch his breath and assess the situation. The fire popped and flared as he watched and listened for fire trucks that might have been dispatched. The two young men had seen his face and his truck. He could not risk their exposing him or his employer to scrutiny. Feeling the urgency to leave the scene of his crime, he made a decision. He limped back over to the bodies and dragged each twin in turn to the edge of the flames, leaving first Brad and then Thad to be consumed by the fire.

Prince then returned to his truck, but when he put his hand in his pocket to fetch his keys, there was nothing there. It was only then that he remembered dropping them when the first boy's ATV took him down. He limped back to the area where he had been hit and searched the leaves, grass, and waning Bluebonnets with the flashlight on his phone. His search was in vain, and when he heard the siren of an approaching fire truck and the grinding sound of another ATV coming closer from the direction of the farmhouse, he jumped into his truck and jerked the wires from beneath the dashboard. He hot-wired the engine, and it sparked and sputtered to a start. Prince threw gravel on his exit from the roadside and headed down the county road, leaving a trail of white caliche dust to mingle with the smoke from the burning field.

2

———————

erit Bridges rushed into the closing elevator from the parking garage and punched the button for the top floor of the sleek high-rise in downtown Austin, Texas, where her law office was located. She impatiently tapped the toe of her right black high-heeled pump as the elevator seemed to creep up to the penthouse. The morning air outside was warm, indicating an early summer, but the conditioned air inside the building was a refreshing seventy-two degrees. She took a deep cleansing breath of refrigerated air and smoothed her navy pencil skirt. She looked more like a supermodel than a lawyer, with her long blond ponytail, designer handbag, and crisp white sleeveless blouse, but her black leather briefcase said no nonsense.

As usual, she was running late, but knew that Betty, her office manager and right hand, would have the office up and running and awaiting her arrival. Merit was not a morning person, but that was okay because Betty was and she ran the office with the efficiency of a drill sergeant disguised as a sweet auntie, from her Ann Richards style bouffant hairdo to her sensible shoes.

When Merit entered the glass doors of her office, Betty met her with a cup of tea and an upbeat, "Good morning, Merit."

"Good morning, Betty. Anything new?" They continued down the hallway to the inner offices, walking side by side as they did every day.

"A few messages sent to your email. Nothing urgent. Val is on his way in."

"Great, hopefully it will stay low key and I can get a few things off my desk."

As if the gods of fate heard her comment, the phone rang. Betty rolled her eyes toward the heavens, handed the tea to Merit, and answered, "Law Office of Merit Bridges."

Merit listened and monitored Betty's demeanor as her face changed. Any semblance of tranquility was swiftly shattered as unmistakable tension radiated from Betty's persona.

Merit's shoulders dropped as she continued to her inner office and put her briefcase, handbag, and cup of tea on her desk. She remained standing until Betty completed the call and entered the room to report the dire news.

"It was John David Lane's farm supervisor. Lane's twin boys were attacked and burned in a fire in the dark hours of the night. Both sustained life-threatening injuries. Lane and his wife are at the hospital with the boys. It was purportedly arson in the greenhouse and growing fields. The house is intact. They think it has something to do with their licensing case. They'd like for you to join them at the hospital."

Merit digested the shocking news. "Oh no. Fire? Of course, of course."

Betty nodded. "I told them you were on the way. I'll call an Uber for you. You'll never find a parking place over there."

Merit grabbed her purse, checking, from habit, to make

sure her phone was inside, and went back out the way she came in. In her rush through the reception area, she bumped into her law clerk, Valentine Lewis. He started to laugh, then gazed at her face and moved aside. Betty followed Merit around the corner and Val looked at Betty with questioning eyes.

Betty gave Val a look that said, "Wait until she's gone."

Merit entered the Dell Seton Medical Center at The University of Texas Hospital on Red River Street, situated on the other side of downtown, and approached the reception desk.

"I'm here to meet the John David Lane family."

The receptionist checked her monitor then pointed. "They're in the acute care unit. Down that hallway, take the elevator to the second floor and follow the signs."

It was unlike Merit to be rude, but she didn't say "thank you" as she hurried to find her clients. She was fond of the Lane family, good people who didn't deserve to be caught up in some arsonist's game.

Merit's involvement in the Lane case had to do with a dry, boring side of the law: agency regulation. Merit didn't do criminal law or litigation, except to strategize. Her expertise was mostly in finance, real estate, general business, and occasionally probate. Somehow, regardless of her specialty in business practice, she often got tangled up in clients' lives and problems, putting her in danger multiple times. She just didn't know how to quit, and once sucked into an issue, she fought until she reached the other side, even when things got out of hand.

Looks like it's going to happen again, Merit thought as she exited the elevator and was hit by the omnipresent smell of antiseptic. She steadied herself and started down the long hallway to face her clients and their tragedy.

When Merit walked toward the end of the hallway, she saw her client, John David Lane, walk through a door, cross the hall, and look through a glassed-in room with two hospital beds, then return through the door. Attendants went in and out of the controlled environment where the Lane twins, Thad and Brad, were being treated. As she reached the glass enclosure, Merit observed that both young men appeared unconscious. Each had tubes coming out of their mouths and IVs going into their arms. Merit could see only one face, she wasn't sure which one, as they were identical twins, but the other's face was wrapped in gauze, completely obscuring his identity.

Lane saw her looking into the glass encasement. "Merit, we're in here."

Merit entered a small waiting room where the Lane family huddled together. She shook hands with John Lane, holding his right hand in both of hers. The matriarch of the family, Gladys Lane, sat in the corner holding an embroidered handkerchief in her hand. She had obviously been crying, but seemed to be holding it together, for now. The twin's younger sister, Cameron, and two adults Merit didn't recognize were sitting quietly on a sofa nearby.

Merit went over to Gladys, sat beside her, and took her hand. "Gladys, how are you holding up?"

"My boys, Merit. My boys." She began to tear up again. "The doctors don't know if they'll make it." Cameron moved to her mother's side, a look of disbelief displayed on her face.

Merit patted Gladys' hand. "I'm so sorry." What else could she say? She had yet to be briefed, and certainly had no medical knowledge to share.

Lane patted his wife on the shoulder and looked at Merit.

"Let's go down to the vending machines. I could use a cup of coffee."

John walked to the end of the hallway nearest the elevator, followed by Merit, into an opening that housed several vending machines and a small dining table that was littered with fast-food debris. Merit cleared the trash, pulled an antibacterial wipe from her handbag, and wiped the table. She never went anywhere without the wipes since the days of COVID-19.

Lane pulled some dollar bills from his pocket. "What would you like?"

Merit sat down. "Nothing, thank you."

Lane sat opposite her and hung his head. "Me either. Just a ploy to get us some privacy."

Merit felt a jab of sympathy for him. "Will you tell me what you know?"

"Last night, the boys went out joyriding on their ATVs. They do it often, against their mother's wishes, but I've never seen much harm in it because I've forbidden them to leave our property."

Merit nodded. She let him speak. She could ask questions later, if necessary. She simply wanted to hear the details for now and to find out how she might assist him.

Lane cleared his throat. "As best we can guess, they came upon someone torching the greenhouse and field closest to the county road. The twins were assaulted and left to burn in the field. The farm supervisor and I, along with firefighters, got to them just in time and pulled them from the blaze. Brad got the worst of it. His face was burned, and he didn't regain consciousness. We're told that Thad revived for a brief moment in the ambulance, but he was in such pain they gave him a sedative before he could explain much. He said the arsonist was one man who looked like Bob Marley, with a can of gasoline. The attendants didn't know if Thad was lucid or delusional when he said it. He hasn't been awake since to tell us anything further."

Merit nodded. "I assume the authorities were called. What did the sheriff say?"

"The arsonist, assuming it was one man, was gone before the fire trucks arrived. My farm supervisor saw an older model pickup truck headed out in a cloud of dust. Didn't get a plate number or description."

Merit felt rage but kept her face neutral. *Bastard.*

"It took the firefighters hours to get and keep the blaze under control. They brought in additional pump trucks from Austin to help out."

Merit nodded. "It wasn't just a cigarette someone threw out?"

Lane shook his head. "No. The firefighters say it was definitely gasoline that started it. Arson for sure."

"Your home is okay?"

"Yes, the fire was down by the county road, away from the house and the bunkhouse. Probably so the arsonist son of a bitch wouldn't be seen by the farm workers and could get away."

Merit looked at Lane as tears welled in his eyes, then he dropped his gaze. "We could lose our boys."

Merit thought of her teenage son, Ace, and couldn't bear the thought of something like this happening to him. The best she could come up with was, "Hospitals these days are so advanced. You're in the best place possible. Let's hang onto hope. Betty is already praying for the boys. You know how powerful she is."

Lane gave her a waning smile.

"Betty said you think it has to do with your regulatory case?"

"What else? It wasn't random, and the vandalism on all the area farms has been increasing over this past year."

"But, this is the first arson, right?"

"Yes, but things have been escalating at a steady pace."

Merit unconsciously twirled her ponytail between her fingers as they both grew quiet, then she said, "Let me get Ag Malone, my investigator, to talk with the sheriff over there. Ag also has contacts in the Austin Police Department. I'll see if we can put together some additional information from authorities and get back with you."

"Thank you, Merit. I really appreciate it. We should warn the other farmers in the co-op."

"I'll have Betty take care of that. We have all the contact information in your files."

"Right. Right."

"Please let us know if anything changes with the boys. We'll have you in our thoughts every minute."

3

Raiden Prince dusted off his work boots and put them in the closet of his Austin rental house next to his brown leather cowboy boots. He didn't wear the pointed-toe variety. He liked the square-toed Ariats, the kind real cowboys used for hard labor. He wore them in Texas to keep up the image of a good ol' boy who wasn't to be trifled with, but in reality, he was from New Jersey and preferred sneakers or Doc Martens.

Prince pulled on a pair of expensive running shoes, jogging pants, and a long-sleeved wick-away shirt and wrapped his exercise armband around his bicep to hold his phone. He was tall and slender with a runner's physique. Muscular, but not bulky. He had shoulder-length dreadlocks that he dyed black, but his face was as pale as the snow in Jersey. He hated that about himself, so he added dark complexion makeup to his face and hands, waterproof and sweat proof. For today, he pulled his dreadlocks into a man bun with a rubber band and stuffed his hair under a burnt orange University of Texas ballcap.

Prince cued up some tunes by Rek Banga, self-proclaimed

king of Jersey rap. He preferred the Jamaican stoner costume as his regular persona most of the time in Austin. The disguise allowed him to show his real hair, although he also had the cowboy, the student, the homeless drifter, and a host of others if he needed them.

That morning, Prince had put on the student outfit to get rid of the truck, taking it to a crusher out on the I-35 bypass. The house he was renting had a garage, where he could have hidden it, but he wasn't one to take chances and he wasn't sure if anyone had seen the truck. Also, he had no keys. He'd have to hot-wire the damn thing every time he drove it, if he kept it. Prince kicked himself for losing the keys in the grass at the Lanes' farm. He had plenty of motor vehicles at his disposal, each one appropriate to his disguise of the moment, so one less truck made little difference. But, the keys—careless. Prince shrugged off the mistake and smiled at himself in the mirror as he admired his Longhorn T-shirt, jeans with holes, and sneakers.

I am so clever.

Prince was in Austin as a gun for hire. He enjoyed his job, not because he was a reckless psychopath, which he was, but because it gave him a lavish lifestyle and allowed him to be anyone he wanted to be. He transformed into a homeboy when in Jersey and fit right in with the HipHop scene and gangsta rap crowd, complete with a million-dollar crib and a chest full of bling. Participation in the music scene made it easy for him to hide his income, though he mostly dealt in cash. Hell, he even paid taxes.

Prince had practiced, and often used, the Texas drawl. He had not adopted it, but some of it had wormed its way into his mouth and wouldn't let go even when he went back to Bloom-field, New Jersey, for weeks at a time. He cursed enough for either state—the universal language in both worlds.

Right now, he was working for a businessman and his cronies in the marijuana growth industry—big business, and they could afford him. Prince's persona for meeting with his current client was the good ol' boy outfit with the cowboy boots, dreads pulled back in a ponytail. His Texas work mobile phone had a 713 area code, which was Houston, so his clients didn't have a clue that his home base was in Yankee land or that he was currently housed in Austin.

Prince knew most people, including his current employer, considered him a monster. A necessary evil. Prince was convinced that people in general didn't have the strength within to do the dirty work. He had the ability to remove all emotion from these types of scenarios and just get the job done. His clients knew that sometimes hurting people was necessary, and there were some people who didn't need to go on living, but clients didn't want that sentiment in their daily lives. Prince was an arm's length tool they could use, then wash their hands of him with simple cash. That suited Prince just fine. He wasn't in it to be admired or loved, just paid.

Some thought that Prince must have had a rude upbringing, suffering all types of abuse and/or neglect, to develop into the monster he'd become, but that was far from the truth. His mother now lived five streets over from his home in New Jersey and he saw her often between jobs. He'd purchased her home for her when he'd made his first million. His father, who was considered a saint, had passed on a few years back, and Prince missed him every day. He'd been reared with love and respect and all good things, except for money. They had been so poor, he often ate only one meal a day, and his clothes were always hand-me-downs or from the local thrift shop. His father's deep shame and being unable to provide for his family created a small wound within Prince's heart that grew and grew until it was a seething resentment.

In the room, that he shared with two brothers, there was a huge crack across the entire ceiling where water dripped in when it rained. He'd lie in his bed for hours pretending the crack was a roadmap out of poverty. He had a full story crafted in his mind about each ruthless step he'd take until he exited his situation. A big part of that exit was emulating the rappers in Jersey, but his main source of income was as a hired gun. It paid more than music, and it gave him an outlet for his dark side.

When he first started rapping was when he'd developed his love of disguises. He would find everything in a Goodwill or Salvation Army store, and the clothes made the man. When he put on a newly configured outfit, he became that persona. It set him free from all the strife around him and gave him hours of pleasure dreaming of how he'd buy his mother the very home she now lived in. He also fantasized about traveling the planet, which he now did often, between jobs. He felt the world owed him for the pain he'd suffered in his youth. He'd paid his dues, and now he collected. Nothing wrong with that. In fact, to him, it was perfect.

He'd been stepping up the shenanigans for this particular client for weeks and had been hired to stay in the area for months, if needed, until he'd terrorized almost every small producer of weed out of business. Except for his boss and his boss's friends, of course. Intimidation was his weapon, and he was good at it. Murder didn't bother him either, although he rarely was given the green light to enjoy it. Occasionally, he killed someone just for the fun of it, if they crossed him.

Last night, at the Lanes' farm, things had gotten out of hand. He had been tasked with burning the greenhouse and field, not putting two young men in the morgue. He knew he'd gone too far, but his work was not an exact science. It came with all types of twists and unexpected turns, and he had to play each hand as it was dealt. How was he to know two kids would be out joyriding in the middle of the night?

It was their fault as much as mine.

Prince, needing to replace his work truck, and craving more anonymity in the field, devised a plan. He took an American Airlines flight out of Austin into Brownsville in the Rio Grande Valley and rented a car at the airport using one of his fake IDs and matching credit card. He drove deep into the cotton belt and observed the comings and goings of farmers and workers around the area. In a couple of hours, he had his target, a boll weevil inspection truck parked on the side of the road. Prince could see the inspector in the field, about a quarter of a mile away, hammering in the traps that were designed to catch and kill the small ugly gray beetles with long snouts. The inspector would work the entire cotton farm, placing the traps about every tenth of a mile or so.

The insects, eradicated in most of Texas, persisted in the Rio Grande Valley where it was warm and humid enough for the beetles to easily survive the winter. Also, new beetles periodically arrived from Mexico, where populations flourished. Texas was still the largest cotton producer in the country, and the last state with the hated, nasty boll weevil.

Yes, there were inspectors in Central Texas, near Austin, and Prince could have stolen a truck there, but the word would go out and the theft would be discovered in no time. Where the boll weevil had been eradicated, trucks were few and far between, but in the Valley, there were legions of trucks and inspectors because of the infestation. One missing vehicle was not going to be noticed, outside the area, for some time.

The blame would probably go to some illegal immigrant

who'd crossed the border to commit the crime of vehicle theft. Prince had a long job ahead and a need for ongoing anonymity in the form of a reason to be in and around the county roads in Bastrop County. Hence the truck.

The idea had come to him when he saw the local boll weevil inspector having lunch in LaGrange at the Town Square Cafe. He could have plucked the truck right out of its parking spot, but that was too close to home. Flying down to The Valley, and stealing the truck, allowed him to distance the theft from his work area, and this vehicle could ensure the success of his mission. Besides, it was fun.

He drove his rental car about half a mile down the road and pulled it off to the side into a grove of trees. He wiped it down, grabbed his travel bag, and walked back to the inspector's truck. He hid the bag in the crops beside the truck. Still hidden, Prince looked out into the cotton field and saw the inspector start hammering another of the cone-shaped traps into the ground.

Prince moved swiftly, ducking low and tracking the edge of the brush to avoid being seen too soon. His heart pounded in his chest, a mix of adrenaline and excitement. As he drew closer, he could see the inspector more clearly: an older Hispanic man, his back bent with age and years of work, oblivious to the danger approaching him.

When he was only a few yards away, Prince straightened up and quickened his pace. The inspector, sensing movement, turned around, his expression shifting from confusion to alarm as he saw Prince rushing toward him.

"What do you want?" the inspector shouted, dropping the trap and hammer he was holding.

Prince didn't answer, but lunged at the inspector, delivering a swift and powerful punch to his jaw. The inspector's eyes widened in shock before he crumpled to the ground, unconscious. Breathing heavily, Prince quickly searched the inspector's pockets, his hands shaking with adrenaline and urgency. He felt the cool metal of the truck keys and pulled them free. Glancing around to make sure no one had seen the altercation, he stood up and sprinted toward the truck.

He grabbed his travel bag from the weeds and went to the truck. His hands fumbled with the keys until he managed to unlock the door and climb inside. The engine roared to life, and Prince took one last look at the unconscious inspector lying in the dirt. Prince slammed his foot on the gas pedal and the truck lurched forward, tires kicking up dust as he sped away from the field, leaving the inspector and the cotton plants behind. He laughed all the way to the county line.

Prince drove the five hours back to Austin without incident and parked the truck in the garage at his temp living quarters. He lowered the garage door and gave himself a mental high five.

Success.

4

———

Merit met with Albert 'Ag' Malone in her downtown office the night after she'd left the Lanes at the hospital. She wanted him to start working the file right away, before the evidence and memories of those involved grew cold.

Ag entered Merit's inner office in his usual Aggie maroon shirt, blue jeans, and boots. He had been Merit's investigator at the firm since she'd set up shop in Austin, years ago. Although Merit was a University of Texas Law grad, and Ag had attended Texas A&M, an archrival school, Ag was willing to work with her because she paid well, was smart, and the work was interesting. Also, he had a secret crush on her that was not so secret, but not directly discussed. Both were equally thrilled when UT and A&M joined the SEC and were able to play football against each other again. Summer could not go by fast enough so that the season could start and their teams could get onto the gridiron. High-priced bets of food, alcohol, and favors would surely ensue.

"Hey, Merit. You really should lock that outer door when you're here alone at night," Ag said.

Merit smiled at him. She couldn't help it. "Yeah, I know. Want a beer?" Merit pointed to a glass of wine sitting on her desk.

"I'll grab it." Ag walked back out of her office and down the hall toward the break room. When he returned, he held a frosty Lone Star longneck.

Merit tipped back in her chair and looked up at him. "Hello, you. Have a seat."

Ag sat in one of the guest chairs before Merit's desk, took a long look at her, then took an equally long pull on his beer.

Merit smiled at him again. "Good to see you. Cheers." They both took another sip. She studied his beautiful eyes with the dark, curly eyelashes as he stretched his long legs out from the chair and relaxed his lean body against the back.

"What's up?"

Merit's demeanor changed. "Have you watched the news today?"

"No, I haven't had a chance."

"Remember that marijuana farm real estate file I had you work on a few months back? John David Lane?"

Ag thought for a moment. "Right."

"Well, it looks like the competition might have decided to derail the Lanes' business. Someone set his large greenhouse and hemp field on fire last night, and Lane thinks it's an escalation of some shenanigans that have been going on over in Bastrop County."

"That seems extreme."

"Yes. What's worse is the Lane twins were either investigating or accidentally stumbled upon the perpetrator and were almost killed. Both are in the hospital on life support."

"Oh man. Tough break. They're sure it's arson?"

"That's what the fire department thinks, but I'd like for you to get with the sheriff over there and make sure. See what you can find out."

"The boys couldn't give any information?"

"One purportedly woke up in the ambulance and said the perpetrator was one man in a pickup who looked like Bob Marley. They're not sure if it was delirium or if he actually saw someone."

Ag scratched his chin in thought. "I don't know the sheriff well, but Chaplain does. My guess is APD is already informed, but if not, okay to read him in?"

"Sure." One of the things Merit relied on with Ag was his connections. Chaplain was the chief of detectives at the Austin Police Department, one of Ag's best contacts and his good friend. Ag often called on Chaplain, who had no first name as far as he knew, when he needed an introduction or behind-the-scenes information.

Ag contemplated the assignment. "If someone out there is playing dirty, and if the twins don't make it, it will go from arson to murder."

Merit shivered. "Let's hope for the best. Lane is expecting you to come by and start snooping around. When you go to the farm, introduce yourself to the farm supervisor and he'll tell you what he knows. He'll probably be in the bunkhouse if he doesn't come out to greet you. For now, can you put some protection on at the hospital, just in case."

"You think someone may want to finish the job on the boys?"

"If they're concerned about being identified, they might. I hope not, but better to be safe than sorry."

"I'll get one of my guys on it tonight."

"Thanks, Ag. I knew I could count on you. Keep me posted."

"Will do." He finished the last of his beer, put the bottle on her desk, and walked out of her office, feeling a tiny ache inside the moment he left her.

The next day, Merit sat again in her office with her law clerk, Valentine Lewis, while Betty minded the phones and popped in and out when it suited her. She and Merit had a shorthand and open-door policy that made them the perfect working duo. Their relationship filled every part of their lives, business and personal. Merit had been matron of honor at Betty's recent wedding when she married Bob Tom Jakes. Betty had been Merit's strength when she lost her husband, Tony, to suicide several years before. The loving matriarch had stepped in and helped care for Merit's son, Ace, when both were too devastated to handle the sorrow.

Betty placed a cup of hot tea with milk on Merit's desk and turned to Val. "Want a refill on that coffee?"

Val looked up from his iPad. "No, thanks. I'm good."

Merit looked at Val and admired his attire. He was particularly dapper today in a vintage Armani suit and Hugo Boss tie. He always found the best secondhand merch, which was what he could afford on a student's part-time income.

"How are classes going?"

"Heavy reading load right now, but I'm getting on top of it. We'll have summer school finals next month, then a break before we start the fall semester."

Val commuted three days a week to San Antonio to St. Mary's Law School. It offered the most flexible program in the area so he could both work and attend classes. Assisting Merit, first as her paralegal and now law clerk, was putting him financially through school. It also didn't hurt to have a practicing lawyer like Merit on hand if he got stuck on something difficult like the rule against perpetuities or double hearsay, two of his most challenging topics to date.

Merit smiled. "Hang in there. It gets easier every year. The first year they scare you to death, the second year they work you to death, and the third year they bore you to death."

Val laughed, although he'd heard it many times before. "So they say."

Merit took a sip of her tea. "Let's get some work done."

Val tapped the iPad screen to bring it back to life. "Shoot."

"I know Betty already briefed you on the recent tragedy at the Lanes' farm. You recall when we helped the Lanes navigate the bureaucracy regulations in order to expand their marijuana and hemp operations."

"Sure."

"Good. Let's make certain all of our new license applications are up to date and still in process with the State. Work with Betty on that."

"Will do."

"In 2015 the state created the Compassionate Use Program for Texans with severe epilepsy. That's the basis for the current law. Start there."

Val tapped notes on the screen. "Got it."

"Don't fall into the trap of confusing the medical marijuana licensure with the state's Hemp Program for businesses that produce low-THC cannabis products. We want to track the legislation that deals with medical cannabis processor licenses primarily, but I'd like the updates on both."

Val started to look like a deer in headlights.

"I know, it's complicated. There are only three licensed medical marijuana dispensaries, each can operate only a single growing facility. They must test their crops monthly and share the results with the Department of Public Safety, not the Department of State Health Services, which oversees the hemp stores. There are thousands and thousands of hemp stores. It's two separate things under the law."

"I'll be precise."

"Next, I want you to update our files on all the votes coming up in the Texas Legislature on cannabis law. The state's crop law is legislated by the Texas Department of Agriculture. It's a regulatory quagmire of layered red tape and rules that require a team of experts to navigate."

"I'll say."

"Search Senator Paige Linden's website. She's on top of all that. Then, call her office and speak to Stuart Lawton. He'll know if there's anything new not yet on the site. Tell him I sent you."

"Will do."

"Give me your best shot at organizing it."

Val added the instructions to his notes. "It's a wonder that Texas allows marijuana cultivation at all with the Bible thumpers in opposition, and Republicans running the legislature."

"Republicans like to make money same as Democrats, maybe more."

Betty entered with a stack of files and put them in Merit's in-box. She gave Val a funny look and he laughed. "I bet you never had a toke, Betty."

Betty huffed a bit, bumped the nape of her Aqua Net coifed hairdo, and said, "The earth is a treasure chest we open to find wonderful things: food, energy, medicines. Marijuana is no different. It's all in what you do with it."

Merit smirked and Val almost spit his coffee. *Yeah, she toked a bit in her day.*

5

Raiden Prince drove to Harrison Farms near LaGrange, in Fayette County, about halfway between Austin and Houston off Highway 71. LaGrange was home to the original Chicken Ranch, which operated from 1905 to 1973, made famous in "The Best Little Whorehouse in Texas." Prince wore his cowboy outfit today, dreadlocks pulled back, and square-toed boots showing beneath Wrangler jeans. No holes.

Prince's boss, Blake Harrison, met him at the cattle guard and opened the gate, swinging it wide enough for the white boll weevil inspection truck to enter. Harrison, the larger of the two men, also in boots and jeans, wore a Stetson to ward off the hot sun.

"What the hell?" Harrison said, looking at the truck.

Prince smiled proudly. "It's my new ride. Picked it up in the Rio Grande Valley."

"The Valley?"

Harrison's face showed delight at the ingenuity of the idea, but he didn't acknowledge it verbally. Instead, he threw his meaty leg over his ATV, started it, and led Prince up the long winding driveway that brought them to the home office. There was no one else near the house. No ranch hand was to see Prince up close, per their agreement, and Harrison made sure he was the only one who met with Prince. Harrison didn't want their connection revealed any more than Prince did.

Prince was not worried at all about law enforcement, he could outsmart them, but it was of paramount importance to him that he keep his identity a secret. Prince never really worried about going to prison for the things he did because businessmen like Blake Harrison had reputations and power to protect, and in turn would hide him in order to stay anonymous themselves.

Prince used his disguises and feigned dialect to give the client the image they wanted most to see when he met with them. Harrison only knew the cowboy. He had no idea about the Rastafarian, the UT student disguise, or any of the other ones for that matter. The dreadlocks were either hanging free, pulled back in a bun, or stuffed under a hat to fit each disguise, but in Austin, the hair wasn't really a problem. There were left-over hippies everywhere and flamboyant students as well.

Prince parked the truck and followed Harrison into the home office, that looked like a hunting lodge. There were dead animal heads, longhorn cattle horns, and maps of local lands hanging on every wall. Harrison sat down in a massive leather office chair, and Prince found his way to an animal print seat near the boss's oversized wooden desk. More and more of the Harrison farmland had been steered away from cattle and toward marijuana growth as the industry developed, but there were plenty of cows around to make Harrison feel like a real cattle baron. A plaque on the wall asked: Did you eat beef today?

Harrison hung his Stetson on a hat rack by the door, then settled behind his desk, his hands steepled together. He looked at Prince who stared back at him. The hired gun wondered what it felt like to have a father who was so rich that his son never had to worry about money.

Harrison had inherited almost everything that he owned, but cannabis growing was his idea. It was Harrison's chance to make a statement outside of his father's legacy, although the fact that he was doing it all with his family's money seemed lost on him.

Harrison had invested a lot in the state's Hemp Program which designated that the product must not contain more than 0.3 percent THC post-decarboxylation. But, that was different than full-strength marijuana. Texas only allowed cannabis cultivation for medical purposes, under one license, the Dispensary Organization license. Any growth of crops for the gummies dispensed in the medical marijuana clinics required one to have the limited, and highly coveted, medical marijuana license. They were so limited that just a handful of people, about ten across the state, held the licenses. That was about to change, and that's why he needed Prince.

A new statute was in the Texas legislature to expand the number of licenses, and a line was forming to get them. That was Harrison's goal, obtaining the new med marijuana licenses that were going to be allowed after the upcoming law was passed.

For now, he made his money through Texas's extensive hemp industry consisting of CBD shops selling delta-9 THC/CBD gummies and tinctures made from the hemp plant, the low THC version of the cannabis plant. These products adhered to the requirements of the Federal 2019 Farm Bill and were legal and easily available for over-the-counter or online purchase in Texas's CBD stores. In actuality, it was a joke, as the levels were not adequately regulated, and most went over the limit.

But, that wasn't enough for Harrison. He wanted the prestige and money of the medical marijuana market, featuring products for a specific list of medical conditions, for example cancer, multiple sclerosis, and epilepsy. That's where the big money was. With the state's large population, it was projected to become the third largest medical cannabis market in the country in a few short years. Harrison's plan, with the new licenses, was to get more than his fair share of the wealth that was expected to pour in as the industry exploded.

The medical processor license application fee was six thousand dollars, and the ongoing license fee was almost half a million per year. Anyone who doubted the value of the market needed only to look at what growers were willing to pay for the licenses to see the potential. Harrison intended to be the top producer, whatever it took. Hence, Raiden Prince had been hired. But right now, Prince was not pleasing him.

"What the hell happened out there?"

"I did exactly what you instructed me to. I lit that place on fire. It's going to take them a while to recover from that; maybe they never will."

"There are two kids in the hospital right now who might not make it. It's already on every damn news station. Drawing that kind of attention wasn't part of the plan."

"It would have been on the news either way."

"Yes, but minus the possible murder charges against the idiot who did it."

Prince bristled but remained cool. "I arrived there unnoticed, or so I thought. I set to work burning the field and the greenhouse, all per your very detailed instructions. It was going swimmingly until the twins showed up." Prince laughed.

Harrison did not laugh. "Do you think this is a joke?"

"No. But sometimes things happen when you light someone's yard on fire. You might not get the usual 'satisfaction guarantee' that you're looking for. I did the job that you asked for despite the complications. I improvised when things changed, had to protect myself, and get out of there."

Harrison stared at him. Prince continued to return the gaze. He knew bad guys and Harrison was one of them; he just dressed in thousand-dollar cowboy boots and a big-ass hat.

"Look, the Lane twins surprised me. I didn't have much of a choice in the moment."

"You almost killed them, for Christ's sake."

"I hope I did. I don't need any witnesses and neither do you. Remember that. The boys tackled me and to be honest, they're huge."

"Yes, they both play on the Giddings football team. They aren't called Buffaloes for nothin'."

"I'm not surprised, but I managed to get the upper hand. Problem solved."

"Well, they didn't die. Sorry to disappoint you, Prince, but they made it to the hospital. They are unconscious and in critical condition, but they might pull through and then what?"

Prince looked worried for a moment. "Do you want me to go there and finish the job?"

Blake shook his head. "No. Are you listening to me? I don't want you anywhere near that hospital. Not yet anyway. If they wake up, are you sure they can't identify you?"

"Probably not. It was dark and I was wearing dark clothing." Prince didn't mention that his dreadlocks had tumbled out of his hat.

"All right, I want you to keep an eye on things. A close eye. Monitor the situation and keep me posted. I'll decide what to do as things develop."

"Is that all?" A tinge of sarcasm crept into Prince's tone.

"For now." Harrison responded with equal sarcasm.

"Have my money for the week?"

"Yep. The envelope is right there." Harrison pointed to a white envelope with a rubber band around it on a small side table.

Prince stood, picked up his cash, left the farm, and decided he would stop in at the hospital after all.

Just a quick visit.

6

Ag, at his home office in Briarcliff on Lake Travis, set up a file on the Lane case and began to assemble the pieces of the puzzle needed to investigate and report to Merit. He needed a kickstart to get the case rolling, until he could interview the Lanes, so he called the APD and set up a meet that morning with his buddy and chief of detectives, Chaplain.

Ag drove into Austin, arrived at APD, checked in, and stored his weapon in the lockers provided for that purpose. He and Chaplain exchanged a hearty handshake upon his entry into the detective's office and settled with coffee and small talk to catch up. They both eventually wound down on the personal topics and Ag turned to business.

"You've heard about the arson at the Lanes' farm over in Bastrop County?"

"Yep. Senator Linden has been on us to help the sheriff over there with anything they need for the investigation."

"Glad to hear you're up to speed. That's why I'm here. Merit Bridges has assigned the investigation for her law firm clients to me, and I need an introduction to Sheriff Burke. I haven't done a lot of work over there, and I doubt he knows who I am."

"Burke. Yeah, I know him. Glad to."

Chaplain reached for the phone's intercom button. "Get me Sheriff Bruce Burke in Bastrop County, please."

"Right away."

In no time, the request had been made and Ag was set up for a meeting that very afternoon. "I knew I came to the right guy." Ag laughed. "Can't thank you enough."

Chaplain's laughter, a deep symbol of camaraderie, resonated through the room as he dismissed Ag with a gesture of goodwill. "Consider it a debt repaid in advance, my friend."

On his way to Bastrop County, Ag rang the office of Sheriff Bruce Burke and asked him if they could meet at the Lane farm instead of the sheriff's office. Chaplain's call had smoothed the way and Sheriff Burke was happy to oblige.

Ag wanted to get a first-hand look at the damage to the greenhouse and field and take photographs for his report for Merit. When he arrived at the Lane farm, the sheriff's vehicle was not visible, but it was obvious where the fire had occurred. Ag pulled his blue F-150 pickup to a stop on the side of the county road next to the charred and post-apocalyptic farm land.

Ag whistled at the sight, then left his truck and walked around the edge of the devastation. He shot multiple photos of the fire-damaged greenhouse and field and took a long-lens shot up to the Lanes' home to show the distance from the house to the fire. He surmised from the evidence that the greenhouse and field, and not the Lanes' home or surrounding buildings, were the targets of the arsonist.

Ag picked up a long, thin branch and broke away the side growth, leaving a stick for poking around. He used the rough tool to flip over some ashes and lift a few plants at the edge of the fire that were wilted and partially charred. Bluebonnets were shriveled and wilted at the edge of the road from the heat. It was said that it's a crime to pick or damage Bluebonnets in Texas. Merit had told Ag that was an urban legend. He still wasn't sure.

About that time, the sheriff arrived, parked his Bastrop County black-and-white SUV, and joined Ag. They shook hands and sized each other up, Ag noticing that Burke's brown uniform was rather snug.

"Thanks for meeting me. What a mess, heh?"

Sheriff Burke pushed his standard beige cowboy hat back on his head. "Yep. Devastating, and senseless."

"Someone didn't think so. Any idea who that could be?"

"Your client, Lane, thinks it's part of some methodical vandalism scheme involving the cannabis industry in the county. I've spoken with Chaplain, at length, and there have not been similar incidents in Travis County or any of the other counties surrounding Austin that he tracks. Only over here."

"He told me the same. I haven't had a chance to interview Lane or his family. Merit Bridges asked me to start putting a file together, but to give the Lanes some space while the twins are in danger."

"Damn shame the boys stumbled into this mess. Come over here and I'll show you where the assaults occurred."

The two men walked back to the county road, Ag carrying his poking stick and Burke hitching up his equipment belt that tended to ride awkwardly on his hips under his belly. They proceeded about five yards down the shoulder to an area where the land had been disturbed by tire marks next to the field. Across the road, a barbed wire fence was partially down and a makeshift repair was containing the neighbor's cattle.

Sheriff Burke pointed. "That's where one of the twin's ATVs came to a halt."

"I see." Ag poked a few more clumps of grass with his stick.

Sheriff Burke pointed again on their side of the road. "That's where we think the arsonist parked his vehicle. You can see the ruts on the roadside. And here's the blood where the boys were struck."

Ag walked around the area. There was yellow crime scene tape laying on the ground, but the scene had been released without clean-up. He plucked at a piece of the yellow plastic with the point of his stick.

"The lab took the tree limb that was used as a weapon to examine it further. Blood samples were taken from the ground, but it looks like the blood belonged to the twins. No third-party blood found, so far."

Ag nosed around the bushes and grass next to the crime scene and took a few pictures of the tire tracks and damaged fence for his report. "You'd think those two big twins could have overtaken one man. Are you sure it was only one perp on the scene?"

"No, we can't be sure, but Thad Lane said one man."

He also said it was Bob Marley, Ag thought.

"We're just getting started on the investigation. Hopefully, I'll have more in a day or two. I'll be happy to share, or you can get updates from Chaplain."

"I appreciate that." Ag walked back toward the area where the perpetrator's truck was supposedly parked, poking along the way with his stick and flicking at the grass as he went. When he drubbed, he flicked something metal that he first thought was a bottle cap or smashed aluminum can, but when the metal glinted in the sunlight and made a rattling sound, he looked more closely. He and Sheriff Burke squatted on their haunches, and both said in unison, "Car keys."

Ag adjusted his stick and stuck it through the ring that held the keys. He stood up, bringing the keys on the stick with him, and both men examined the find dangling in the air.

Sheriff Burke spoke first. "Well, I'll be damned."

Ag dialed Merit's number as he drove from Bastrop County back to Austin. He caught her at her desk and gave her an update on the information gleaned from Chaplain and Sheriff Burke, the state of the scene, and the finding of the keys.

He promised a written report with pictures after he had a chance to interview John David Lane and hopefully the Lane twins.

Neither realized that was not going to happen.

7

———————

Senator Paige Linden stormed through her office door at the Texas State Capitol barking orders to the young female assistant who trotted beside her, trying to keep up. The people who worked in the senator's office were smart and as passionate about their jobs as she was. If they weren't, they didn't last long. Not with this senator.

Lindy, as she was called by her constituents, was tough, but fair, and relished being in the power position of heading up the Senate Committee on Agriculture as well as the Committee on Health and Human Services. They were the committees that governed the sale and supply of cannabis in Texas. Current estimates were that there were over five thousand hemp, CBD, and cannabinoid retailers, manufacturers, and distributors in Texas that employed more than fifty thousand workers and generated more than eight billion in annual revenue. Those statistics brought a lot of power to the door of those who sat on the committees regulating the so-called Mary Jane.

She was also on the Senate Committees on Finance, Water,

Rural Affairs, and the Texas Windstorm Advisory Board. As anyone could see from these appointments, her primary interests were in health, agriculture, and land use. With all her committees combined, Lindy was at the point of the spear.

"Find Stuart Lawton."

"Yes, ma'am. I mean yes, Lindy."

Lindy was christened Paige because her family owned a large portion of Bastrop County and had a lovely old craftsman home on a high hill at the edge of Paige, Texas, an unincorporated area with a population of less than two thousand hardworking folks. Those residents were mostly farmers, ranchers, and an occasional oil producer where the geology fell into place just right. Lately, a few seeking to flee the Austin traffic and prices had found their way to the county.

Lindy had been the Texas Senator in District 14 for over ten years following four successful terms in the Texas House of Representatives. The district served Bastrop County, home of the Lanes' farm, and a portion of Travis County, home of Austin and the State Capitol. She was only the eighth female to serve in the Texas Senate since 1845. Good ol' boys surrounded her daily, but she was not intimidated and, in fact, enjoyed the camaraderie having grown up the only girl in a family with four male siblings. She could also hit a three-point basketball shot from outside the paint when she was in college and might still, if she practiced a little.

Lindy slammed her purse down on her desk, pulled out her rolling chair, and continued barking orders. "I want to speak with Sheriff Bruce Burke. Get him for me, now."

"On it."

As she sat and waited for the call, Stuart Lawton walked in.

"You looking for me?"

"Yes. Have a seat. I want to know everything about the fire that happened last night on the Lanes' farm."

"Yes, Lindy. I'm already on it. I've got a few more calls to make and I'll email a report to you. Should take less than an hour."

As Lawton stood to return to his office, Robert Ersery, senator from Dallas, rudely walked past Lindy's receptionist and tapped on her door. He was a gangly sort who looked like he'd lost twenty pounds since he'd purchased his suit. His wing tips were so big, they stretched out in front like scuba fins, causing them to make a slapping sound when he walked.

Lindy looked up at the man who was a constant thorn in her side, put on her proper etiquette smile, and said, "Come in, Bob. How are you today?"

"Senator Linden, I heard about the fire in your district. More trouble."

Lindy rolled her eyes at, then nodded her dismissal of, Stuart Lawton who gladly slipped out the door while Ersery continued to suck all the air out of the room.

"Kind of you to come by and check on things. It is troublesome, Bob. A few of my constituents were hurt, along with a substantial loss of property."

"Do you now see the problem with legalizing marijuana? We have people out there no better than drug dealers burning down each other's farms. It's like pissing to mark your territory."

Lindy leaned back in her chair and measured her response. "I'm sorry, Senator, but I don't think anyone knows exactly what happened. I'm reaching out to the sheriff to get more information. If you'd like, I can have my staff report to your staff about what we learn. But, I do take offense at your comparing farmers to drug dealers, especially since most of them are friends of mine."

Ersery huffed. "This is going to be your undoing, Senator. I assure you. Marijuana should never have been legalized in this state."

It was interesting to Lindy that medical marijuana was not legalized in Texas prior to 1973 when possession of any type was considered a felony. It was actually 2015 when a religious case was made by a guy named David Simpson who introduced House Bill 2165 to legalize the use of cannabis for recreational use. Simpson was an avid follower of Sid Miller, an outlier politician who had been advocating education leading to legalization for decades. Sid Miller became so popular, he'd become the Commissioner of the Texas Department of Agriculture, which oversaw the administration of the Texas Industrial Hemp Program.

Simpson had argued, "I don't believe that when God made marijuana, he made a mistake that the government needs to fix."

That year, medical use had been legalized allowing for low-THC cannabis oil use. Of course, the Texas governor was dead set against it and thought that it would open the door for every hippie smoking pot user to sit on a curb and light up, or oil up, as the case may be.

Lindy had become involved because Bastrop County had some of the biggest cannabis facilities compared to others in the state. She no longer tried to argue her position with the close minded, especially Senator Robert Ersery. She knew by heart the statistics and mountains of evidence that showed the good that marijuana did for people in pain, with epilepsy, or those diagnosed with cancer. She chose not to cast her pearls before swine and just kept quiet, allowing him to talk, which is what he wanted anyway. Ersery went on about misuse of medical marijuana cards and a myriad of other tired old arguments, then wound down and finally ran out of steam.

The young assistant popped her head in the door. "Sheriff Burke on line two, Lindy."

Lindy turned to Ersery. "Senator, we'll keep you up to date."

The assistant held the door open for him until he got the hint and went through it.

Lindy gave him a finger wave. "Have a good day."

"Hrmph."

8

M erit, wearing her favorite little black dress, entered Pot Luck Restaurant downtown on West 4th Street in the Austin Warehouse District. The aroma of garlic and spices hit her nostrils like an Italian freight train. She checked in with the hostess and was directed to a small table by the window where her buddies waited for her. It was girls' night out with her two best friends and fellow wine enthusiasts.

Clover Thibodeaux, a beautiful Asian goddess was the mayor of Austin. Clover was married to Merit's colleague, Kim Wan Thibodeaux, the litigator she used for most cases involving courtroom antics and some criminal defense work. Next to Clover sat Red Thallon. Merit had known Red, a journalist for KNEW 9 TV, even longer than she'd known Clover. Red's distinctive auburn hair and form-fitting clothing made her memorable on camera. She wrote the online news for the station as well, giving her a chance to scoop a story before the nightly news aired. Red was currently off the market with a new boyfriend, giving him a test drive to see if he could tolerate her schedule. Reporting took her out into the city at all hours of the day and night, and she was not the type to cook and clean. Maybe he'd stick around, maybe not. So far, none other had tolerated her chaotic lifestyle, on which she thrived.

The three women had been through some tough times, and it had bonded them for life. They supported each other's careers, kept each other's secrets, and respected each other's need to keep business information to themselves when their respective code of ethics required it.

Merit had once brought in a prospective new member for an audition to the group, named Natalie, who'd turned out to be a psychopath and had hung Merit on a meat hook at the direction of a Russian mobster. Since that brief foray into expanding the group, no new members had become the rule.

Merit found her way to a round high-top table and observed a nice bottle of red wine that was breathing its perfumed scent. The cork rested beside it and three empty long-stemmed wine bowls stood at the ready. There were hugs all around and the three sat in a circle, facing the wine bottle, and each other.

Clover started. "We waited for you."

"Thank you. I see that." All three laughed. Good therapy, starting the evening off right.

"Sorry I'm late. Work."

"Not at all, we just got settled in. I hear you have a lot on your plate these days."

The three knew how to make chitchat, but when something huge was brewing, like the Lane case, there was no strained waiting between them. They just dug right in.

Merit nodded. "So, you heard about the arsonist at the Lanes' farm. Figured you did."

Clover poured the wine for all three. "Yes, it was in my daily briefing. It included the fact that you represent John David Lane."

Red tasted the rich red. "Mmm, good one. I wrote a story on it. Should be online in about..." she looked at her watch. "...ten minutes. I plan to do a follow up. May I call you about it?"

Merit also tasted the wine and smiled with approval. "Sure. I'll share what I can. I have Ag working on it. Maybe I'll have something more in a day or two."

"Great."

Clover looked thoughtful. "How unfortunate about the Lane children."

"Very sad. The Lanes are beside themselves with worry. There's a constant vigil at the hospital with the twins. I've been down there off and on. Betty, too. Ag has a man on guard, just in case the perp comes back."

"That bad, huh?"

"Yes. They may not make it."

"Let me know if you need some extra coverage."

"Thanks, Clover."

Red nodded. "My inside guy at APD said the perp tried to burn the boys alive."

Merit shuddered. "It's true. They were knocked out and couldn't fight back."

"He thinks it may have been to cover evidence."

"Yes, one of the boys, Thad, may have seen him. Said he looked like Bob Marley, before he passed out."

Clover looked surprised. "Bob Marley?"

"Yep. The prince of peace himself. I need you to keep that to yourself until APD releases it."

Red made a zipping motion across her mouth. "My lips are sealed."

At that moment, the waiter arrived and Merit did a double-take. He was about ten years younger than the women, all in their late thirties and early forties. His ponytail was blond and almost as long as Merit's.

He handed a menu to each woman and took a minute longer to give Merit hers, then topped off the wine in each of their glasses.

He looked directly at Merit. "A server will be out to take your order in a few minutes. May I do anything for you in the meantime?"

Merit blushed a bit under the intensity of his gaze. "We could breathe another bottle of Malbec while we look these over."

"Coming right up." He walked over to the bar and gave instructions to the bartender. All three watched him as he walked away and appreciated his behind as he moved.

Chris Pine's got nothing on you, Merit thought.

All three looked back at each other and laughed. The women had had their backsides gawked at over the years. Turn about was fair play.

In a few moments, a pretty young woman, probably a UT student working part-time, came over and took their order. Merit ordered bruschetta, and Red a charcuterie board. Clover opted to share theirs as she still had dinner at home with Kim Wan and the children. She tried not to keep her security team out too late. They had families too. When Clover was first elected mayor, security was at a minimum. She drove herself to and from work and only had guards when attending official events. Now, since she'd been kidnapped by a domestic terrorist group, she had round-the-clock security and hadn't driven a car in months.

When the food was ready, the handsome waiter, not the pretty young co-ed, brought it out to the women and served them. He lingered again on Merit, and this time, she returned his gaze.

When he left, Clover said, "Merit, you are shameless."

"Just looking."

Red laughed. She knew about Merit's taste for younger men. She also knew it had cost her in the past, but judging her friend was not her style. Besides, she'd made enough mistakes of her own, probably more than Merit. Clover was the settled one. Her heart belonged to one man, and her children, of course. Good traits for a mayor to have.

Merit excused herself to the ladies' room and when she returned, the girls had funky smiles on their faces.

Merit quizzed them. "What's going on?"

"Oh, nothing," Clover said and changed the subject. "What's Ag think of the Lane case?"

"He's seen Chaplain at APD and the sheriff in Bastrop County, a guy named Burke. So far, nothing you don't already know. I hope Ag and the sheriff can get a lead on the arsonist."

Red nodded. "I interviewed Burke for my news piece."

Clover looked concerned. "Just don't get yourself in too deep, Merit. You know what happened before. Your life has been in danger more often than it should when you get yourself too tangled up with your clients. Believe it or not, you're not Wonder Woman and one of these days you're going to get yourself into something you can't get out of."

"Yeah, yeah. It's not like I purposely try to get myself sucked in. Sometimes my clients have really bad enemies. Besides, both of you are the pot calling the kettle black," Merit said with a shrug.

"Yes, well not exactly the same, and I have security. Besides, Ace needs you, remember that."

"How could I forget."

The student server approached. "May I bring you another bottle of wine?"

All three said, "No thanks." They'd reached their limit. She left the bill and Merit collected it before one of the other two could grab it.

"It's my turn." Merit looked over at the handsome waiter who was now behind the bar. "I wonder how long he's worked here."

Red burst out laughing. "Merit, he's not a waiter."

"Ugh, I knew it. You guys got him to play a joke on me."

Now both of them were bowled over with laughter. She was going to have to come up with some pretty good revenge. They had gone too far this time.

Clover touched her arm. "Oh my word, Merit; he's not a jokester or a waiter. He's the main chef and co-owner of this place."

"What?"

Red smiled. "That's Patrick Herbert. He was a James Beard Best New Chef Nominee last year."

Merit looked incredulous. "That doesn't make sense. Why would he be waiting on tables? It's not like there isn't staff here."

Clover laughed again. "He wanted to meet you, Silly. I think he has a thing for you."

A light blush sprouted on Merit's cheeks. They were getting up to leave and Merit spotted the chef coming toward them. He walked them to the front, opened the door for them, and cast a smile that made Merit's knees weak. She couldn't help but be flattered; however, she was going home alone tonight.

The next afternoon, Merit sat at her desk, deeply engrossed in a file about land usage that she was trying to understand without falling asleep. It was the end of a tiring day, and nothing was sinking in. Just about the time she decided to knock off, go home, and take Pepper for a run, Betty tapped on the door and entered carrying a vase with a beautiful bouquet of huge pink peonies.

Betty laughed. "Delivery for Merit Bridges from Freytag's Florist."

Merit looked at the flowers and smiled.

"Secret admirer?"

"No idea. Who's it from?"

Betty set the flowers down on the corner of Merit's desk, took the card off the little plastic fork, and handed it to Merit. It was too late for Merit to hide the truth, so she shared the card, feeling like a confessor.

"How nice. From Chef Herbert at Pot Luck." *Wonder how he knew I liked peonies?*

"What's going on with that?"

Merit blushed. "Nothing. I don't really know him. We met on girls' wine night."

"Well, looks like he wants to know you."

Merit smelled the lovely fragrance. "Maybe."

Betty went back to the door. "Those are as beautiful as all git out."

After she left, Merit picked up the phone, dialed Pot Luck, identified herself, and asked for Chef Herbert.

He came to the phone immediately. "Merit, it's wonderful to hear from you."

"Thank you for the flowers, Chef Herbert. It was such a surprise."

"It's Patrick. I'm glad you liked them."

"Like is a mild word. They're gorgeous."

"I was hoping they might get me a dinner date with you."

"I have a lot on my schedule right now. Let me see what opens up."

"I'll take what I can get. Or just stop by Pot Luck any night and see me."

"I'll think about it. Thanks again."

After they hung up, Merit looked up to see Betty by the door. Merit wasn't sure if she was listening or just passing by.

Betty walked away and Merit thought she heard Betty swear under her breath, "Holy shit. Here we go again."

9

———————

John and Gladys Lane took a break from the hospital and returned to the family farm to check on the property, change clothes, and have a much-needed nap.

Merit had arranged to meet them there with Ag so he could ask questions regarding the vandalism that had been going on in the county. It was far more extensive than Merit had realized, as the Lanes had played it down until the fire incident. There was some confusion, at first, as to whether it could be random, but now that seemed unlikely.

Merit and Ag left her office in his blue F-150 and drove half an hour out Highway 71, then cut over at the intersection of Highway 21 where the largest Buc-ee's Merit had ever seen was located. The mega travel stores, based in Texas, were known for their food shopping, multi gasoline pumps, and clean bathrooms. Merit had never been a fan because the snacks were too hard to resist, and they were often crowded.

They turned off 21 onto the county road that ran out to the Lanes' farm and found themselves transformed to another space and time. There were fields of hay, open pastures, some

55

lovely homes and some falling down. Both Merit and Ag took a breath of the fresh air, when they drove onto the winding lane that led up to the majestic restored farmhouse. So close to Austin, yet so far.

Merit had been representing the Lane family, for both business and personal matters, for over ten years. Most recently, she had guided them through the application process to acquire additional licenses for cannabis cultivation, which would expand their current operation three times over. With the popularity of the commodity, new permits were in high demand and harder for the Lanes and their co-op to obtain. Lobbying certain regulatory agencies and officials was part of Merit's job, and tracking legislation was imperative to support the task.

Merit admired Lane and his family. They were traditional Texas farmers who believed in the American way of hard work, legacy wealth, and family traditions. She knew that Brad and Thad would be sorely missed during their recovery, if they recovered. At age seventeen, they were old enough and strong enough to be integral to the farm work and often joined the hired hands doing common labor to keep the farm running. She hoped against hope that they would heal soon.

The Lanes came out the door of the home onto the palatial wrap-around porch, as Ag parked in one of the many parking spaces, and he and Merit got out of the truck. Merit introduced Ag and hugged Gladys. The wear and tear on the couple was evident.

"We won't take much of your time. I know you need to rest."

Lane nodded. "Shall we go inside?"

Once inside the Lanes' lovely home, Gladys offered tea or coffee, but Merit and Ag politely declined. The woman did not need another chore. They sat at the huge kitchen table, large enough for the Lanes' extended family during holidays and birthdays.

Lane sat at the head of the table. "We want to thank you for sending your man over to the hospital. It gave us peace of mind and allowed us to leave today for a much-needed break."

Gladys looked at Ag. "Yes, thank you so much."

Ag replied, "You can thank Merit for that. She instructed me to send someone over."

Merit smiled. "No thanks needed. Do you mind if Ag asks you a few questions to flesh out the picture of what happened?"

"Shoot."

Ag flipped open his file. "I've been through the, uh, area with Sheriff Burke." He almost said crime scene but caught himself in time. "There's no doubt that it was arson. Merit tells me this is the culmination of a lot of dirty tricks that have been going on in the area for some time. Can you give me details of the other incidents?"

Lane nodded. "For starters, some of the farms that are part of the co-op have been vandalized. Tools missing, sheds and bunkhouses torn up. At first, it was assumed to be kids getting out of hand or lowlifes looking for a quick buck."

Ag took notes and Merit listened.

"Next, it became more serious. Escalating. Chemicals poured onto crops, greenhouse windows broken out, fields run through with trucks, destroying plants. The arson appears to be the next stage of intimidation."

Ag looked sympathetic. "Is there security?"

"To a point, but we can't police thousands of acres. We also have a couple of absentee owners who have houses that are not occupied at all times. The copper wiring was stripped out of both houses and appliances removed. That is a common occurrence these days, so we didn't necessarily attribute it to the same vandal, but that's when the co-op pooled some funds to hire a security company to roam the area. A few extra motion cameras were installed like those used for game observation, deer and the like."

Ag nodded. "Sounds like a good response on par with the level of threat."

"Next, large farm equipment disappeared on two farms, not ours. One piece was a hay-baler, and the other was a combine. It's not easy to transport that type of equipment. It requires some planning, and a large flatbed."

Merit nodded. "They would also have needed to avoid the security cameras and guards to get those transported."

"Right, but farm equipment is moved in and out of this area all the time, especially this time of year, so the guards could have driven right past them and not been alarmed. Now, we have the guards on the lookout, but we're one step behind what the perpetrators might do next. There are miles and miles of country roads out here and lots of places to hide. We just don't know how they're staying so well hidden."

Merit looked sympathetic but was angry underneath. "The fire here was the first one?"

"Yes, it's a whole new level of terrorization. It cuts into the profits to deal with these heavy losses and it's expensive to clean up and replant."

Ag scratched his chin. "And, you've never had anything like this happen until just this year?"

Lane nodded. "Right."

"How did you get into the business?"

Lane took on the look of someone remembering a long story. "Marijuana use in Texas started off as part of a hippie culture before it was taken over by big money. There are still some hidden crops around, but legal cultivation has turned into a money-making machine for those who bought CBD and/or medical marijuana growth permits. We were lucky to get both types of licenses early, but then the legislature clamped down on any new medical marijuana ones for a long time. Now, with additional licenses coming online soon, every farmer and wannabe farmer in the state, and some out of the state, have come out of the woodwork to try and get their hands on them."

Merit looked at Ag. "Senator Linden is trying to keep farming in Texas under control and she supports increasing the licenses to mostly existing farmers in lieu of out-of-state strangers swooping in and taking over the industry."

Ag swept his arm wide. "This farm is vast. I can't see from end to end. How many buildings are on your property?"

Lane pointed out a big picture window. "Over that way is the greenhouse and open fields. Over there is the bunkhouse and supervisor's quarters. There are drying sheds and barns along the back of the property that way. Our goal is to start and cycle through as many crops per year as possible to keep overhead down and income up. Still, it's a lean margin and we have to watch every dime. Vandalism can cut deeply into our profits, especially if it slows crop production. We also have cattle and they're moved between the fields that aren't cultivated with hemp."

Gladys, who had been quiet, obviously thinking of her boys, came to life for a moment. "Once, a cow had gotten around the cattle guard and into one of the drying sheds. It chowed down on some prime cannabis, and by the time the twins had chased her out of the building, she was so stoned she could barely walk and kept falling over and getting up again."

Merit and Ag laughed, until the memory of the twins brought tears to Gladys' eyes, and their faces became somber again. Lane got up and went to his wife's chair, stood behind it, and put his hands on her shoulders. Merit and Ag, feeling they'd overstayed their welcome, rose and began to make their way to the front door. Gladys stayed seated at the table while Lane escorted them out.

Lane and Ag shook hands. "Thank you for your time. I know it's tough right now."

Lane looked worn out. "We'll be back at the hospital later tonight, if anything else comes up."

At that moment, Ag's phone screen indicated a 911 text message and he turned to Merit. "I better address this."

While Merit lingered and said goodbye to her client, Ag stepped outside and returned the call. When Merit followed Ag out, Lane retreated inside and closed the door. Ag relayed the news.

"It's my man at the hospital. Something's happened. We better get down there."

Merit looked back at the door. "Should we alert the Lanes?"

Ag looked stricken. "It sounds bad, but I don't have details."

Merit nodded gravely. "Then, let's let the doctors talk to them when appropriate."

10

———

Merit and Ag went immediately to the hospital, where Ag dropped her at the front door and went to park. Merit's heart raced as she rushed through the sterile corridors, anxious to reach the intensive care unit where the twin brothers were being treated. A man wearing a hospital security uniform was standing at the door, not Ag's guard.

Ag walked in a few moments later and looked around for his security guard. He started down the hall to find him. "Let me get with my guy for a briefing and I'll fill you in after."

Merit nodded. "Thanks."

Merit went into the family waiting room while Ag inquired about his man at the reception desk. When he found the guard, a burly man with a stern demeanor, he bore an expression that was grim and troubled.

"Ag, I left for less than five minutes for the toilet. I asked hospital security to spell me, and he promised to stand at the door until I returned. When I got back, he was gone and a doctor I hadn't seen before was fiddling with the wires and tubing."

Merit came down the hall, joined the conversation, and heard the last of the report. Merit and Ag exchanged alarmed glances. Merit's voice trembled. "Did you try to stop him? Did you call for help?"

The guard looked like he'd failed a test. "By the time I confronted him, the monitors were going crazy, beeping and flashing. The intruder ran out and real doctors came running in yelling 'code blue.'"

"Did you try to find him?"

"Yes, after the doctors took over, I searched this floor, but didn't see him again. There are a million places in this hospital he could hide. I thought I should get back here and make sure he didn't return. That's when I texted you."

"What are you doing here now?"

"After I made sure we had coverage on the door, I came to view the security tapes."

Ag nodded. "We'll talk about it later. Go back to your post at the door and I'll get someone to spell you. Don't rely on hospital security. Coverage might be redundant, but we can't take any chances with them. After that, you can check the security tapes and see if you recognize the perp or can see where he went."

Glad for a task and for someone to take charge, the guard said, "Will do."

Lane and Gladys came rushing down the corridor, past reception, and ran into the intensive care area. "Someone called us. What's happened?"

Merit and Ag left reception, stood outside the open door of the hospital room, and eavesdropped as inconspicuously as possible. Classmates of the twins huddled behind them with horror-stricken faces. The young students had started a daily vigil since the boys were hospitalized. Some wore Buffaloes football jerseys bearing Brad and Thad's numbers, others cheerleader uniforms, all trying to process the situation, dealing with sadness and disbelief. The news of the accident that had brought Brad and Thad to this place had spread like the arsonist's wildfire, leaving their community in distress. Even more important to the Giddings community was the fact that the boys had a choice whether to go to Giddings or Bastrop High School. They'd both chosen their father's alma mater, and played for the Buffaloes.

One of the nurses turned to the parents, her expression grave and voice strained. "We're not sure yet. It seems that someone tampered with the tubes connected to the IVs. We're doing all we can to stabilize both boys. A hospital administrator is on his way down now."

Lane hung his head. "We should never have left them."

The nurse tried to comfort them. "There were people everywhere. You're not to blame."

A few moments later, hospital security gathered up all of the students and took them to the elevator with the plan of putting them in the main downstairs waiting area.

Merit turned to Ag. "Who would do such a thing?"

Ag put his arm around her shoulders. "This is far worse than we feared. I'll stay here until my additional security people arrive. My crew is small, but I contract with a local security service. They're top notch and can come in on a moment's notice. I'll also ask hospital security for some extra coverage. They're probably already arranging it."

As the medical team worked tirelessly to save Brad and Thad, Merit and Ag stood by helplessly, vowing to find whoever was responsible for the treacherous act. As the world outside continued to spin, those who loved the twins could only wait and pray for a miracle that might never come.

Prince, in his doctor disguise, exited the hospital through the laundry area. When he reached the uplifted doors at the dock, he shucked the white jacket, pulled out his shirt tail, and mussed his dreadlocks loose from the band. He stepped out into the Austin sunshine as if nothing at all had happened.

Prince hoped he had done enough to get rid of both witnesses. He had spent plenty of time on the first twin's IV, the sicker one with the gauze on his face. But he only had a couple of seconds on the second boy's medical trappings. Maybe it would be enough. If not, he could always try again.

That was fun.

Upstairs, in the sterile, fluorescent-lit hospital room, the air was thick with despair as the twins lay side by side in their hospital beds. Thad lay motionless, his face pale and peaceful, but his breaths shallow and erratic. The tubes and wires that snaked from his body still connected to machines that continued to monitor his fragile state.

Beside him, Brad's bed was eerily still. His once vibrant blue eyes were now closed forever, his chest unmoving. The steady beep of the heart monitor beside him had flatlined, signaling his departure from this world. Brad and Thad, once inseparable twins, now found themselves alone, one in the world of his unconsciousness, and one in an unknown heavenly place where they may or may not reunite.

In the silence of the room, the only sound was the soft whirring of medical equipment and the muffled sobs of the Lanes, gathered nearby. Brad's parents stood at his bedside; their grief palpable as they clung to each other for support.

Merit and Ag stood in the hallway, shock showing on their faces. A nurse stayed in the room; her expression solemn as she monitored Thad's vital signs. With a heavy heart, she shook her head, knowing that Thad's fight was far from over and that he could follow his brother at any moment.

11

Merit approached the Texas State Capitol, the largest in the United States, and marveled at its grandeur of Renaissance revival architecture, a massive three-story structure comprised of red Texas granite. She took a long stroll through the rotunda, a spectacle of white Texas limestone, with the famous Texas star in the middle of the dome above her head. As she passed into the east wing, and entered the office of Senator Paige Linden, she continued to marvel at the wooded interiors as she reported her arrival to the receptionist.

"Please take a seat. She'll be right with you."

In a few moments, Lindy came out of her office and greeted Merit warmly. She invited her into the inner sanctum, more heavily wooded, with floor-to-ceiling windows and the seal of Texas on every possible surface.

"Thank you for seeing me on short notice."

Lindy pointed to a guest chair before her desk, with the seal of Texas across the tanned leather back, of course. Both women sat. "Not at all. How are the Lane children?"

"Unfortunately, the Lanes lost Brad this morning."

Lindy's hand flew to her mouth. "Oh no. I'm so sorry."

"Thad is hanging on by a thread."

"How tragic."

"Yes, the situation is far worse than it first appeared. Someone may have intentionally tried to end the boys' lives again at the hospital. We've beefed up security."

Lindy composed herself. "Good Lord. What can I do to help?"

"My investigator has put together a picture of increasing vandalism and destruction on and near the Lanes' farm. He's been able to isolate the incidents to the Bastrop and Fayette County areas, so far. All the victims have been cannabis farmers or landowners leasing land to cannabis growers. Since I represent the Lane family farm and the grower's co-op that they belong to, I'm organizing an investigation with my in-house PI."

"Good."

"We're in the process of compiling a list of which cannabis farmers have not been targeted. We hope there's a pattern."

"That doesn't mean that the untouched farms are the homes of the perpetrators."

"Of course not, but it might give us an idea who to focus on."

"I see."

"It would help if we knew who had license applications pending for approval in the next round of permits."

"You know I can't divulge that. Your client would have an unfair advantage in the process."

"I don't see how. It will be public information soon enough." Merit was fudging with the facts, and she knew it.

"But, not yet. I can't help you with that. Isn't there something else I can do?"

"Yes, you can speak with the senator from District 18,

covering Fayette County. Maybe he has an idea about what's going on in his territory. We have not been able to compile information from that area as easily since I have no clients over there and they have not formed a co-op that we know of."

"That I can do. I know Senator Jacobson very well. We're neighbors at home and here. His office is right next door. He's also pro cannabis farming. He's of the Bill Murray school of thought. Legalize cannabis in all fifty states, use the taxes to repair roads and highways, and call it Operation Pothole."

Merit laughed although she'd seen the comment on Facebook several times. "Great. Glad to hear we have some support for the growers."

"To an extent. I'm sure you're aware that Senator Robert Ersery, from Dallas, is hell-bent on closing down the permitting process again as we did in 2019."

"Yes, I'm aware, but I thought the political tides were turning."

"They are, but they can turn back. It would be a shame, and I'm doing all I can to open up the industry to further development."

"Thank you."

"I'll reach out and let you know if anything similar is going on over in Fayette County. I can also introduce your investigator to someone at the LaGrange Police Department. Would that help?"

"Very likely, yes. One more thing."

"Listening."

"The Lanes have even more need for approval of their application for new growth licenses. I want to assure you that the loss of one field and greenhouse will not affect their ability to deliver product under the new permits. Their farm supervisor has already started rebuilding their greenhouse, and they have other fields currently under cultivation that remain healthy. Please don't let the committee be swayed to diminish their chances when we eventually arrive at a vote. Don't kick a man while he's down."

"I understand. I'll keep an eye on things. For now, I'll send over that contact info."

Merit rose to leave and shook hands with Lindy, who stood as well. "Thank you, Senator."

She turned toward the door and ran into a young man coming in with an armful of files.

"Merit Bridges, meet Stuart Lawton, my legislative aide on all things marijuana and hemp related."

Lawton juggled the stack of files to attempt a handshake, shrugged, and said, "Pleasure to meet you. Just call me the weed whisperer."

Merit laughed. "Looks like you've got your hands full there."

Lindy smiled at Merit. "Stuart is currently researching the widening gap between federal and state marijuana legislation. You may have read that the DEA is set to reschedule cannabis from a Schedule 1 drug to a Schedule 3 drug. It would no longer be classified with deadly drugs like heroin and methamphetamines—those with high potential for addiction, abuse, and little or no medical uses."

Lawton chimed in. "Texas has traditionally followed federal guidelines, but with these changes the legislature may leave marijuana where it is. The two laws would conflict. I'm trying to write up a report for the senator about the gap between the two."

Merit had some knowledge of the proposed regulatory changes but hadn't considered the issues that would be created between state and federal statutes. "Will you introduce legislation to change the state classification?"

"That's what we're looking into. I need Stuart's research to make an informed decision."

"Well, I better let you get to work then. I'll look for that information on LaGrange PD."

"Right. Thanks, Merit."

"No, thank you, Lindy."

When she arrived back at her office, Merit received the text from Senator Linden's assistant with the contact information for the chief of police of LaGrange. The text indicated that the senator had made an introduction, and that Ag was expected and needed no appointment.

It's not what you know, it's who you know. At least in Texas.

Merit forwarded the information to Ag and asked him to go over and see if the chief could shed any light on the issues of vandalism in Fayette County.

Ag drove to LaGrange that afternoon and checked in at LPD.

"I'm here to see Chief Troy. I think he's expecting me."

"May I have your name, Sir?"

"Ag Malone."

The woman's demeanor shifted, and she looked at the door in the foyer behind her. "Chief Troy is out, but I've been instructed to put you in touch with Officer Twitty. If you'll have a seat, I'll call him in for you. He's out in his cruiser right now."

"No need to disturb him. Please let him know I'm at the coffee shop on the square when he gets back."

"I'll be happy to."

Ag could read people like a book and when he thought

something was hinky, it usually was. He also knew that the fastest way to get the skinny on what was going on in a town was to hang out at the local diner and listen.

Ag wanted to inquire deeply into the vandalism in Fayette County. It seemed to be a mere trifling compared to what was going on in Bastrop County, just a half hour's drive away. Why was that?

Ag nodded politely, left the police station, and walked over to the Town Square Cafe. He pushed open the door, the bell above it jingling softly. The place was cozy, filled with the rich aroma of frying bacon, fresh brew, and the low hum of conversation. He garnered a casual once over from a few local patrons who seemed satisfied with his boots and jeans and went back to minding their own business.

He spotted an empty stool at the counter and made his way over, sliding onto it with a sigh.

"Morning, hon. What can I get ya?" A young waitress in a short uniform with a nametag that read "Brandy" greeted him with a bright smile.

"Just coffee, thanks. Black. And maybe a little information."

Brandy nodded and turned to grab a mug from the shelf. As she poured the steaming liquid, Ag noticed her glancing around nervously. "I'm not supposed to gossip, but what do you need to know?"

Ag assumed she was bucking for a nice tip. "I hear there's a lot of hemp and marijuana being grown around here. Know anything about that?"

"You a cop? DEA?"

Ag laughed using his typical charm and shook his head. He

paused, taking a cautious sip of the hot coffee. "Nope. Just a curious sort. Might buy some land around here."

"Well." Brandy began, her eyes sparkling with the thrill of sharing news with a stranger. "The police got a tip that Old Man Jenkins was growing medical marijuana on his property. So, they organized this big raid, rolled up in a bunch of cruisers, all serious and ready to bust him."

Ag raised an eyebrow, intrigued. "And did they?"

Brandy laughed, a light, melodious sound that filled the diner. "Not exactly. Turns out, Jenkins was growing hemp, not marijuana. I heard they felt pretty silly once they figured it out."

Ag chuckled, shaking his head. "Bet the local authorities didn't like that."

"Not one bit," Brandy confirmed, her smile widening. "They had egg on their faces, that's for sure. Jenkins was mad as a hornet, too. He said it was politically motivated by some big growers trying to get the best of the little guys. The whole town's been buzzing about it ever since."

Ag took another sip of his coffee, the warmth spreading through him. "Sounds like I've been missing all the excitement."

Brandy shrugged, a playful glint in her eyes. "Small towns, you know? We take our entertainment where we can get it."

Ag nodded, appreciating the humor in her words. "Thanks for the coffee, Brandy. And the story."

"Anytime," she replied, giving him a wink before turning to greet another customer.

Ag moved to a booth in the corner, and after about twenty minutes, a tall, lanky man in a police uniform walked in. His eyes scanned the room before landing on Ag. With a slow, deliberate stride, he made his way over.

"Mr. Malone?" the officer asked, extending a hand.

"Ag," he replied, shaking it firmly. "You must be Officer Twitty."

"That's right," Twitty said, taking a seat across from him. "Chief Troy sends his apologies. He got called out on an urgent matter."

"No problem. I'm looking into the recent incidents of vandalism in Fayette County. Senator Linden thought your department might have some useful insights."

Twitty leaned back, crossing his arms. "Well, vandalism's always a nuisance. But nothing out of the ordinary for a place like Fayette County."

"Really?" Ag raised an eyebrow. "I've heard it's been a lot worse here lately and wanted to compare it to the upturn in Bastrop County. Maybe establish a pattern of some sort. Can you give me some specifics?"

Twitty's eyes flickered, a slight hesitation before he spoke. "We've had a few incidents. Graffiti, some broken windows, that sort of thing. Small-town stuff."

Ag scribbled in his notebook, then looked up. "How many incidents, exactly?"

Twitty shrugged, his evasiveness becoming more apparent. "I'd have to check the reports to give you an exact number. But, like I said, it's not been anything we can't handle."

Ag nodded slowly. "That's interesting. Because Bastrop's seen a significant uptick in vandalism. Almost seems like a coordinated effort. Any chance it's the same here?"

"Couldn't say," Twitty replied, his tone carefully neutral. "Each county has its own issues. What happens in Bastrop doesn't necessarily spill over into Fayette."

Ag watched him closely, sensing there was more beneath the surface. "It just seems odd. Two neighboring counties, one with a spike in vandalism and the other claiming business as usual. Mind if I take a look at those reports?"

Twitty stiffened slightly. "I'll have to clear that with the chief. But I can tell you, there's nothing in them that points to anything unusual."

"Sure," Ag said, a nonchalant smile playing on his lips. "I'll wait to hear from Chief Troy, then. In the meantime, any patterns you've noticed? Specific targets? Anything calling medical marijuana or hemp growing into the equation?"

Twitty shook his head. "Nothing that stands out. Random spots mostly. Like I said, typical small-town stuff."

"Alright," Ag said, closing his notebook. "Thanks for your time, Officer Twitty. Here's my card if you think of anything else."

Twitty nodded, standing up. "I'll keep it in mind."

As Twitty left, Ag couldn't shake the feeling that the officer was hiding something. He sipped his coffee, deep in thought. Whatever was going on in Fayette County, it was clear that getting to the bottom of it would take more than just a few casual conversations, or even a call from a senator.

12

———

M erit, working in her office, was determined to catch up on the stack of files that Betty had left for her the night before. Merit heard a tap at the door and turned to see Val, her law clerk, standing outside the office sheepishly waiting for permission to enter.

"Val, what is it? You're not usually shy about coming in here."

"May I speak to you for a moment about something personal?"

"Sure, have a seat." Val closed the door behind him and sat in one of the guest chairs, looking more like a client than her law clerk.

"My grandmother is having some problems that I hope you can help us with."

"I don't have a lot of time today, Val, but let me hear what's bothering you and we'll see if and how I can help."

Val had been Merit's paralegal, turned law clerk when he started law school, for many years and she really valued him.

He was a hard worker and was killer at research. He was an invaluable part of the firm, but she also genuinely liked him.

Merit flipped the top page of a legal pad over and took some notes.

"What's her name?"

"Constance Stanhope."

"Giddings, right?"

"Right. Just outside the city limits. I don't talk much about her, but my grandmother is a sweet woman. She suffers from a touch of dementia. We deal with it as a family and try to take care of her as best we can. She's still able to live alone and is very independent."

"Of course. I remember your speaking of her."

"I believe that someone is trying to steal her land. It's been in the family for years. The land was once farmland, but it's not cultivated anymore since my grandfather died. She has a small home on the property that looks like something out of the seventies, with avocado-green appliances and linoleum floors."

Merit nodded and smiled. She knew the type of home he was referencing. They were sprinkled all over the state.

"I don't know exactly what or who is involved, but something is definitely happening and I'm starting to become concerned for her. After what occurred at the Lanes' farm, I see the lengths that some people will go to get what they're after. I don't want something bad happening to my grandmother or her land."

"Okay. Has something specific happened? What's alerted you to the problem? People can't just steal land from others. It's not like you can pack it in a suitcase. You know notarized documentation has to be filed to transfer title to land and very specific laws followed."

"There's this contract."

Merit felt her stomach drop. Elderly people were constantly

getting scammed out of money or property due to signing something they didn't read, or thinking they were signing something when it turned out to be something entirely different.

"What contract? Tell me more."

"I don't know the specifics of it but after talking to my mother, she said she visited with Grands and it seems underhanded. I know this is what you do, Merit, so I'm asking for your help. The land is very important to us as a legacy, and my family does not want it to be sold. It's one of the very few large tracts still left around the perimeter of Austin."

"I understand. I would certainly like to see the contract."

"My mother and I are going to meet at Grands'. I'll pick it up then and bring it in for you to look at, if you're willing. I was hoping to tell them tonight that you'd agreed to take a look."

"I'll be glad to review it. Has anything been considered with regard to putting the land in trust or appointing a guardian ad litem for your grandmother's affairs?"

"My mother has been reluctant to challenge her mother's independence, but we may have to sooner than later. Did I ever tell you that back in her heyday my grandmother was married to Texas State Senator John Stanhope? She sometimes slips back in time and goes on and on about their love story and how smitten he was with her."

Merit looked up from her note taking and smiled. "Is that right? I think I remember the name."

Val nodded. "They acquired the land together. The two were inseparable until he died of cancer years ago. She never remarried or even dated anyone else. Sometimes I wonder if his early death was a good thing because he would have been so sad to see her slowly succumbing to dementia."

"I'm sorry, Val. There's nothing about that situation that is easy."

"Thank you. What do you think about the man trying to get her to sign a contract?"

"Well, I would like to look into it a little further, but I'd guess these people are trying to acquire the land so that they can use it for development, either real estate or oil. These types of people may use unscrupulous ways to get whatever they want. Money is never an object to them, and they certainly don't worry about morals."

"What should I do?"

"Get the contract and we'll go from there."

"Will do."

He left the office and Betty entered with a cup of tea, light with milk. She set it on the desk. "Is everything okay with Val?"

"I'm not sure yet. It's his grandmother. Someone may be trying to take advantage of her. I'm going to check it out."

"If they are, you give them a good talkin' to."

"Yes, ma'am."

13

The cemetery was shrouded in a heavy summer drizzle, casting a gray pall over the already somber scene. The family plot on the Lanes' farm was surrounded by a waist-high black metal fence with points at the top of each stake. It was obvious that there had not been a funeral there in a while as most of the headstones were aged, and the ground undisturbed, except for the plot dug for Brad. The closed mahogany coffin was held above the ground by straps stretched between metal poles over the dark hole in the earth. A spray of Texas grasses and wildflowers was spread over the casket, starting to bead with raindrops. Only the immediate family could fit inside the fence, but the surrounding meadow was filled with mourners, most hiding under umbrellas and trying to stay out of the increasing drizzle and resultant mud.

Brad's funeral drew a crowd that seemed to stretch on endlessly through the field, a testament to the profound impact he had on the tight-knit community. Obviously missing from the crowd was Thad, still in the hospital and fighting for his life. The thought that the mourners might have to do this ritual again, if Thad died, added to the cloak of grief that held them in darkness.

The pain was felt most deeply by Brad's parents. Mother and father stood side by side, their grief palpable in the air around them. Lane, usually a pillar of strength, now seemed to falter under the weight of their loss. Gladys, her eyes brimming with tears, leaned into her husband for support, their hands intertwined in a silent gesture of solidarity. Lane's free arm was stretched around the shoulder of their daughter, Cameron. She looked straight ahead, unblinking and without emotion, her face a blank slate of shock. Her naive youth diminishing her ability to process what was happening around her.

Among the mourners just outside the fence stood Merit, Betty, and Ag. Sadness and compassion for the Lanes frozen on their faces. Senator Linden walked into the group and shook hands with a few of the other dignitaries, who were in attendance, before taking her place at the other edge of the fence. She and Merit exchanged a surreptitious nod.

Brad's schoolmates stood a few yards back in silence, their expressions etched with grief, as they struggled to come to terms with the loss of their friend. His fellow football players and coaches were wearing their team jerseys, their usually confident demeanor now replaced by expressions of profound sadness. They had fought alongside him on the field, their bonds forged in the shared tradition of competition and camaraderie. The cheerleaders, too, stood among the mourners, their pompoms missing and forgotten, as they grappled with the reality of a world without Brad's infectious enthusiasm.

Even the debate team, usually so focused on the art of argumentation, found themselves at a loss for words in the face of such a devastating circumstance. Brad had been one of them. Many thought he'd grow up to be a fine lawyer, or maybe a congressman, or both. The team stood together, their heads bowed in silent reverence, a testament to the universality of grief that transcended school cliques and social circles.

As the service began to unfold, a hushed reverence settled over the crowd, broken only by the occasional sob that escaped unchecked. A voice rose from the sea of mourners. It was a voice trembling with emotion but determined to be heard. It was one of Brad's debate teammates, a young man whose name was lost to Merit in the blur of tears and sorrow. He stepped forward tentatively, his gaze fixed on the casket before him, his words a fragile offering in the face of overwhelming grief, his voice wavering but resolute.

"Brad was more than just a friend. He was a beacon of light in a world that often feels dark and unwelcoming. He was the kind of person who made you believe in goodness, even when everything around you seemed to be falling apart. His laugh was infectious and easily given."

As he spoke, memories of Brad flooded back to the crowd. They remembered his laughter ringing out across the school halls, his unwavering determination on the football field, and the countless lives he had touched in both big and small ways.

"Although he may be gone from this world," the young man continued, his voice breaking with emotion, "his spirit will live on in each and every one of us. We carry his memory with us, a guiding light in the darkness, a reminder of the power of love and friendship to transcend even the deepest of sorrows."

With those words, the crowd stood united in their grief, their hearts heavy but their spirits lifted by the memory of a young man who had left an indelible mark on their lives. And as they said their final goodbyes, they did so not with despair, but with a quiet sense of gratitude for having known and loved Brad, if only for a fleeting moment in time.

As the crowd dispersed, Merit, Ag, and Betty walked down the path to the area where the cars were parked. Ag walked between them and took Merit and Betty's hands on each side. Betty choked out, "Only the good die young."

With that, Merit let the first tear escape and her lips parted in a quiet gasp of grief.

Merit, Betty, and Ag drove up to the Lanes' home in Merit's car for the funeral reception, leaving Ag's pickup near the pasture by the graveyard. Upon entering the living room, Merit saw several of the waiters from Pot Luck. She had not realized they would be catering the event. She hoped against hope that Patrick was not present, or at least would be in the kitchen preparing food. She circumvented the room carefully, looking for her client, but also preparing herself for the possible encounter with Patrick. When he walked into the room, carrying a tray and directing his staff to the setup of a long table, laden with a selection of food, he caught Merit's eye. They exchanged a cordial nod and returned to their tasks. Merit glanced at Ag, and he looked irritated as he stared at Patrick. Betty held her counsel but did not appear surprised. When Patrick looked back at Merit, Betty gave him the side eye. They weren't fooling her one bit.

Merit walked away from Betty and Ag toward the Lane family, putting some distance between herself and them. Did Ag suspect that she was involved with Patrick? He was acting odd, but she couldn't imagine how he would know. Betty probably knew. She always was one step ahead. It was none of their business, so why did she feel so guilty? Merit tried not to think about it as she approached John and Gladys.

Across the room, Ag whispered in Betty's ear, "Let Merit know I need to leave. I'll see you at the office tomorrow."

Betty looked at Ag with sympathy and understanding. She

knew he had fallen for Merit and seeing her interested in another man was hard to take, so Betty didn't try to stop him, and joined Merit, Gladys, and John.

Lane looked at Merit, his gaze like stone. "We need to find these people, Merit. That was my boy. I won't let them get away with this."

"They won't. I'll do everything that I can to help."

"They murdered my son over marijuana."

"Over money. Not that it's any better. Brad was a fine young man." Merit felt lame as she said the words.

"I don't know how I'm going to tell Thad when he wakes up, if he wakes up. They were inseparable. He didn't even get to say goodbye."

Tears welled up in Merit's eyes. She could not imagine what John was going through. If anything ever happened to Ace, she didn't think that she would be able to go on. Losing her husband, Tony, was enough. Her empathy for the Lane family was limitless.

At the edge of the driveway, Ag accepted a golf cart ride to the far end of the Lanes' farm where his pickup was parked on the roadside. He thanked and tipped the driver, who left to shuttle another attendee. Ag took out his keys to open his door, but his thoughts were focused on Merit. He knew she had a new boy toy and that it wouldn't be the last, but it didn't make it any easier for him to know that it was probably a fling.

Since Tony's death, Merit had not invested true emotion into any relationship as far as Ag knew, and he knew most, if not all. He tortured himself by keeping track of her boy toys, partially to protect her and partially because he could not stop himself. He was humiliated that Betty knew of his feelings for

Merit, but they rarely discussed it. Each of their natures prohibited being disloyal to Merit by talking about her private life behind her back. Besides, what would it change?

Why won't Merit play with me? She seems to play with everyone else.

That wasn't really fair. She was very selective and most of the time discreet, because of the differences in ages between herself and the men she selected.

He'd tried often enough to play with Merit, but even as he asked the question, Ag knew why she would not go out with him. If they ever came together, there would be no turning back to friendship and camaraderie. It would be everlasting love, or nothing at all. If it ended, they'd never see each other again. It would be too painful.

Ag, preoccupied with his thoughts, pulled open the truck door into the road and, in his absentminded state, put himself in the path of an oncoming speeding vehicle. Ag jumped out of the way just in time to avoid the collision and turned to see a gray SUV whose driver didn't try to stop. Through the back windshield of the vehicle, there appeared to Ag to be a lone driver, a cascade of dreadlocks showing above the headrest.

Ag quickly focused on the license plate, seeing only that it was a Texas plate, black and white, with four and six as the last two numbers. Ag remembered Thad's statement to his ambulance attendants that the arsonist looked like Bob Marley. *Dreadlocks.*

Ag jumped in his truck, did a quick U-turn, and headed in the direction of the fleeing SUV. Ag drove as fast as he could over the bumpy, unpaved road and gained on the vehicle ahead. He strained to see through the flying white dust from the caliche, but could not see any more of the license plate or the type of vehicle he was following. He sped to catch up, but the faster he drove, the faster the vehicle in front of him moved.

Ag and his prey eventually reached a stop sign at the intersection of the caliche and paved roads. The driver ahead of him stopped, got out of his vehicle, and walked back toward Ag with a shotgun over his arm. Ag instinctively placed his hand on the console that contained his Glock 19, but didn't remove it. Instincts told him not to.

The man was an old codger, obviously from the country, and driving a black pickup truck, not a gray SUV. Ag had been following the wrong vehicle.

Ag rolled down the window, and the codger leaned in. "What are you doing riding on my tail like that? You could have killed us both. Does anybody follow the law on this road anymore?"

"I'm so sorry. I didn't realize. I'm so sorry." Ag couldn't manage any further excuse. "Did you see a gray SUV?"

"He almost mowed me down before you did the same. What business is it of yours, anyway?"

"I'm sorry. I thought you were that SUV."

"Don't let it happen again. My neighbors don't take kindly to aggressive driving. The next stop might be your last."

The old man walked back to his truck, got in, hung the shotgun on the gun rack, put on his blinker, sat a moment longer, then turned right onto the feeder road.

Ag didn't move for a full minute.

Prince had seen Ag, whom he did not know, getting into his truck by the road at the funeral gathering. Prince knew he wasn't going to hit him, but it was fun giving the guy a scare. He was joyriding to celebrate his win in finishing off Brad at the hospital. He had been driving up and down the road for hours, watching the sad-faced mourners park and leave their cars and head up to the cemetery plot for the funeral of his victim. To them it was a somber event, to him it was a party.

"One down, one to go." He cranked up the music in his gray SUV. He loved the vibe of Babyxsosa. Her moody tunes mixed with her unmistakable rap style blared out from his playlist, fitting the occasion perfectly.

Prince was surprised to see the pickup truck make a U-turn and start to follow him. He sped up, kicking up as much caliche dust as possible. He watched behind him, the truck was a ways back but still coming. Prince swerved back and forth in the road until he came up behind another vehicle in his lane, a black pickup truck. He stayed on the truck's tail, continuing to swerve, creating as much camouflage dust as possible. At a wide spot in the road, he dove around the black truck, almost putting it in the ditch and sped away in a cloud of white caliche.

The driver of the truck raised a fist in the air, the country version of flipping the bird, but Prince didn't see it. He was long gone and headed back to Austin. Ag unknowingly took his place, following and further irritating the old codger until they both stopped at the intersection of the paved road.

The next day, Val knocked on the door of Merit's office. He had a manila file folder in his hands.

"Is this a good time?"

"Sure, take a seat."

Val settled in and pulled a document out of the file. "This is the contract that my grandmother received from the guy who said he wanted to buy her land in Lee County."

He passed over the contract and Merit flipped through it. Her brow furrowed. She perused the last page and was relieved to see that it was not executed.

"Is this the original?"

"Yes."

"So, she didn't sign another copy?"

"She said she didn't."

"Do you know who brought it over?"

"Just some guy. She can't remember his name and he didn't leave a card. As you can see, there's no name on the contract for the buyer, yet."

"Yes. Just a blank to be filled in. That seems fishy." Something was definitely not right.

"Thought so, too."

"Until I meet with her, make sure she doesn't speak to him further, and especially that she doesn't sign anything."

"I've already told my mother to keep an eye on her, but I'll warn them again. Sad to have to monitor her. My grandmother was such a dynamo in her day. So full of life. Even though she's old fashioned, she's never judged me or my lifestyle choices."

Merit smiled. "Your biggest fan?"

Val nodded. "Something like that. She paved the way with the rest of the family when I came out."

"Have you considered moving her into a relative's home or having someone live with her?"

"Yes, but she won't have it. She stopped talking to my mother for weeks when last it was discussed."

Merit looked back at the contract. "Well, I would like to look into this a little further. I need to read this thoroughly and get back with you. May I keep this?"

"Of course."

"My guess is that these people are trying to acquire the land so they can use it for development. If that's the case, they can make her an offer and she can reject it, but once they tie her up in a contract, they can sue her for specific performance. In other words, force her to sign the full contract and sell under the agreement. Once she signs, it's difficult to prove they defrauded her without going to court. It probably wouldn't hold up, but it could be an expensive fight."

"So, it's a contract to make a contract. She may not be able to testify to anything she did. She probably wouldn't remember."

"I understand. I'd like to speak to your grandmother myself. It is her land and she's the one that's had direct dealings with these people, so I need to hear it from her. You can talk to Betty about my availability and pick a time that works best for her to come in."

"Absolutely. Thank you so much. I'll get Grands' schedule and set it up as soon as possible. Thank you so much."

"No problem. Let's start with the meeting. I might do a little digging on my own until then, but I want to see what your grandmother has to say before we proceed."

He left the office and Betty entered with a cup of tea. She set it on the desk. "Is everything okay with Val?"

"I'm not sure yet. We'll have to see. He'll be setting up an appointment. Make it sooner than later."

Betty winced. "More trouble around here than you can shake a stick at."

Merit looked back at the file she was already working on, but something about Val's desperation made her prioritize his file instead. She opened a new email, put in Ag's address, and called out to Betty.

"Would you come back in here, please."

Betty entered the office. "What's up?"

"Would you scan this and email it to me and copy Ag?"

"Need it now?"

"Yes, please."

Betty laughed. "I aim to please. You must be worried."

"I am a little. Thank you. Hopefully, Ag can help me sort it out."

Betty took the contract from her and went down the hall to the copy room which was also the scanner room, the office supply room, and the cleaning supplies room. Small office, expensive rent per square foot.

Merit returned her attention to the email and typed a note asking Ag to research the chain of title of the Stanhope property in the property records in Lee County. She emphasized that he also track the oil and gas history, any leases, units that may have been formed, current state of availability for leasing, and so forth. She indicated that Betty would be forwarding a property description attached to an unexecuted contract via separate email.

Status: Urgent!

15

Merit and Red went for a short run around Lady Bird Lake then cut through downtown Austin and took a turn around the Texas State Capitol. It was a sultry night until the heat broke when the sun went down. As the season shifted into full summer heat, they were running later and later when it was cooler.

Merit saw lightning in the distance and looked up at the sky. "Is it supposed to rain?"

Red followed her gaze. "I checked the KNEW 9 site. It's storming over near Dripping Springs, but it should be clear here until around midnight."

When they reached the Congress side of the Capitol, they slowed to a walk to cool down. Merit looked up at the east wing. The uplighting and landscaping made the entire campus look beautiful.

Red admired it. "I never get tired of looking at the architecture."

"Neither do I. I hope Senator Linden is up there working on the Lanes' file."

Red laughed. "You think she is?"

Merit laughed. "Maybe, but I think she has a lot more on her plate than cannabis licenses."

"We're lucky to have her. One of the last truly principled holdouts in the Senate."

"I don't agree with all of her politics, but I've grown to admire her more over the years."

As the women turned on Eleventh Street toward the Governor's Mansion, they noticed what appeared to be a homeless man standing at the end of the long sidewalk, just outside the black wrought iron gates of the Capitol grounds.

The man set up a cardboard sign featuring a large cross, on a makeshift easel, with writing that was illegible, and pulled a book from his knapsack.

As the women walked on, and the wind began to whip up, the homeless man started to preach. His long, hooded rain cape swirled out as he turned 180 degrees from the majestic building and faced Congress Avenue. He raised an arm skyward, his hand holding a version of the King James Bible.

The women turned back to see what he was up to.

"Ladies and gentlemen of Texas, saved Christians and lost souls, I say to you the time has come to reclaim our state from the darkness that threatens to engulf us!" The preacher's voice boomed through the chilly evening air, carried by a gust of wind that sent his cape billowing again. Dark clouds gathering above seemed to echo his ominous tone, as if nature itself were lending credence to his words. Locals and sightseers, who were out on the town, began to gather and listen.

With fervor burning in his eyes, he scanned the crowd gathered before him, a congregation of both believers and skeptics, drawn in by the spectacle unfolding outside the seat of power. He also surveyed the Capitol building behind him, appearing paranoid about any security or police that might appear.

"For too long, we've allowed corruption to fester within these hallowed halls!" His voice rose, punctuated by the crack of thunder in the distance. "But I tell you now, my brothers and sisters, we hold the power to cleanse this land of its sins! We hold the power to restore righteousness and justice to our beloved Texas!"

His message carried a weight that resonated with many, tapping into their fears and frustrations, while simultaneously kindling a flame of hope for change. Others blew him off and walked on by to the nearest bar or tourist destination. Red, who was always looking for a new angle on a story, took out her phone and shot a video of the preacher man.

"You going to broadcast that?" Merit looked incredulous.

"Probably not. But I catch footage all over town. Never know when something might fit in with another story."

"We will not be swayed by the temptations of greed and deceit," the man proclaimed, his voice unwavering in its conviction. "Together, we will stand firm against the forces of darkness that seek to divide us! Together, we will reclaim our state and usher in a new era of righteousness and prosperity!"

The preacher's gaze hardened, his brow furrowing. "And let us not forget the insidious influence of the devil's weed, marijuana, that the state has sanctioned for growth within our borders!" he thundered, brandishing the Bible as if it were a weapon against the perceived moral decay. "We must reject this perversion of God's creation, this poison that dulls the mind and weakens the spirit!"

The preacher's condemnation of marijuana struck a chord with some, tapping into deep-seated religious beliefs about morality and righteousness. Most just watched out of curiosity without agreeing with the message. Austin, being a blue heart in the middle of a red state, mostly supported liberal thinking and cannabis use.

"Do not be deceived by the lies of those who would profit from our suffering," the preacher continued, his voice rising above the gathering storm. "We must resist the allure of easy pleasures and stand firm in our commitment to God's will! For only through righteousness and steadfastness can we hope to overcome the trials that beset us!"

With a final flourish, he raised his arm, the Bible held aloft like a beacon of hope that his message was heard. Lightning struck above the dome of the Capitol to punctuate the message. Apparently running out of steam, the preacher grabbed his makeshift easel and cardboard sign, then stood staring out into the crowd, in the direction of Merit and Red.

The crowd slowly dispersed, looking for the next interesting thing to observe and digest. Merit rolled her eyes at Red, and the two women walked on toward Merit's condo.

As the preacher's fervent sermon came to an end, and the rain started earlier than expected, he drifted away from the Capitol, carrying his sign and easel, his long rain cape flapping behind him. When he was out of sight, he made his way toward his sleek gray SUV parked at the curb of a side street. He threw the cardboard sign into the grass beside the sidewalk, removed a small electronic device from the top of the makeshift easel, and threw the pieces of wood on top of the sign.

Once inside the vehicle, the preacher's facade began to crack as he shed his disguise, revealing the true identity of the man beneath. He pushed his hood away from his face, exposing eyes that gleamed with a dangerous intelligence. With practiced ease, he removed a stocking cap, allowing his shock of dark dreadlocks to be loosened and exposed.

Prince glanced at his reflection in the rearview mirror. Gone was the guise of the homeless preacher, replaced by the cold, calculated visage of a man who lived by his own rules. With a sense of purpose driving him forward, he started the SUV and the engine roared to life.

As he merged into the flow of traffic, Prince's mind buzzed with thoughts of the mission ahead. He made some mental notes about the security at the Capitol, the various entrances he had reconnoitered, and the video cameras that were obvious and those that weren't so obvious. He planned to download the video from his hidden camera when he arrived at the temp house.

He would decide how the assignment was best served, and Blake Harrison could like it or lump it. There were rivals to be dealt with, enemies to be neutralized, and power to be seized. Only he knew by instinct and experience the necessary next move. And Prince was more than interested in the next step to ensure the success of their dark endeavors.

16

———

Merit had the television on the credenza in her office tuned to KNEW 9. She was awaiting the results of the vote by the Texas Senate on the expansion of the Texas Farm Bill that would allow for the increased licensure for growing medical marijuana in Texas. She had the sound on mute, but occasionally looked up to see if the results were in.

The house had already passed the bill, and it was expected to pass in the senate today, and be forwarded on to the governor for his signature, but Merit had learned not to count chickens. She looked up to check the screen again and saw Red Thallon standing in a hallway in the State Capitol with a microphone in her hand.

"Betty, it's on." Merit yelled toward the hallway, grabbed the remote, and turned the volume on and up.

Red spoke into the microphone and reported on the vote. "The Texas Senate is composed of thirty-one members who represent thirty-one separate geographical districts in the state. Today, twenty-four of these members voted to expand the licensure of medical marijuana in the state, marking a significant shift in Texas's agricultural and medical landscape.

"This bill, officially titled the Texas Agricultural and Medical Cannabis Act, seeks to increase the number of licenses available to farmers for the cultivation of medical marijuana. The expansion is aimed at providing more access to patients in need, promoting agricultural diversity, and boosting the state's economy through the burgeoning cannabis industry. Proponents of the bill argue that it will offer relief to patients suffering from chronic conditions, including epilepsy, cancer, and PTSD, while also creating new jobs and tax revenues for the state."

Betty came in and sat in one of the guest chairs. Merit rolled her desk chair to the side so Betty could see the screen.

Red continued. "Opponents, however, have raised concerns about the potential for increased recreational use and the challenges of regulating a rapidly growing industry. Despite these concerns, the Senate has followed the House's lead in endorsing the bill, which now moves to the governor's desk for final approval."

Onscreen, a group of senators streamed out of the chamber doors and into the hallway.

"And here comes one of the bill's primary advocates, Senator Paige Linden."

The camera panned to Senator Linden, exiting the chamber, striking as ever in a tan summer knee-length suit. Red swiftly approached her, microphone extended.

"Senator Linden! Red Thallon, KNEW 9. Can you share your thoughts on the passing of the Texas Agricultural and Medical Cannabis Act?"

Senator Linden smiled broadly, clearly elated. "Of course, Red. Today is a historic day for Texas. The passing of this bill is a huge step forward in supporting our farmers, our economy, and most importantly, our patients. We've worked tirelessly to ensure that this legislation addresses the needs of those who can benefit most from medical marijuana, and I'm thrilled that my colleagues have recognized the importance of this issue."

Red pressed further. "What do you say to those who are still skeptical about the expansion?"

Linden nodded thoughtfully. "I understand their concerns, and they are valid. That's why the bill includes stringent regulatory measures to monitor cultivation and distribution. We've also allocated funds for research and education to ensure that the implementation is as smooth and as safe as possible. This is about helping people, and I believe this legislation is a balanced approach that addresses both the opportunities and the challenges."

"Thank you, Senator Linden. Congratulations on the passage of the bill."

"Thank you, Red."

The camera returned to Red as she concluded. "There you have it. The act is one step away from becoming law. This is Red Thallon, KNEW 9, reporting live from the State Capitol."

Shortly after Red went off camera, Merit's phone rang.

"Hey, Red. She knows your name now."

Betty got up and gave Merit a wave and left the office. She had more important things to do than listen to the ladies' chatter.

Red laughed. "Imagine that. I must be big time now."

"Seriously, good job on the reporting, and great for my clients. They'll be tipping some bourbon tonight in Bastrop County."

"Cheers."

Merit, Lane, and the group of farmers known as the Bastrop County Growers' Co-op met at the Lanes' farm to celebrate the passage of the Farm Bill expanding medical marijuana licenses. Gladys was at the hospital with Thad, and Lane had his mobile phone in his denim shirt pocket, alert for any news. He had plenty of back-up hosts at the gathering and could leave at a moment's notice if anything changed in Thad's condition. The twin had been showing signs of improvement but had yet to regain consciousness. It was obviously not the best time to throw a party, but this was business and time would not wait for mourning or any other reason.

As the afternoon sun bathed the farm in a warm golden glow, the atmosphere buzzed with the chatter of excited guests. Huge kegs of ice-cold beer lined two tables on the wraparound porch. Stacks of red plastic cups stretched sky-high beside each keg. Several open tents with misting fans were set up where guests gathered to avoid the heat. Laughter and the sounds of Shinyribs playing under a gazebo in the adjacent side yard. The lyrics of "East TX Rust" provided a lively soundtrack to the gathering.

Senator Linden was the guest of honor. Most attendees knew her well enough to call her Lindy, which she encouraged. She wore cowboy boots and jeans with a Stetson perched on her perfectly blow-dried brunette hair. Her earrings were silver spurs that caught the light and danced when she spoke. Merit looked just as good in a long denim skirt with boots and a colorful hand embroidered Mexican blouse pulled down around her creamy white shoulders. Her earrings were dangling longhorns. The two looked at each other and nodded their approval.

When the guests arrived, they were met with a spread of BBQ that few experienced, even in the best BBQ restaurants in the state. The table was laden with vast amounts of potato salad, coleslaw, a cauldron of beans, fifty loaves of Mrs. Baird's white bread, sliced dill pickles, heaping rings of raw onions, and gallons of barbecue sauce. Dispersed between the sides were huge cutting boards awaiting the main attraction—meat.

From the porch and through the windows, guests could see the ranch hands nearby tending smokers, grills, and pits dug into the ground, where cabrito was being tenderized after a two-day process that made young goat meat fall off the bone. They were smoking up the air with brisket as well, and sending a sweet aroma that made the guests' mouths water.

Betty and Bob Tom Jakes were in attendance, one of their rare political outings. Bob Tom usually worked the weekends at the golf course, and Betty liked puttering around her garden more than she liked socializing. They both baby sat their new grandsons any time they got the chance. Today, it was important to fly the flag and show the colors for the law firm.

Ag wore his usual maroon shirt, jeans, and boots. He didn't have to change much for anything he attended. Although he gave her plenty of space, he was always aware of where Merit was and who was near her. In turn, Betty was always aware of both of them and the energy that connected them.

Senator Linden navigated the crowd with ease, engaging in animated conversations with guests and co-op members alike. Her presence exuded a blend of authority and approachability, earning her admiration from all who crossed her path. Meanwhile, Merit and Lane, the gracious hosts, moved among their guests, ensuring everyone felt welcome and appropriately catered to. With a practiced finesse, they orchestrated the festivities, their hospitality as warm as the Texas sun overhead.

Merit stepped up to the highest spot on the porch and Lane rang a cast iron triangle dinner bell hanging from an eave. When they had everyone's attention, Merit spoke.

"Ladies and gentlemen, cowboys and cowgirls, howdy y'all.

Thank you for being here today to honor Senator Paige Linden. Lindy, as we affectionately call her, has been bringing attention to your little gang of farmers for several years, and we're finally ready to see some fruits of her labors, and yours. We appreciate her hard work on behalf of the growers' co-op and particularly thank her for her hard work in passing legislation expanding the Farm Bill. Lindy, will you say a few words?"

Senator Linden gracefully took her position beside Merit on the porch with a big smile as the guests' applause signaled approval. "Thank you for inviting me here today. I believe that this is the finest looking bunch of farmers I've ever seen."

Everyone laughed. A few whooped and hollered. Merit moved to the side and out of the limelight.

"Thank you, Merit and John, for inviting me here today, and to all of you, I want y'all to know that you are the backbone of our community, and it's an honor to stand before you. Your hard work and dedication are what keep Bastrop County and my senatorial district thriving. Without you, our local economy would falter, and our community would lose a vital part of its soul."

She knew the votes that kept her in office came primarily from this group, not to mention a lot of the money in her reelection coffers. So far, she'd been able to avoid seeking dark money, and intended to keep it that way. But, beyond politics, she genuinely felt a deep connection to these people and their way of life, stemming from generations of her family residing and working beside them. Amidst shared meals and shared stories, bonds were strengthened, and friendships forged, reaffirming the timeless values of kinship and collaboration between them.

Sure, there were a few haughty ones, like Mike and Joanna James, who lorded their wealth over their staff and never got their hands dirty. But they were a rarity and tended to associate with a different crowd. When their money was involved, they played the game and pretended to enjoy their neighbors.

Lindy resumed her stump speech. "The challenges you face are not small, and I want to assure you that I am committed to fighting for the support and resources you need. Whether it's securing better subsidies, improving access to agricultural technology, or ensuring fair market prices, I am here for you."

The crowd nodded in agreement, murmuring their approval. Some exchanged glances, their expressions reflecting a mix of gratitude and determination.

"You know, it's easy to stand up here and talk, but the real work happens out in those fields and barns. I've walked the fields, seen the sweat on your brows, and I want to say, from the bottom of my heart, thank you. You are the heroes."

Applause erupted, echoing through the trees. Senator Linden's words seemed to resonate deeply with the crowd, touching the core of their shared experiences.

"And let's not forget, this isn't just about work. It's about family, heritage, and preserving a way of life that's been passed down through generations. Together, we can ensure that our children and grandchildren can enjoy the same beautiful, prosperous life that we do today."

With that, she stepped down from the porch, joining the crowd as one of them.

Reverend Thomas Weatherland from the local Presbyterian church stepped up on the porch and said, "Let us pray." He blessed the food and all in attendance. He expressed gratitude for Senator Linden and ended with a plea to the Almighty and his son, Jesus Christ, for the healing of Thad Lane.

As he stepped off the porch, the sun began to set, casting a warm, golden glow over the gathering. It was a moment of unity, a testament to the enduring spirit of the community, and a reminder that they were all in this together, deep in the heart of Texas.

As drinks were refreshed, the meats were laid out on the table and carved by the ranch hands. Merit and Lane resumed their positions on the porch and roles as hosts and said, "Let's eat!"

Merit moved around her kitchen on Sunday morning in her robe and slippers, sans make-up, making tea and heating up a blueberry muffin from Texas French Bread. She'd splurged on Door Dash delivery that morning because she was craving the comfort of carbs and missing Ace. With her food prepped, she sat at the dining room, facing the view of downtown Austin through the wall of glass.

After a few bites, she called Ace at his high school, as she did every Sunday. It was the best she could do to keep in touch between their visits in Houston, breaks in Austin, and trips to the coast. Ace had been in the Rawson Saunders School for Dyslexic Students for several years, and it had proved to be the best decision Merit had made on his behalf.

"How's it going down there in H-Town?"

"Great. Missing you and Pepper. How's Austin?"

"All good here. Pepper is sitting on my foot right now looking out at the tall buildings. She never seems to tire of that."

Pepper's ears perked up at the use of her name, then she settled back down with her head on the toe of Merit's slipper.

"Give her a scratch on the belly for me."

"Will do. How's school going? Any news on your big test last week in English lit?" Merit knew that anything with lots of words and sentence structure was challenging for Ace, but he had tutors, and could advocate for extended time if he needed it.

"Nope. I'm still waiting. In the meantime, I've got an algebra test tomorrow, and I think I'll do better with that."

"Excellent. So, no partying in the dorms tonight?" Merit laughed.

Ace laughed too, as both knew the school was strictly business on the nights before classes. For the price Merit paid for tuition, it better be.

"How are your hippie, pot-growing clients doing?" Ace had often teased Merit about her representation of marijuana growers.

"Trouble at every turn, but we're planning to win out in the end, I hope."

"Legalize marinara." Ace laughed.

"Just keep rollin'." Merit laughed.

"Weed my lips."

"Should be a joint decision."

"I think you're dope."

"You're my best bud."

Merit and Ace had been playing word games since he was a small boy and had been diagnosed with dyslexia. Now, it was like a ritual.

"Objection, Counselor. I've had enough." Ace finally stopped the punning, still laughing.

"Hey, that's my line. I'm the lawyer."

"Have a good day, Mom."

"You too, Peach. Love you."

17

Prince drove his stolen boll weevil inspector's truck to Harrison Farm near LaGrange. He had been called in for another meeting and he hoped that this one was going to be better than the last. He didn't need Harrison raging again. It was starting to become irritating. Harrison should be a happy client. He was getting everything he wanted, and it was all happening on a really fast timetable.

Prince pulled into the driveway and drove up to the lodge. After he parked the vehicle, got out, and walked into the building, he noticed that Harrison had made sure no one else was around. Just like he liked it. It was a condition of his employment, although he took no chances and still wore his disguises when in public. He sat down in the chair in front of Harrison's desk.

"What can I do for you?"

"Things aren't moving in the direction that I would have liked. I thought burning down the farm would have kicked out the chance for the permits, but my informant tells me that Lane and the co-op's licenses are probably going to be approved anyway. They have Senator Paige Linden in their back pocket."

Prince rolled his eyes. "I could have told you that wasn't going to be enough to deter them." He didn't tell Harrison that he had visited the hospital and put the icing on the cake by killing Brad. That, too, had not been enough to shut down Lane and the co-op farmers.

Harrison pouted. "I thought between burning down the farm, and putting one of those brats down, that we would have done all we could do to ensure that Lane was knocked out of his spot. But he's still probably going to move ahead."

"We could take out the second twin."

"If it didn't work with the first one, the second one won't tip the scales. Besides, that might make it a little too hot to handle around here. I can only go so far with bought-off law enforcement before they get nervous."

Prince scratched his chin in thought. "What law enforcement? They don't know about me, do they?"

"Not specifically."

Prince looked relieved. "If the senator is the deciding factor, take out the factor."

"That's a bold move. If we do, it can't be seen to be connected to the cannabis industry. She has a lot of other legislation, but this is the most lucrative. We'd need to make it look like something else."

"We can do that. I've done recon and I'm ready to move at a moment's notice."

"Let me think about it. For now, let's try the male plants."

"Male plants?"

"Yeah, I've arranged for you to pick them up in Austin. Go straight to the Bastrop farms with them. Don't bring them anywhere near my crops. Wash your truck before you come back out here."

"Okay. What do I do with them?"

"Place them in the greenhouses if you can get in without leaving a trail or put them next to the fields where the hemp plants are growing."

"Okay. What's the goal?"

"Male plants produce seeds that will pollinate the female plants. The wind will carry the seeds across the fields."

"Don't cannabis plants produce male and female plants naturally?"

"Yes, but farmers rip out and destroy the male plants immediately. If not, we can't control getting the female plants to flower. That's the part that's cultivated and cured for the marijuana."

Prince nodded. "Learn something new every day."

Harrison reached over, lifted, and set a box with two-gallon jugs inside, containing some liquid, on the desk. "Take these with you and hang onto them until I give you the go ahead."

"Will do."

"Remember, take no unnecessary risks. It's imperative that you not be caught."

"No chance of that." Prince didn't mind playing a little dirty pool to up the ante on the job, but his skill set went way beyond male plants. "Let me know about the senator."

Prince drove along the dark, winding roads of the Texas countryside, the truck's headlights cutting through the thick blanket of night. The GPS on his phone guided him toward a greenhouse on the outskirts of Austin where the male hemp plants waited. The plan was simple, yet its implications were vast.

Prince arrived at a nondescript warehouse, killed the

engine, and stepped out, the cool night air hitting his face. A single light flickered above the entrance, casting eerie shadows across the parking lot. He approached the door, knocked twice, and waited.

A burly man with a scruffy beard and a baseball cap answered, eyeing Prince suspiciously. "You Prince?" the man grunted.

"Yeah. You got the plants?"

The man nodded and led him inside. Rows upon rows of potted male hemp plants filled the space, their spindly leaves reaching toward the overhead fluorescent lights. Prince's contact gestured toward a pallet stacked with several trays of plants.

"These are yours. Get them loaded and get out of here," he said curtly.

Prince wasted no time. He hoisted the trays into the back of his truck, securing them with bungee cords to prevent any damage during the drive. Once everything was in place, he closed the truck bed and gave a final nod to the man, who merely grunted in response before disappearing back into the warehouse.

Prince drove home and hid the truck full of plants in the garage. He needed daylight to perform the task and intended to head to Bastrop County the next morning.

Early the next day Prince's drive to Bastrop County was uneventful, though his mind raced with thoughts of what he was about to do. He knew the risks—if caught, the consequences would be severe. But the payoff, the power shift, was worth it. As he neared his destination, he turned off the rap music he was playing and looked around for any farmers who might be working.

Seeing none, Prince drove down the easement by the cotton field for boll weevil inspection, as close as he could get to the hemp pasture. He parked and proceeded the rest of the way on foot, carrying the trays of plants carefully. He navigated the perimeter of the field, his eyes scanning for any signs of security.

He circled around the edge of a drying shed and placed the plants on the ground by the entrance. He found the door easy to break into by pushing the wood at the edge of the lock. He went inside, located the driest buds, took a plastic zip-lock bag from his pocket, and selected about a half pound for his personal use. Chill pill was one of his favorite varieties, and his stash at home was getting low. He put the filled baggie in his pocket and proceeded out the door, closing it behind him. He skirted the shed and proceeded with the task at hand.

Reaching the first greenhouse, he set down the plants, tried the door, and found it locked, just as he had expected, and decided to skip trying to pick the lock. He moved along the edge of the property until he found a spot where the hemp field began. He placed the male plants strategically, weaving them in and out of the outer row of hemp plants. He knew the wind would do the rest, carrying the pollen from the male plants across to the female ones, effectively sabotaging the crop.

He went back to the truck for additional trays of plants and repeated the same process. As he worked, he kept a watchful eye on his surroundings. The last thing he needed was to be caught in the act. The task took longer than he anticipated, but he finally placed the last of the plants and stood back, wiping the sweat from his brow. The fields, bathed in sunlight, looked serene and undisturbed, but Prince knew the chaos that would ensue in a matter of days.

Satisfied with his work, he made his way back to the truck. The drive to Austin felt lighter, the tension easing from his shoulders. He had done it. Now, it was only a matter of time before the effects of his actions rippled through the farm, and if he was lucky, through a few of the nearby farms as well.

Prince couldn't help but smirk as he thought of the chaos that would ensue. The farmers would be furious, the crops ruined. And in the end, his boss would have one less competitor to worry about.

Hell, maybe I'll get a bonus.

18

Lindy sat in her office chair at the Capitol, exhaustion weighing heavy on her shoulders like a lead cloak. The day had stretched on endlessly, dragging its feet into the night. All she wanted was to escape to the comfort of her home, crack open a bottle of wine, and forget the chaos that was ever present in the Texas Senate. But duty tethered her to her desk, a relentless taskmaster demanding completion of her paperwork before she could surrender to a glass of wine and a good night's sleep.

Lindy studied a brief prepared by her staff on the Ogallala Aquifer that ran beneath the Llano Estacado and the Great Plains from Nebraska to Texas. She had been working on a bill to join with other state governments to support the health of one of the world's largest aquifers underlying approximately one hundred seventy-four thousand square miles. The aquifer ran under eight states, including Texas, as part of the High Plains Aquifer System starting in Ogallala, Nebraska. Although none of the land in her district was in the aquifer, Lindy was on the committee for Water Rights in Texas placing her, and fellow senators, squarely in the middle of diverging opinions.

There were those interested in preserving the vitality of the aquifer against those for using more of the water as part of irrigation and other purposes through groundwater wells. The aquifer, at risk of over-extraction and pollution beginning around 1950, stood at risk of depletion which would endanger the livelihood of citizens of the panhandle counties, and thereby all of Texas. She recorded her notes on the bill in the margins of the document and placed it in the outbox for her staff to work on the next day.

She hoped to trade her vote on the aquifer for votes from several senators on other upcoming legislation. She would not sell out her protection of the aquifer for the votes, but she could certainly bend a little around the edges in the interest of expediency to obtain advancement of both bills. She was a master strategist and often found a path to get her way while making it look like the other side was winning.

Next, she turned to the committee regulations for granting the medical marijuana licenses. Each day this week had been a relentless march through bureaucratic trenches, all in preparation for the committee's next meeting. The weight of responsibility bore down on her. The threat of burning marijuana farms and destruction of crops cast a pall over her thoughts, a harbinger of further potential catastrophe. She still intended to support the Lanes and the other farmers in her district in obtaining the new licenses.

Several of her committees were about to endure some extreme scrutiny from the press and the public. It wasn't just about optics; it was about the fragile balance of power and the precarious direction of their committee's endeavors. Paige vowed to wield her influence like a hammer, to crush dissent and ensure this would be the last farm torched in her county.

The faster the matter was settled, and the licenses issued, the sooner things would calm down and farmers could farm without fear of interference.

A weary yawn escaped her lips as she contemplated food, her stomach growling in protest against the neglect of sustenance. It was past nine, and though she longed for the comforts of a home-cooked meal, reality dictated otherwise. Stir fry seemed a fitting compromise, a beacon of flavor in the sea of choices in the Austin foodie scene. As she scrolled through the Grubhub app, searching for a delivery option, a sudden noise shattered the silence, causing her to send her phone tumbling to the floor.

"Damn," she cursed under her breath. The empty corridors of the Texas Capitol now echoed with an eerie silence, devoid of the usual bustle of activity. Paige's unease prickled at the edges of her consciousness, a whisper of paranoia urging caution. She hit the first speed dial button on her desk phone and heard, "Security, Senator Linden. How may we help you?"

Lindy was brave, but not stupid. She often had Security escort her to her car in the parking lot when she worked late. This wasn't that. "Just heard a strange noise in the corridor. Would you send somebody for a walk-by, just as a precaution? I'm a little jumpy tonight."

"Of course, they'll be right up."

"Thanks." She hung up, waited a few moments, then heard a sound again. *Footsteps? No, heavier, some type of banging.* She stood, froze and listened again.

With hesitant steps, she went past the empty receptionist's desk and peeked into the hallway, senses alert for any sign of intrusion. As she strained to discern the source of the disturbance, her mind raced with possibilities. Was there real danger, or merely a trick of the imagination, a figment of exhaustion playing cruel tricks on her senses?

She breathed a sigh of relief when she heard the elevator ding and saw a uniformed silhouette wearing a guard hat exit into the corridor. She walked toward the figure, laughing at herself.

"Great, it's you. Thanks for coming. I must have the jitters tonight."

"No problem, ma'am."

The guard advanced toward her while removing his gloves from his hands. Without warning, the world tilted on its axis and she felt the grip of fear. The guard was coming too close for comfort, and she didn't recognize him. She backed up one step at a time without realizing it as the guard advanced further toward her. When her back was against the corridor wall, he struck. A vice-like grip closed around her throat, cutting off her breath in a cruel embrace.

No gloves. Better for the feel of it.

Panic surged through her veins, a primal instinct urging her to fight or flee. But her assailant was too strong. She tried to claw his face, desperation lending strength to her trembling limbs, but the hands held fast. Darkness encroached upon her vision, a veil of oblivion descending like a shroud. The sustained pressure caused blood vessels in her face and eyes to burst.

In those final moments, as her life slipped away like grains of sand, Senator Paige Linden knew one truth: *In the hallowed halls of power, even the mighty could fall.*

19

Merit sat at her desk, in the early morning, with the television tuned to KNEW 9. As usual, she had the sound muted and looked up occasionally from her computer screen to check for Red Thallon's daily broadcast. Her mouth dropped open when she read the crawl below the image: *Senator Paige Linden murdered at Texas State Capitol.* Onscreen there were police cars surrounding the campus and leading up the drive to the east side entrance. Every news station in town had a van that was evident in the background. Merit reached for the remote about the same time Red's image appeared, microphone in hand, standing in front of the east wing.

Red's familiar voice reported. "Senator Paige Linden was found today, in the wee hours of the morning, in the hallway of the east wing of the Texas State Capitol by campus security. We are still waiting for a press conference, and what we know now is very little."

The crawl under Red's image continued to convince viewers that the news was actually true. The camera angle shifted to show the windows on the east side of the building.

Red shifted to a profile shot. "Here you can see the senatorial wing of the Capitol on the east side. The windows to the far left are to Senator Linden's office. She was purportedly found in the corridor just outside her office doors."

Betty heard the television and came into the office to find out what was important enough for Merit to unmute the sound. She stared in shock as the scene unfolded in front of her eyes.

"My Lord," whispered Betty as her hand flew to her mouth.

Merit just stared at the screen.

A spokesperson, in a dark suit and tie, came out onto the Capitol steps and walked up to a podium placed there for his use. The camera crew adjusted their shot from Red to him.

"My name is Jonathon Anderson. I am the liaison for the press in the Texas State Senate. We do not have a lot of information at this time. We have been told that Senator Linden was strangled, I mean killed, around 10:00 p.m. when her last staffer had left for the day. She was discovered in the corridor, just outside her office doors, after having called Security when she'd heard a disturbance. Unofficial sources say that she was strangled. More information will be forthcoming about the cause of death when a full autopsy has been performed."

Red yelled a question up at Anderson. "How did someone get in the building?"

"We're uncertain as to access. As you know, this is one of the most secure buildings in the state. Police are reviewing CCTV footage and the guards on duty are being questioned at this time."

Several more questions were asked by reporters, but Anderson deflected. "We will have another briefing this afternoon if any additional information is available. APD will join us at that time if they have any findings to report. Thank you."

With that, he turned and went back into the Capitol.

Betty turned to Merit and posed the question, "Who would want the senator dead?"

"I can't imagine. I wonder if it was personal or business?"

"Either way, if she was strangled, how she died is barbaric."

Merit shuddered as she thought about Red informing the city that the senator was strangled to death. "It seems so personal, being strangled."

"It is. What a terrible way to die, she must have been so scared."

Betty made a tsking sound. "It's absolutely repulsive."

The next weekend, Senator Paige Linden was laid to rest in Bastrop County in her family's plot, next to her parents and her baby boy who had died in childbirth. Her husband, college aged daughter, and a small group of friends were in attendance. A memorial service on the Capitol grounds was planned for later the next week.

Lindy's murder had shocked the state and the nation. What made the situation even more alarming was the fact that the perpetrator had managed to infiltrate the Texas Capitol. The security breach at such a significant and supposedly secure location added an unsettling layer to the tragedy. The assailant had not only taken the life of a respected senator but had also exposed vulnerabilities in the protection of public officials and government buildings. This raised serious concerns about the safety protocols in place and sparked a nationwide conversation about the need for enhanced security measures.

The investigation into Senator Linden's murder was swift and comprehensive. Law enforcement agencies, including the Texas Rangers and the FBI, worked tirelessly to piece together the events leading up to the crime. Forensic experts combed through the evidence, and security footage from the Capitol was meticulously reviewed. The hunt for the perpetrator became a top priority, with authorities leaving no stone unturned in their pursuit of justice.

As the investigation unfolded, the public's grief and outrage were palpable. Vigils were held across the state, with communities coming together to honor Senator Linden's legacy and demand accountability for her death. All weekend, flowers, letters, and tributes piled up outside her office and at the Capitol steps, a testament to the profound impact she had on those she served. Her dedication to her constituents and her unwavering commitment to justice and equality were celebrated, even as her untimely death cast a long shadow over her achievements.

According to Red in a follow up story: "Senator Paige Linden's murder not only robbed the community of a passionate leader but also left an indelible mark on the state's political landscape."

Her legacy of advocacy and public service would continue to inspire others, but the haunting memory of her violent end served as a somber reminder of the fragility of life and the ever-present need to safeguard those who dedicated their lives to serving the public.

20

Merit and Ag met in Merit's office at the end of the next workday. Betty had already gone home, and the wooden floor in the hall echoed Ag's footsteps as he approached Merit's door. It was creepy.

"Ag?" Merit called out to make sure it was him.

"It's me."

"Great. Grab a beer. I'm in my office."

Ag retraced his steps through the reception area, stopping to lock the door to the office, and went into the break room. He grabbed a Lone Star longneck from the refrigerator and doubled back to Merit's office.

"I locked the door. Betty should have secured it on the way out."

"I told her you were coming in."

Ag sat, took a long pull on his beer, and made a face. He didn't say she could wind up just like Senator Linden if she wasn't careful.

Merit tried to ignore the expression and sipped her wine. "Sad about Lindy."

"Very. Tragic. Be careful, Merit."

"I will. Her death is going to cause a mess with Lane and the co-op."

Ag went into business mode. "How so?"

"His permits were dependent on her political clout. It's the Agriculture Committee that governs regulations and licensing for marijuana cultivation and manages the implementation of the Farm Bill. Now the chair of the committee is gone."

"You think that's why she was killed? Does this have something to do with what happened on Lane's farm?"

"I have no idea, but I intend to find out. It's curious that the murder was after the vote expanding the licenses, but before choosing who would receive them."

"Could be motive. I wonder which senator will take over as chair."

"We're making a big leap here. There could be many motives. We need some proof as to who was behind her death. Either way, we need to find a way to keep Lane and the co-op in good graces with the committee."

"What's the next step?"

"I'll work on lobbying the next senator in line on the committee. You try to find out who killed her."

"Chaplain should have some information by now. I'll drop by and see what I can get from him."

"Thanks, Ag."

"In the meantime, I've been looking into the research Senator Linden sent to us about other vandalism in and around LaGrange and Fayette County. I'll try to find a connection between what's going on with the Bastrop area farms and the murder of the senator. If they're connected at all."

"You think they are now?"

"I'm becoming more convinced. Officer Twitty, a real shady

character, I met with in LaGrange seems intent on hiding something. If we're good for now, I need more time to look into it."

"Yep. I guess that about wraps it up for today. I'm beat." Merit looked down at her phone as a text message came through from Patrick. She smiled, and Ag pretended not to notice.

"Don't you ever take a night off anymore?" Ag slumped further into the guest chair and slid his long legs under the edge of her desk.

"Yep. Just not today."

"How about we go grab a drink somewhere besides the office? Give ourselves a break."

Merit looked at Ag's handsome face. He was charming, but they needed to stay friends, not become lovers.

"Rain check? I'm tired and it's getting late. I need to let Pepper Dog out for a pee, and I have an early day tomorrow. Let yourself out. I need to wrap up a couple of things before I head out."

Ag rose to leave. "Sure. Get some rest. I'll get back to you when I know more."

Merit noticed his disappointment although he tried to hide it. "Thanks, Ag. Night."

Ag took the elevator to his truck in the garage and sat for a moment. He knew Merit wouldn't lock the door behind him. She took so many chances, it scared him. A few minutes later, he saw Merit exit the same elevator and get into her cherry-red BMW SUV. The fact that she still had it was a miracle to him. She'd lost a vehicle on almost every major case since he'd known her. He waited until she left the garage, then followed.

I'm not stalking her. I'm keeping her safe. Sure. Keep telling yourself that.

Ag actually wasn't stalking her. He didn't follow her around, and lived his life fully without her, but every now and again, an opportunity presented itself to keep an eye on her and he took advantage of it.

When Merit pulled onto the street, she headed in the direction of her condo, then took a right and veered off course. Ag followed her, blending into the traffic. His plan was to see her safely home, then head out to his house at Lake Travis. Ag's brow furrowed when he realized she wasn't heading to her condo as she'd said.

They wove around the one-way streets in downtown Austin until she pulled up to Pot Luck Restaurant and valeted her car. She walked inside with a bounce in her step.

Guess she's not tired anymore.

Ag knew she was there to see the chef from the funeral. He had felt the energy between them, and Betty's look of disapproval had confirmed that something was afoot. Ag felt slighted, but knew he had no reason to. She was an independent woman, owed him nothing but friendship and professionalism, and had made her feelings clear. The strength of the pang of jealousy that swept through his gut surprised him.

Now, I'm stalking. Time to go home.

21

Merit drove her car from the garage toward Pot Luck even though she had told Ag that she wasn't up to going out. She wasn't sure why she lied to him, it just seemed awkward to turn him down and then tell him that she was going to meet someone else for drinks. She felt like it would be some kind of betrayal to him, even though they weren't dating, and she owed him no explanation. It was just easier to tell him that she was beat and going home, but she needed to blow off some steam.

Besides, she hadn't been one hundred percent sure she was going to Pot Luck. She was deeply disturbed about Senator Linden's death, and she wanted company and comfort without attachments. She was still debating the whole younger man chef in her mind, and her car just drove over to the restaurant on its own.

Sure. Keep telling yourself that.

She wasn't sure what she was doing but she didn't want to think about it. Maybe Betty was right to disapprove. Merit didn't really need a man in her life at the moment, but she had a weakness for the younger guys, and this one seemed to have taken a shine to her. Regardless, it was her decision to make.

She certainly wasn't interested in anything serious, but a little fun had gotten her into trouble before. How did Betty put it? 'If you go for the sweet honey, you might get stung by the bee.'

Merit walked into Pot Luck and headed for the bar, sat down, and ordered her favorite Malbec. She didn't bother to tell the bartender that she was there to see Chef Herbert. She figured if Patrick wanted to see her, he would find her. She sipped her wine and was considering getting up and leaving when a warm hand rested on her shoulder. She turned and found a set of beautiful green eyes attached to the handsome chef. He was wearing the traditional white double-breasted jacket and pants. *Pot Luck* was embroidered on the chest pocket.

"I'm glad you were able to make it." He sat down on the barstool beside her and signaled her glass for another pour. "It's on the house." The bartender raised her eyebrows but complied.

"Thank you, and thank you again for the flowers. You look busy. How is your night going?"

"Better, now that you're here."

She smiled. She felt good around him. She pointed to the wine. "Nice. You're not joining me?"

"I have to finish a couple of quick things in the kitchen. You okay here for a minute?"

"Sure."

"Order anything you want."

"Wine's fine."

"You're fine." Patrick stood, touched her shoulder, then went through the restaurant and into the service doors.

It was the end of food service, and the staff was cleaning up and doing their closing tasks. She knew she should be careful about public displays of affection. The food industry was notorious for gossiping, especially about one of their own. She waited and enjoyed the last of her wine while Patrick finished his duties.

Merit watched as the cute student bartender, from the girls' night out, counted the bills in her till. A man that Merit didn't recognize approached the bartender with an envelope. Merit squinted at what was in his hand then diverted her eyes to hide her prying. Maybe it was part of the close-out, but something seemed clandestine about it.

The bartender took the envelope from him, looked around the room, then lifted the change container from the register and took something from beneath it. She slyly handed it to the man, and he put it in his pocket, too quickly for Merit to identify what it was.

Merit's armpits prickled, her body's way of communicating that something was off. What just happened? Did she just watch a drug deal go down right in front of her eyes, or maybe it was some type of payoff? Were they stealing from Patrick? No, that was ridiculous. It wasn't until the bartender turned and realized that Merit was watching her, a blush rising to her cheeks, that Merit was sure something untoward had just transpired.

Merit smiled at the bartender but didn't get anything in return. Did the staffer feel in that moment that she had been caught? Merit sipped the wine as the girl turned and finished her tasks. Merit watched as one by one the staff started filtering out of the restaurant. She felt a hand on her shoulder again and jumped.

"Oh, I'm sorry, I didn't mean to startle you."

She turned and smiled. The chef was behind her. "I guess I'm just a little jumpy. Are you finished?"

"Yes, everyone's gone. Would you like a tour of the kitchen?"

"Sure, I would love that." She got up from the stool and followed him through the service doors. It was a standard kitchen, but she knew that was where he made his magic and was clearly proud of it. Pots hung from hooks above a massive cooking surface, and stacks of pots and pans lined the shelves behind it. A commercial-grade dishwasher was steaming on the other side of the room.

"Looks great. Now I'll be able to picture you while you're at work."

"My favorite place."

"I can see why."

He indicated the back corner of the kitchen. "Let me show you the brick oven."

They walked over and looked into the cave formed by the opening. Heat still emanated from the bricks. "Impressive."

"Pot Luck is my pride and joy."

"I can see why. Look, I want to tell you something in the spirit of protecting how much you love this place."

"What do you mean?"

"I might have seen something at the bar that you should know about."

He stopped the tour. "What's that?"

"I think one of your bartenders was taking something from the register. I saw it right in front of my eyes."

He stared at her for a beat, then started laughing. "No, you must have misunderstood. There's no way."

"I'm pretty sure I know what I saw. She took something from underneath the change drawer."

"Merit, I appreciate the concern, but I know my staff pretty well and they just wouldn't do that. You probably saw someone pay her for better tables."

"Better tables?"

"Yes, they do that sometimes. A server will share tips with a hostess, for example, to make sure she gets more tables than another. It's frowned upon, but I try not to get too involved in it. Unless it becomes unfair, I stay out of the servers' politics. The better servers always end up winning out anyway."

"I don't know if that's what I saw."

"It's fine, Merit. I think you just misunderstood."

"Maybe." Merit wasn't convinced but it wasn't her place, and she wasn't going to argue with him. He clearly wasn't concerned, and it really was none of her business. It was entirely possible that she did misunderstand something. She accepted that and felt relieved, but that tiny voice was still whispering in her ear.

Patrick turned to her and tipped her chin with his hand. She smiled up at him. He kissed her softly on the lips and she felt a stir inside. She forgot all about the waitstaff.

He led her over to a couple of chairs at a small table at the back of the kitchen. "Let's sit here and talk." He pulled a bottle of the same Malbec she had been drinking at the bar from a case of wine stacked in the corner.

"Okay." She sat and watched with dreamy eyes as he opened and poured the wine.

"So, tell me, Merit, what is keeping you so busy that you won't go out on a date with me?"

"I'm here, aren't I? Tell me more about Pot Luck. How long have you owned this place?" Merit needed a moment to breathe and settle, so she diverted him with small talk.

"I've always loved to cook, even when I was younger. It was my dream to have my own place and feature the things that I wanted to serve."

"The food definitely is delicious."

"Thank you. I take pride in our menu and the locally sourced ingredients. I believe in having the best things in life," he said with a wink.

"Is that right?"

"Of course. Now all I have to do is convince you to go out on a date with me and I will have everything I've ever wanted."

He was laying it on thick, and she was loving every minute of it. He was easy to like, and she enjoyed a man with ambition and a dream. He liked her and she liked him and maybe that was enough for the moment.

"Let me think about that date. For now, I should probably get home and let you lock up." She finished her wine. "I need to take the dog out, and I have a long day ahead of me tomorrow."

"I won't keep you then. How would you feel about going out on the water with me next week? I can't take a weekend night off, but I can sometimes slip out on Tuesdays or Wednesdays. A little relaxation might do us both some good."

She smiled. He was probably right. She could use some time off, with a young, handsome gentleman, and she loved the water.

"Well, that sounds lovely. Call me at the office and we'll pick a date." She got up from her chair. "Thank you for the wine."

He took her hand and kissed it. Something she didn't expect from someone so young. He was courting her and that worried her a bit. She didn't want him to get the idea that she was emotionally available to him. Still, he was intoxicating and she was drawn in.

22

———

Val escorted his grandmother, Constance Stanhope, into the conference room of Merit's office. He introduced Constance to Betty who came in behind them. After hands were shook and dresses admired, Val pulled out a chair for each to sit.

Betty offered tea or coffee, and Val said, "I'll get it."

Constance smoothed her skirt and crossed her ankles. She was a classy woman, with plenty of wrinkles to reflect her experience, but high cheekbones and a straight spine, showing her good bones and breeding. She looked out the window. "What a view."

"Thank you. Make yourself comfortable. I'll let Merit know you're here and be right back."

Betty stood and went down the hall to fetch Merit from her office. Val returned from the break room with a tray holding a tea pot, two teacups on saucers, a small pitcher of milk, and one steaming mug of dark roast coffee.

"Here, Grands. Hot tea, just the way you like it." He poured both cups from the teapot, added milk, served her, then set the second cup of tea at the end of the conference table for Merit. He sat beside his grandmother with his coffee and patted her hand.

She smiled at him with pride. "Thank you. This smells delicious."

Merit joined the meeting with a legal pad and pen in her hands. Val stood and introduced them. He raised his voice just a bit so the older woman could hear him. "Merit, this is my grandmother, Constance Stanhope. Grands, this is my boss, Merit Bridges. She's the lawyer I told you about."

Constance put her cup down. "Nice to meet you."

"Pleasure's mine." She shook Constance's fragile hand.

Merit sat, took a sip of tea, and leaned forward, her tone gentle yet determined.

"Thank you for coming in Mrs. Stanhope. I understand you've had some recent visitors asking about purchasing your land."

"Yes. Please call me Constance."

"Then, please call me Merit. How many times has someone visited you, and has it been the same person or more than one person?"

"Just one man that I recall."

"We're here to ensure that your wishes are respected and that you're not taken advantage of. Do you recall any specific details about the visits from the man? Any names or companies he represented?"

Constance paused, her brow furrowing as she struggled to recall. "I remember a young man, nice suit, very polite, but persistent. He kept asking about the land, offering more money the second time he came by. I couldn't tell you his name."

Val listened intently, his jaw tightening slightly at the

mention of the persistent visitor. "We'll need to gather as much information as we can to build a file about them, Grands."

Merit nodded in agreement. "Absolutely. And don't worry, we'll do everything we can to protect your interests."

Val refilled the cups of tea for the ladies, bringing a sense of warmth to the room. "Here you go, Grands."

Constance smiled gratefully, taking a sip of her tea before continuing. "Well, first of all, he never made an appointment, which I thought was rude."

Merit and Val exchanged glances.

"He didn't say who he was working for?"

"No, I assumed he was working for himself. He didn't mention anyone else."

As they delved deeper into the conversation, Merit took detailed notes, piecing together the fragments of Constance's memory.

"Hmm. Did he say what he wanted to do with the land?"

"No. But I didn't get the impression he planned to live there. He didn't look at the house at all. I saw him looking out at the pasture. He might have taken a few pictures with his phone the first time he came by."

Val looked disturbed. "You didn't tell me that."

Constance's shoulders slumped. "Didn't I?"

Val patted her hand again. "That's okay, Grands."

A clearer picture of the situation emerged, and Merit reassured her new client. "Valentine and I will sort all this out for you. Don't worry about a thing. If he comes back, or if anyone else shows up, it may be best not to let them in. Call Valentine or your daughter immediately. Okay?"

"I'll try to remember that."

After the meeting concluded, Val escorted his grandmother toward the door, a sense of reassurance settling over them.

"We'll get through this, Grands," he said, squeezing her hand gently.

She smiled up at him, her eyes reflecting a mixture of gratitude and resilience. "With you by my side, dear, I know we will."

23

———————

Merit met Patrick just before sunset, as requested, at the parking lot near the recreational dock on Lady Bird Lake. When Patrick had suggested that he take Merit on the water that week, she had assumed that he was going to take her on a booze cruise or maybe a dinner cruise on one of the riverboats. That was not the case at all. He had advised her to wear shorts and either deck shoes or running shoes, which she thankfully had done. He escorted her to the water's edge, handed her a life jacket, and pointed to a two-person red kayak attached to the dock. The guides had various colored kayaks lined up for others waiting to depart.

Austin Boat Tours was in the process of organizing six couples to go out on the water for what they called the 'Sunset Boats and Bats Tour.' The guide, a thin athletic-looking sort, started his spiel as the couples settled into the kayaks.

"Welcome, kayakers. My name is Hudson. I am a certified lifeguard, on the swim team at the University of Texas, and I'm a strong swimmer, if you get into trouble. If you get stuck or run out of steam, and are unable to paddle back, I can tie your kayak to mine and get us both back here. So, you can relax, even if you're not a great swimmer or strong enough to paddle all the way, and enjoy the evening."

One of the couples looked particularly relieved to hear about safety first.

Hudson continued. "You're in luck, as we have a clear night and a thumbnail moon. It will allow the stars and the city lights to shine brightly."

Several couples stopped to look at the guide while others fiddled with life jacket buckles and boat oars. Hudson steadied one of the kayaks for a couple to enter, got them settled, and then went to the next couple, all the while talking about the itinerary for the evening.

"First, we paddle from here along Lady Bird Lake the entire length of downtown during the golden hour. Then, we stop to catch the sunset over the water. Next, on the way back, the bats will be the main event as they fly out from under the Congress Avenue Bridge. After the bats do their thing, we'll paddle back here along the skyline, noting architecture by night and star gazing. The entire tour is a bit over two hours long."

Merit had heard about the tours from friends but had never gotten the chance to go on one. With one and a half million bats about to fly out from under the Congress Avenue Bridge, she thought it would be a great adventure.

She smiled at Patrick. "You sure are full of surprises."

He smiled. "It's not easy to surprise or delight a woman like you."

She smiled and he held her hand as she balanced herself into her seat. He climbed into the cockpit behind her as she held onto the dock to steady the kayak, mimicking what she saw the guide do with others.

The tour began as the group started making their way out to

the main body of the lake. Merit and Patrick quickly figured out the balance and paddling routine. It was the perfect night to be out on the water and the cool breeze that flowed through her hair made it easier to withstand the heat of the waning day. She loved Austin and this was a special treat. There was just nothing like it in all of Texas, and it did not disappoint. The highlight was the bats darkening the night sky with their vast numbers.

When they headed back and were viewing the stars overhead and the lighted skyline, Patrick put his hand on her shoulder in a particularly romantic moment.

When the tour ended, Merit and Patrick put away their life jackets and paddles, thanked and tipped Hudson, and left the dock for their vehicles. They drove separately back to her condo, having agreed to re-join there. She clicked the gate to the garage open, then waited for Patrick to pull up behind her. He tailgated her SUV into the parking garage and they parked in her reserved spots. They made their way up the elevator and into the high-rise building, his arm around her waist. The kissing in the elevator was hot and exciting.

After they walked down the hall, she unlocked the door and motioned him to go inside. Pepper, Ace's brindle Cairn Terrier, met them at the door and turned over on her back so Merit could bend down and rub her belly. Patrick chuckled at the antics and Merit looked up at him and smiled.

"I'm going to have to take her out."

"Sure, that's fine. Should I go with you?"

"No, just help yourself to a drink."

"Okay. Do you have wine? I can get a bottle opened and breathing while I wait."

"Yes, that sounds great. In the wine fridge. I'll be back shortly."

Patrick whistled when he moved into the living room and saw the view and decor, including a black baby grand piano. "Wow."

"Make yourself at home." Merit reached into the coat closet in the entry for a leash and went back out the door with Pepper. At times like this, she missed her old home because it hadn't required an elevator to take the dog out. Her house had been burned down at the direction of a mega sign company trying to scare her off a case, and every time she thought about that house, she grew sad. That was the home where she lived with her husband, Tony, and where her son, Ace, had grown up.

The beautiful high-rise was the logical choice after all the villains that she'd come up against in her legal career, and Betty had pressed her to move there. Security was the building's number one priority, followed closely by privacy.

Once downstairs, Pepper was kind enough to quickly do her business so that Merit could get back up to Patrick. When Merit and Pepper entered her condo again, she found Patrick in the living room looking out the wall of glass windows over downtown.

"You have a beautiful view, and what a kitchen. I could almost run the restaurant out of there."

"Yeah, it's great here. I'll give you the tour. It's quick. You found the kitchen." She began to point at each door in turn. "That door is the powder room. There's the laundry and storage. That open door is my son's room." She turned around and pointed the other direction. "That door goes to my bedroom."

Patrick picked up two glasses he'd found in the kitchen, now containing red wine. "That's the room I'd like to see."

Merit laughed and walked through her bedroom door. He followed. She stood at the end of the bed, and he handed her a glass of wine. She took a sip as he stared at her, and her smile grew bigger. He put the wine glasses on the nightstand, returned his attention to Merit, and stared into her eyes, making her feel like she was the only woman alive. Within seconds, his mouth was on hers with a passion she hadn't felt in a long while.

Oh boy.

He grabbed her by the waist and pulled her into him. They kissed again and she could taste the wine on their lips, which added sweetness. He moved his mouth to her ear and began whispering his plans for the evening. Everything about Patrick was intoxicating, and she couldn't get enough of his lips or his voice.

Pepper came to the door and stood watching them.

Patrick sat on the side of Merit's bed and pulled her into his lap. She grabbed his blond ponytail and gently tugged on it, then laughed.

He pulled her shirt over her head and unhooked her bra.

He whispered in her ear again. "You are so beautiful, Merit."

She grinned, loving the sound of his words and kissed him harder.

Pepper watched for a few more minutes, then trotted across the condo and found her spot in Ace's room for a nap. Pepper didn't wake up until Patrick slipped out just before dawn and Merit locked the door behind him.

24

Val sat down to compile the research Merit had requested on the updates to the 2015 Farm Bill, focusing on the implications for hemp versus marijuana in Texas. He was surprised by what he found. The 2018 congressional updates aimed to close loopholes in the original bill, but in Texas, the distinctions between hemp and marijuana had become blurred.

Under the law, any cannabis plant with less than 0.3% delta-9 THC is considered hemp and thus not subject to the Federal Controlled Substances Act. Texas adopted these definitions in 2019, making hemp legal in the state. However, Val discovered that many believed this created a loophole large enough to drive a truck through, allowing the sale of marijuana in Texas comparable to that in California and Colorado.

What astonished Val further was the claim that Texas had inadvertently become the largest unregulated drug market in the country. Critics argued that hemp containing THCa, which transforms into THC-delta-9 when burned, effectively mimicked the high of marijuana. The hemp industry insisted their products were legal under the letter of the law, but the U.S. Drug Enforcement Administration disagreed. The DEA suspected that much of the hemp was genetically modified to produce high THC levels and then infused with hash oil, a cannabis extract.

Val noted by researching Senator Linden's website the significant regulatory challenges Texas faced. The Texas Department of State Health Services reported that it had only four inspectors to oversee more than 7,000 registered hemp dispensaries. This lack of oversight worried authorities, who feared that if THC levels weren't properly tested, neither were contaminants like pesticides, heavy metals and molds such as aspergillus.

Val found it intriguing that many in the industry supported better regulation, including testing and age limits, to avoid a black market surge. As it stood, Texas had no laws preventing the sale of hemp to minors. Most industry insiders felt that Texas had progressed too far to turn back and preferred legislative solutions leading to legalization over the risks of unregulated sales.

Val plunked around several other sites and garnered a few more details. He put all of the information in a memo and marked it DRAFT. He noted that he'd put in a call to Stuart Lawton in Senator Linden's office. He attached the report to an email addressed to Merit and copied Betty.

Merit saw the email from Val in her inbox, at the end of the day, and chose to ignore it. It was wine night, and she was running late. She hustled down to her SUV and drove out 2244 to The Grove in Westlake. Fortunately, Red and Clover were parking their cars in the lot when Merit arrived. Everyone was running late. The neon sign outside The Grove flickered intermittently, casting a quirky glow over the trio of women as they sauntered onto the patio, shaded by huge live oaks, ready for their wine night escapade. Merit dropped into a chair at a table covered by a lime-green umbrella, with a sigh of relief. Red and Clover settled in beside her, their faces expressing equal pleasure that the day was done.

Their favorite waitress came around from behind the bar, held up a familiar bottle of Caymus Cabernet Sauvignon from Napa, and looked over at the women. She pointed to the bottle and raised her eyebrows as if to say: The usual? Merit nodded and then turned back to Red and Clover.

Clover looked at Red and smiled. "How's our tenacious reporter doing? Still on the hunt for the next exclusive scoop?"

Red smiled in return. "Yes, always scanning the horizon for the next big thing. How's the mayor job going?"

"I'm up to my ears in these campus political protests."

Merit perked up and looked at Red. "I saw you reporting about it on KNEW 9. Looked dangerous."

"It felt dangerous. The students seemed to be protesting peacefully, but the police reported outside agitators were causing most of the trouble." She then turned to Clover. "What will you do?"

"Off the record, I hate to shut down the students expressing their views, but they've overflowed the university campus onto the streets and alleys around it and it's causing traffic and crime issues, not to mention unhealthy conditions."

Merit thought of her law school alma mater. "The forty acres can't contain them anymore?"

"Apparently not," Clover responded. "What's going on with you? Still dealing with your hippie pot farmers?"

All three laughed because they knew it was far beyond that. "Yep."

The waitress came over with three glasses and the wine, opened it, handed the cork to Merit, and poured a sip for her to taste. Merit nodded her approval, and the waitress poured all three glasses. She placed the bottle on the table and left immediately. She knew better than to eavesdrop on their conversation; after all, what happened at The Grove stayed at The Grove.

As they clinked their glasses together in a toast to another successful work week, Red asked Merit with a twinkle in her eye, "How's your love life?"

Merit laughed. "You heard already?"

"A little gossip, but mostly I guessed. You look like you did when you were seeing the last boy toy."

Clover laughed. "Tell all. I'm out of the loop on this one."

Merit reminded the women of the night they had wine night at Pot Luck and she met Chef Herbert. "He took me on a Boats and Bats kayak tour to watch the bats fly out at sunset. Very romantic."

Clover smiled. "Well, toss an old married lady a bone. How was it?"

Merit blushed. "Amazing. Freeing. Long overdue."

Red and Clover exchanged amused glances, their eyes twinkling with mischief. They were not the type to offer sappy, sentimental support; instead, they chose humor and irreverence. The wine kicked in and they got a little rowdy at Merit's expense.

Red leaned in, her voice dripping with sarcasm. "Well, well, Ms. Bridges, very liberated of you."

"Have fun but be careful." Clover said. "I always said you had a hidden talent for drama, Merit. I just never thought it would involve a hot, young thing half your age."

Merit rolled her eyes but couldn't suppress a smile. Leave it to her friends to turn her love life into a comedy routine. "He's not half my age. About ten years younger, that's all."

Red raised her glass in mock salute. "To Merit, the cougar of downtown Austin. May your conquests be many and your alibis airtight."

Clover joined in. "Your secret's safe with us."

The three women enjoyed the camaraderie, their worries momentarily forgotten in the haze of wine and laughter. In that dimly lit corner of The Grove, beneath the neon glow of the Texas night, they found solace in each other's company, their bond stronger than ever.

25

The midday sun hung high in the sky, casting a bright, almost sterile light over the sprawling greenhouse on the edge of the Joneses' farm in Bastrop County. Prince had selected the target because the Joneses were very active in the co-op with Lane. In addition, they also farmed cotton, and the farmhouse where the Joneses lived was acres away from the greenhouse, giving him privacy. Prince had now committed arson and murder, twice. The next step, today, was child's play, but it was what Harrison wanted, so he set about the task and tried to enjoy it. He'd find some mischief later, more to his liking.

It was an ordinary day for the farm's workers, bustling about their tasks, unaware of the dark intentions of the man who had just arrived. They were accustomed to seeing the white boll weevil inspector's truck in and around the cotton fields and took no special notice today as Prince was parked between the cotton field and the greenhouse. He grabbed his tools from the back of the truck and went into the first row of the cotton field. He planted the boll weevil trap in the usual manner that he'd learned, hammering the cone-shaped device into the ground. He looked back at the workers who were still busy. Next, Prince walked toward the marijuana greenhouse with a confident stride, as if he belonged there, although inspection of any crop other than cotton was not in his fake purview. When he arrived at the back of the greenhouse, he cut a long gash in the heavy plastic with a box cutter, opened the gap, and slipped inside.

Prince looked around at the rows of medical marijuana plants that stood in vibrant green splendor. The carefully regulated warmth seeped into the walls, creating a humid atmosphere that nurtured the various varieties, including apple fritter, northern lights, and bubble gum. Each step brought him closer to his goal, the vial of spider mites tucked securely in his khaki pants pocket.

He reached the heart of the greenhouse, where the most mature and valuable plants were housed. Their leaves were a deep, healthy green, a testament to the care they received. Prince paused, feigning interest in one particularly tall plant. He ran his fingers over the leaves then pulled them aside and found the heart of the vegetation. Carefully, he pulled the vial from his pocket, put it against the stalk of the plant, and with a flick of his thumb, he uncapped it, allowing a few mites to escape onto the leaves. They began to crawl immediately, tiny harbingers of doom.

Prince moved from plant to plant, repeating the process with clinical efficiency. Each touch was precise, calculated to maximize the spread of the mites. The plants seemed oblivious to their fate, standing tall and proud even as the mites began their silent invasion. Beneath his professional facade lay a sinister intent.

After what felt like hours but was only a matter of minutes, Prince straightened up, his task complete. The vial was empty, its contents now hidden among the lush greenery. He took a final look around, satisfaction curling his lips into a brief cruel smile, and clapped his hands to dust off any remaining bugs.

With a quick look through the cut in the plastic, and seeing no one, Prince walked out of the greenhouse, his heart still racing from the thrill of the deception. The sun seemed brighter, the air fresher as he stepped outside, leaving the doomed plants behind.

He walked across the cotton field toward his truck, bent down as if to inspect the boll weevil trap he'd set, looked at the workers one last time, and left. As he drove away, Prince allowed himself a moment of satisfaction. The mites would soon multiply, turning the thriving greenhouse into a scene of devastation. The thought of the chaos and despair that would follow brought a dark joy to his heart. The world continued to move on, blissfully unaware of the destruction that had just been set in motion under the guise of a routine inspection.

Officer Twitty squinted against the setting sun as he maneuvered his official patrol car down the dusty gravel road leading to Harrison's farm. The property was miles away from downtown LaGrange, but he had the perfect cover, as it was in his jurisdiction and he was responsible for it, if prying eyes made an explanation necessary.

Twitty approached the gate, then waited outside it as he watched Harrison, wearing his Stetson, ride his ATV down from the house. Harrison opened the lock, and the gate swung open, allowing Twitty to follow the ATV up the winding road past rows of weathered oaks and perfectly manicured pastures. Twitty parked near the main house, and stepped out of the car, his boots crunching on the gravel. The two men made their way to the office, the smell of earth and hay mingling with the faint hint of something meaty smoking on the outdoor grill.

Once inside, Twitty could hear the sounds of activity in the adjacent rooms, probably the kitchen, but no one disturbed their meeting. Harrison hung his hat on a rack by the door, sat in his big puffy leather chair, and indicated that Twitty should sit in front of the desk.

"Okay, Twitty," Harrison greeted. "You asked for this meeting. What brings you out here?"

Twitty didn't waste time. "We need to talk about your recent activities in Bastrop and Fayette Counties."

Harrison's lips curled into a smirk as he leaned against the desk. "Effective, aren't they? Sends a real message."

Twitty's face remained stern. He lowered his voice. "Effective, yes. But you're drawing too much attention. People are starting to notice. They're asking questions."

Harrison shrugged, his smirk unwavering. "Let them. They'll never figure out what's going on. I'm only doing a few things here in Fayette County to make it look like we're targets, too. Bastrop is my main focus, but we can't just do things over there. It would make it too obvious."

"Maybe," Twitty replied, his tone measured. "But too much heat, and it won't be just the locals sniffing around. The higher-ups are starting to catch wind of it. Chief Troy has been asking more question. We can't afford that kind of scrutiny. Besides, that investigator of Merit Bridges, Ag Malone, is no fool. He's going to eventually circle back."

Harrison's eyes narrowed, a flicker of annoyance crossing his face. "Are you telling me you're out?"

"I'm suggesting you tone it down a little, just in Fayette County," Twitty said, choosing his words carefully. "Continue sending your message but do it over there in Bastrop County. I can't keep telling people I'm unable to solve these crimes in

LaGrange. Pretty soon, I need to arrest someone or at least make it stop."

Harrison pushed off the desk, standing tall. "And what if I don't?"

Twitty met his gaze, unflinching. "Then you're on your own. I've covered for you more times than I care to count, but there's a limit to what I can do. If you bring too much heat, I won't be able to protect you."

The room fell silent, the tension thickening the air. Harrison's smirk faded, replaced by a look of contemplation. Finally, he nodded, a reluctant agreement.

"Fine," he said, his voice tight. "I'll tone it down."

Twitty gave a curt nod. "Good. Thanks, Harrison."

Harrison walked to the door and paused with his hand on the handle. "Just make sure you hold up your end, Twitty. Keep me posted on every move that APD or the sheriff in Bastrop makes."

Twitty was obviously thinking of his continuing extra paycheck. "You can count on it."

26

Merit, Betty, and Val sat in the conference room surrounded by blue balloons and streamers, courtesy of Val's great taste in decorating. On the table was a blueberry cake with blue buttercream frosting, courtesy of Betty's baking skills. Next to the cake was a cake slicer, small blue checkered plates, and a stack of blue-colored party napkins. Coffee and tea on one end of the credenza provided a nice aroma. About a dozen gifts wrapped in shiny silver paper with baby blue bows and ribbons were stacked on the other end of the credenza.

Bob Tom Jakes, Betty's husband and new proud granddad, held his two-week-old grandson wrapped in a pale blue blanket and wearing a blue beanie. It looked like a Smurf had thrown up in the conference room.

Bobby, Bob Tom's son, and his wife, Emily had given birth just two weeks before, to the delight of all concerned. The baby's full name was Bob Ethan Jakes. He was called Ethan, though no one knew exactly why. He cooed and appeared to smile, a new skill he'd just developed, to the delight of his parents and grandparents.

Bobby hugged his new stepmother, Betty. "I didn't know this was a baby shower. Gifts are always nice, but certainly unexpected."

Betty had developed a soft spot for Bobby as he'd cleaned up his act, married Emily, had a child, and become a somewhat upstanding citizen. "Men can have baby showers, too."

Merit beamed at the baby, remembering when Ace was born. "It's a family shower to celebrate everyone's new role in Ethan's life. Let's open those presents."

Emily, who was fairly new to the group, beamed as she opened and unpacked a large stack of cloth diapers and a one-year subscription to a diaper service.

"Who's this from?"

Merit said, "They're all from all of us."

Emily got a little teary, hormones or gratitude. Either way, she was moved. "Thank you so much! This is a godsend. Bobby, you open one."

Bobby picked up a squarish box about the size of a microwave and shook it gently. "Sounds like a baby bowling ball."

Everyone laughed, partly at his joke, and partly at his blue lips from eating the icing.

When he stripped off the paper, he revealed a MamaRoo multi motion baby swing. "Awesome."

On it went from there through onesies, baby blankets, bibs, and multiple gift cards to both practical and fancy baby stores. Ethan was officially the most spoiled baby in Austin. He was passed from relative to friend and back again until he conked out.

As the festivities wound down, Betty stood. "I hate to end the fun, but we do have a law firm to run."

Merit was standing by the wall of glass windows, having her

turn holding baby Ethan, who was now purring in his sleep. "I think Ethan's done for the day."

Bob Tom stood and walked over to Merit. "Yep. I think he's had it. I can't thank you enough, Merit." He looked over at Betty and Merit knew the gratitude was as much for her as the new baby. Betty had always wanted little ones around, and never dreamed that she'd have a grandchild from her late in life marriage to Bob Tom.

Val disappeared, then re-appeared with a book cart from the mailroom, and loaded up the gifts. Betty put the remainder of the cake into a plastic container and added that to the cart. Val tied about half of the balloons onto the cart handle and rolled it out into the hall.

When they all moved to the reception area to say goodbye, Ethan let free a tiny little fart to punctuate the meet-up. All laughed with delight, none of them knowing why gas was so funny. They were just happy.

After Bob Tom and the rest of the family left, Merit and Betty were once again watching KNEW 9, keeping up with the latest from Red Thallon. Onscreen, Red stood in front of the camera, her fiery red hair catching the light as the wind lifted it. In the summer heat, she wore even less clothing than usual, if that was legally possible. She was on Guadalupe Street, called The Drag, in front of a coffee shop with protestors both inside and outside. She held the microphone with a steady hand, her eyes sharp and focused as she reported on the pot pardons in Maryland following recent legalization of marijuana.

"What happens with the new environment of tolerance may change things for those positioned in the market," she began, her voice clear and authoritative. "Eleven hundred licensed

Texas hemp growers are poised to take advantage of a legal adult-use market, if and when Texas chooses to go down the path of legalization."

The scene behind her was bustling, with people milling about, some celebrating the news while others seemed deep in thought, contemplating what this development meant for their future. Red turned and asked a question of a young man standing on the sidewalk with a 'Decriminalize Pot' sign in his hands.

"Why are you out here today?"

"We're trying to make people aware of what's going on with so many carrying the scars of marijuana convictions. There are people with criminal records who can't vote, go to college, buy a house, or get a credit card because they used a substance no more dangerous than a cold beer."

The camera panned over to a group of protestors huddled together, discussing strategies and possibilities. They looked hopeful yet cautious, aware that the future was uncertain. Red continued, her tone becoming more intense as she delved deeper into the implications of the pardons.

"Pot pardons are not just a gesture of goodwill, they are a seismic shift in the landscape of cannabis legislation. Thousands of individuals previously convicted for minor marijuana offenses are now seeing their records cleared in Maryland with other states planning to follow. This is a monumental step toward rectifying past injustices and a signal to the market that change is on the horizon."

Red glanced at her notes, then back at the camera. "But the question remains: how will this affect the broader industry, especially here in Texas? Legalization and the pardons in Maryland could be a precursor to more widespread changes, but the path to legalization in most states is still fraught with political and social challenges. People familiar with Texas's cannabis market believe that adult-use is a ways down the road for the Lone Star State and that near-term focus needs to be on achieving an unencumbered medical cannabis system."

As she spoke, Red's passion for uncovering the truth and shedding light on complex issues was evident. Her reporting wasn't just about conveying facts; it was about painting a picture of the human stories behind the headlines. She knew that for many, these pardons represented hope and a second chance.

"The ripple effects of Maryland's decisions are just beginning to be felt," she concluded. "For those in the industry, it's a waiting game, one that requires patience, resilience, and a readiness to act swiftly when the time comes. This is Red Thallon, reporting live from The Drag, where these protestors are hoping for history to be rewritten, one pardon at a time."

Merit looked at Betty. "This industry is getting more and more attention, and I don't know how long our clients can hold on to their advantage."

"I know. There's an article every day online about some new California conglomerate trying to shoehorn their way into the local market."

"Without Lindy, I don't know how we're going to influence the committee. I need a new plan."

"You'll come up with something, darlin'. You always do. It'll happen, come hell or high water."

27

Merit found herself back at Pot Luck near closing time. She didn't bother to fool herself as to why she was there. She could use a little escape after witnessing what the Lanes were going through. She or Betty had checked on Thad Lane every day, and the news was depressing every time. She still hadn't come up with a plan on how to help the Lanes' business and ensure the receipt of the new licenses. Her brain was tired of thinking about it, and she wanted a distraction.

She perched at the bar on the same stool as last time, and Patrick came over. "Good to see you, Merit."

Merit looked at him and smiled. "So glad you're here. I hoped you would be."

He signaled to the same bartender to pour Merit a glass of wine, then said to the staffer, "You can go when your station is clean."

The bartender nodded, poured the same brand of Malbec, and did a final wipe of the bar.

Patrick whispered to Merit, "Give me a few minutes, then meet me in the kitchen."

Merit looked at her watch, timed five minutes exactly, then took her wine and went through the serving doors. Inside, it was almost dark with only the lights from the various appliances casting streams of color across the stainless-steel tables and recently mopped floor.

Patrick slipped up behind her and startled her in the most tantalizing way. He pulled her over by the prep station, grabbed her by the waist, and lifted her up on the steel counter. His lips found hers and they kissed, their tongues finding one another.

She knew what he looked like naked, but she wanted to see him again. He obviously had the same idea. Clothes went flying, and they were off to the races. This time, it was fast and furious, not like the night at her place which was much more romantic. Neither needed much foreplay nor took long to reach satisfaction. When they were satiated, they slumped down to the damp floor, their backs to a counter, and Patrick pulled a white tablecloth over them.

After their breathing returned to normal, Merit heard a phone ringing. It was late, really late. Who would call the restaurant at that hour? Patrick hugged her, helped her up off the floor, and wrapped the tablecloth around her. He then went to answer the call, his broad shoulders and perfect behind displayed in the glow of the appliance lights. She checked her watch and was surprised to learn that it was two in the morning. Her brow furrowed as she wondered why he didn't just ignore the call.

He picked up the landline in the kitchen office and she heard the mumbling sound of his voice. She suddenly felt uncomfortable when her armpits prickled, and she didn't know why. She found her clothes, dressed, sat at the small break table, and waited.

When he finished the call, he walked back to where she was sitting. He pulled on his chef pants and sat down, shirtless, without another word. She just stared at him dumbly for a moment, then she laughed nervously. "It's an unusual time for a call. Is everything okay?"

He nodded. "Yes, sorry. I probably should have just left it."

She didn't respond.

The silence was uncomfortable. He sighed. "Okay. I didn't want to tell you, but I'm waiting on some information that I can't ignore. Pot Luck isn't doing well."

She blinked. "What? How could that be? It's packed every time I come in."

"Yeah. For the most part it's an illusion, I'm afraid."

She had no idea what that meant. "An illusion?"

"You don't understand the business, Merit."

She was taken aback. "Excuse me?"

"Everyone in Austin seems to want to open their own restaurant. Competition right now is fierce. I'm barely keeping my head above water. The employees are starting to give notice."

"But you're already established. Award winning. New restaurants wouldn't affect you that much. Would they?"

Merit heard a door close at the back of the restaurant, and she froze.

What the hell was that?

She looked at Patrick who didn't seem bothered at all and started laughing. She looked down at herself, partially dressed. If someone came into the kitchen, it was still pretty obvious what they had been up to. She brushed at her clothing self-consciously.

"I don't think whoever that was is going to come in the kitchen."

"Aren't you curious about who that was?"

"I know who it was. Just a few things being dropped off at

the loading dock in the alley. Easier to unload a delivery truck in the early morning when the streets are empty."

She stared at him. The date was turning weird.

"Don't worry. I've got it under control. Just need a little time to sort some things out."

Merit nodded but didn't believe him. "I think it's time I head home. It's quite late and I have a big day tomorrow."

He started to embrace her which turned into a half hug. "I'm so glad you came by. I had fun."

She smiled. "Yes, it was." They got up from the table and he walked her to the front door and unlocked the deadbolt.

"Good night, Merit."

She pecked him on the cheek, waved as she left, and walked to where her BMW was parked. She was looking over her shoulder and totally creeped out.

Odd. *He didn't walk me to my car.*

28

Merit had a huge day and had no time to think about the Lanes or even getting a bite to eat until the end of the day. Ag arrived after Betty left and the building quieted down. It was Ag's and Merit's favorite time to gather and strategize when they were working on a case. Ag pushed the glass hallway door without response, then knocked loudly enough for Merit to hear in her office. She walked down the hall, barefoot, having slipped out of her heels right after Betty left for the day. She looked through the sidelight and saw that it was Ag, turned the lock at the bottom of the right glass door, and let him in.

"Hey, Ag. Welcome."

"Hi, Merit, glad to see you're locking that door when you're alone in here."

"Warning heeded. Things have been creepier around town ever since Lindy was murdered. I don't even walk to my car without security anymore."

"Good. If it takes fear to make you careful, so be it."

Merit laughed. "Bully."

Ag laughed. "Headstrong."

"Want a beer? I have wine open."

"Either one."

Ag followed Merit down the hall to the break room where she retrieved a longneck from the refrigerator and handed it to him. He popped off the top and they both went back down the hall, past reception, and into her office. Only now did he appear to realize how short she seemed and looked at her bare feet.

Merit noticed his look. "Informal today. My feet are killing me. New heels."

"The price of being a beautiful woman."

She blushed ever so slightly. "Have a seat."

Ag took a long pull on his beer. "I haven't written up my report yet, but I found some interesting things while researching Constance Stanhope's land history in Lee County."

"Val will be happy to hear that. He's been skulking around waiting for something to happen on his grandmother's case."

"It appears that Blake Harrison, a wealthy landowner over near LaGrange, has been buying up land in Fayette County, where he lives, and some of the surrounding counties. His purchases include the area around Constance Stanhope's property. He's amassed thousands of acres over the last two to three years. The Stanhope tract is completely surrounded by his recent purchases."

"Any evidence that it's actually his representative who approached Constance?"

"No, it could be a competitor, but I'd lay money that it's him. It fits the pattern I uncovered. He has an organization called BH Investments, LLC. I had to dig through a few layers to find the owners. He has over fifty-one percent, but there are others with smaller interests in the company with him, probably backing him with cash for the purchases."

"Really? I've heard of Blake Harrison, but I didn't think he was a big player."

"He flies a bit under the radar with Austin businesses. Has a small-town image in LaGrange, but underneath it all, he's got fingers in lots of pies. I think the LaGrange Police Department might be protecting him."

"What is he doing with the land?"

"That's the interesting part. Those in the company all have other properties with cannabis licenses and are growing some high-class weed and hemp around the area. It's possible they need more land for cultivation. I drove by several tracts. One in Bastrop County, near the Lanes' farm, has a big greenhouse already set up on it."

Merit looked thoughtful. "Or, maybe they're just buying up the property to hold the competition at bay."

Ag nodded. "Or both. Harrison's latest acquisition, the farm off Dandelion Lane with the big greenhouse, makes me think growing is his priority. Crops are already cultivated, so part of his purchase price was the weed."

"Interesting. Could you give me a few more hours on the file and see if Harrison and the others have made any political contributions?"

"Good idea. I'll look into it and add it to the report before I send it over."

"Thanks, Ag."

"Would you like a quick verbal update if I find anything interesting?"

"Yes, please."

Ag winked, and in his sexiest voice said, "I like the way you say please."

This time, Merit blushed all the way to her bare toes.

✶

Prince stepped out of his sleek gray SUV, the night air as hot and muggy as a Louisiana swamp, and approached Constance Stanhope's quaint farmhouse. His sharp features were set in a mask of determination as he climbed the steps to her front door, his mind already plotting the best way to persuade her to sign the contract.

Knocking firmly, he waited, the sound echoing through the quiet countryside. After a moment, the door creaked open, revealing Constance, her frail form silhouetted in the dim light from within.

"May I help you?"

"Mrs. Stanhope," Prince acknowledged with a nod, his voice smooth as silk. "I spoke with you last week about the proposition on your land. May I come in?"

Constance hesitated, her hand trembling slightly on the doorknob, but ultimately stepped aside, allowing him entry into her home. As Prince crossed the threshold, he looked around to make sure they were alone.

Constance untied her apron and hung it on a hook on the kitchen side of the shared sitting room wall. "Would you like some tea?"

"No, thank you."

They settled in the sitting room, him in a chair and her on the sofa, the air heavy with his words dripping persuasive charm.

"Have you had a chance to look over the contract I left with you? You told me you'd sign it before I came back." He lied.

"I spoke to my grandson, Valentine. He works for a lawyer, Merit Bridges. If you need to discuss this further, I was told to tell you to contact their office. I have her card here somewhere." Nervously, Constance got up, went over to a sideboard, and opened the top drawer which contained a loaded Walther

Model PP, her deceased husband's pistol from World War II. "I know it's in here."

The pistol was small, and probably a little under powered compared to the arsenal locked up by her dead husband and left in the garage gun safe, but it was relatively light, easy to carry and conceal, and it wasn't intimidating to Constance.

She found the card, not taking the pistol, but leaving the drawer open. She walked back, handed the card to Prince, re-seated herself on the sofa, and asked, "Do you have a card?"

Prince's facade cracked, a surge of frustration and anger coursing through him as he looked at the name on the card. *That Bridges bitch has become a real thorn in my side.*

Prince had hoped Constance would be cooperative, but now it seemed he would have to resort to more drastic measures to ensure his plans remained intact. Harrison needed this last tract of land to consolidate the acreage he'd already purchased. Prince didn't plan to take no for an answer. He could force her to sign the contract and let Harrison worry about whether it would stick later. It was better than nothing.

"If you don't have a card, my daughter can write it down for me. I called her when I saw you drive up. She told me to let her know if you came back." Constance smiled sweetly. "She really wants to meet you."

Prince took on the same look he had when he preyed on Senator Linden. The adrenaline rush felt calming and pleasing to him. As he leaned closer to her frail figure, his hands curled into fists at his sides.

Constance blanched white. "You know, my grandson will be a lawyer someday. My husband was a senator. Did you know that? You remember him, don't you, Val? You haven't been to see me in so long. I planted some petunias. How's your mother? Where's Connie?" Constance began to ramble, her words disjointed and nonsensical. She went on and on, while looking around the room as if she didn't know where she was.

Prince paused, his gaze narrowing as he studied her, realizing with a sinking feeling that her mind was slipping into the depths of dementia. With a curse under his breath, he recoiled, the momentary urge for violence subsided. There would be no fun in it. She'd break like a twig with no recognition of his treachery. He looked at his watch. He had to get back down the farm road and onto the county road before the daughter showed up.

Better get moving. Shouldn't have come in my personal car.

He took a moment to reconsider violence against her. She couldn't identify him. Not in her present state. If she did, who would believe her? And, he had on his businessman disguise, his dreadlocks neatly hidden under the salt-and-pepper gray wig. He knew he couldn't risk leaving a trail of this type of violence behind him, especially not in such a close-knit community. And now, Merit Bridges was involved. Regret gnawed at him as he stood and turned on his heel, abandoning his plans to force Constance's compliance.

He knew he would have to find another way to achieve his goals, but for now, he had to limit his exposure. Someone might start connecting the dots. Surely, Merit Bridges would put two and two together if he resorted to violence. With one last glance at Constance, still mumbling and lost in her own world of confusion, Prince slipped out into the steamy night.

Val and his mother, called Connie to differentiate her from her namesake, pulled into the yard before the farmhouse, crunching gravel. Unbeknownst to them, they had missed Prince's gray SUV on the road by only minutes.

Constance met them at the door. "He was here. You just missed him."

Val touched her shoulder and Connie hugged her. "Are you all right? I brought Val, just in case."

"He really scared me. I thought he would hurt me when I told him that we had hired Merit Bridges."

Val took her hand. "Oh, Grands."

The three went into the kitchen and stood beside the vintage yellow Formica table.

"I could see he was really angry. I should never have let him in, but I thought he might force the door if I didn't."

Val controlled his anger. He saw the open drawer of the sideboard and walked over to look inside, where he saw the Walther. "How did you get rid of him? You didn't shoot him, did you?"

"No. I never took the pistol out of the drawer. I pretended I was losing my mind."

Connie pulled out a chair at the table and sat. Val helped Constance take a seat and stood beside the two women. "Why?"

"At first, I just froze, then I made up sentences that didn't make sense. I couldn't think of anything else to do."

Connie was incredulous. "What?"

"I rambled on about your dad and Valentine going to law school and anything else I could think of. I tried to wet myself, but I couldn't go, I was so afraid."

Val dropped down into a kitchen chair and laughed. "Good job, Grands."

Connie was not as amused. "I think you should come spend the night at my house. We'll sort this out with the lawyer tomorrow."

Constance nodded. "For once, I won't disagree with you. Val, help me pack a bag, will you?"

"With pleasure."

29

Merit, sitting at her desk, opened her email and found a note from Ag. Rather than attaching his report, he advised that because of its confidentiality, he had zipped the file and added it to the firm's secure portal. Only Merit and Betty could access the files therein. Only Ag, Val, and a few others could add documents.

This must be sensitive.

Merit opened the security portal and located the file. When she unzipped it, she found the report from Ag with the information they had discussed, plus an attachment entitled: POLITICAL CONTRIBUTIONS OF MEDICAL MARIJUANA GROWERS.

The document contained a list of names in order from highest contributors to lowest. Beside the amount of each contribution was the name of a senate or house member who received the donation. All were on either the senate or house committees controlling the licensure for medical marijuana. At the top of the list was BH Investments, LLC. It wasn't exactly a smoking gun, and the next on the list was close in contributions, so names could have climbed the list, especially if several were combined. Still, seeing the name of the company that was circling the Stanhope land being the same company that made the most medical marijuana contributions was a big coincidence, if it was one.

John David Lane's name was about halfway down the list with the farmers belonging to the co-op populating some of the last entries. The amounts, when Lane's contributions were combined with the others in the co-op, would have placed them second on the list behind BH Investments, LLC.

Merit took a quick scan through the rest of the report to make sure she hadn't missed anything and closed down the portal.

Next, she pulled up a website reporting donations to particular state senators, and researched Senator Robert Ersery. She scrolled through the list of top donors to the last Ersery campaign, and there it was. BH Investments, LLC was in his top five contributors. Millions had been donated to keep incumbent Ersery in his senate seat. He wasn't shy at all about receiving money from lobbyists either. Merit did a cross check on the lobbyists who had managed contributions in exchange for influence.

The Lane group did not use lobbyists, Merit served that purpose, but that didn't mean someone else didn't. She noodled around the site into layers of information and eventually found what she was looking for. Blake Harrison was right there again. This time making contributions from his personal position, not the LLC, probably to stay under the contribution limits legislated by Texas statute. She made some notes with talking points for a meeting with Lane and the co-op.

Merit eventually put aside the Lane file and started culling through a fresh stack of correspondence that Betty had cued up for her to approve before she left for the night.

Ugh.

Her mind was elsewhere. She was angry that Harrison might have gone after her clients, and he was certainly double-dipping on influencing those in positions of power. After a few frustrating minutes, she shut it down and called Security for an escort.

Tomorrow is another day.

30

The next day, Merit began the morning in her condo, as usual. When she was dressed and almost ready to go, she received a text from Red asking her to call. Merit patted Pepper on the head on her way out the door and waited until she got into her SUV to hit speed dial to call her friend's mobile. It went to voicemail, so she left a message.

"Hey, Red. You rang?"

Merit drove her SUV out of the garage, listened to a Hayes Carll song, "Naked Checkers," and tried to chill out on the ride to work. She was conflicted about her time with Patrick. She'd had a great night with him, but there was also something not right about the situation, and her circumstances of her departure was totally weird. She was getting a strange vibe from him, but she couldn't put her finger on what it could be. Her armpits prickled and she decided right then and there that she would not sleep with him again until she got to the bottom of what was setting off her warning system.

Maybe I shouldn't see him at all.

It made no sense to her that Pot Luck wasn't doing well. She had numerous restaurant clients, most celebrity owned, and she didn't see them going under. Maybe he was overfinanced. She had made sure her clients had a balanced budget and actually qualified for a loan with a reputable lender if they needed capital. Maybe it was nothing, but her intuition told her it was something. She decided she would talk to him about it. Give him the benefit of the doubt. Maybe even offer to help. She had tons of banking contacts. Maybe she could hook him up.

Merit arrived at her office, said good morning to Betty, and dug into the day's paperwork. She managed to edit a few draft contracts and do some legal research, but her mind kept returning to Patrick.

At that moment, she received another text from Red: *Sorry, I had no idea.*

Merit let out a deep sigh. "What now?"

Betty apparently heard her and entered Merit's office. "What is it?"

"Red is onto something." Merit flipped over a thick legal book on her desk, found the remote for the television, turned it on, and changed the channel to KNEW 9.

Betty's shoulders dropped. "I hope it's not the Lanes. I don't think they can take anymore."

Merit couldn't imagine what could be going on either. She hoped that another farm hadn't burned down, or worse Thad had passed away. She wasn't sure if she could handle it. Red had apologized in her text. What on earth would she feel sorry about?

While Merit waited for a commercial to clear, unfortunately, she went online and checked Red's posts on social media. There it was: *Pot Luck's doors have been locked for breaching its lease and not paying rent.*

Another post showed: *Patrick Herbert is floundering in his award-winning restaurant, Pot Luck. Employee paychecks have bounced, and employees have reported a demeaning work environment to the Texas Workforce Commission.* Several posts went on to enumerate similar issues as the first posts she had found. The worst was: *Pot Luck's Pots Filled with Pot!*

What the Fritos?

Merit looked up; her heart felt like it was seizing in her chest when she saw what was on the screen. She just stared; no words would form.

"Oh no," Betty whispered. "Oh no."

Merit couldn't believe it. Red was reporting the news and now Merit understood why she felt she needed to say she was sorry. Red was standing in front of Pot Luck, doors chained and locked, reporting the arrest of Patrick.

"Due to a recent report to KNEW 9, we are investigating the arrest of the chef and owner of Pot Luck Restaurant, Patrick Herbert."

Merit was sure that she was going to throw up. She watched as Patrick was being taken away in handcuffs from the restaurant.

Betty sighed. "Oh, Merit."

"This can't be true. It can't be. I was just with him."

Red continued. "According to law enforcement sources, Chef Herbert has been arrested for selling drugs out of his award-winning restaurant. Law enforcement apparently sent in a ringer to act as a waitress and get information on the operation. The undercover agent was able to obtain evidence implicating the award-winning chef and several of his staff."

Was that what the late-night call had been to Patrick? She had been right when she saw the bartender dealing drugs and it appeared that Patrick had lied to her about it. All the pieces were falling into place.

Merit launched herself from the room and ran down the hall to the restroom. She slammed the door behind her and heaved what little she had in her stomach. How could this be? She had attached herself to a criminal. Would anyone connect them? Her girlfriends knew, and Betty's suspicions were now confirmed, but who else?

There was a soft knock at the bathroom door and Betty asked. "Merit, are you okay?"

Merit wiped at her mouth and stood up. She grabbed some paper towels from the dispenser and wiped her face, then proceeded to wash her hands. She needed to keep a lid on this. Tight.

"Yes, I'm fine. I'll be right out."

She opened the bathroom door and Betty hugged her.

Merit was tearing up. "I know exactly what you're thinking, so don't bother saying it."

"I wasn't going to say a thing."

"I know, but you'd be right to."

Merit went back to her office and texted Red: *No warning? What gives?*

Red didn't text her back, only adding to Merit's frustration.

31

———

A few days later, Merit got on the road to Houston to fetch Ace for a long weekend at the beach in Port Aransas. It was comforting to have Pepper Dog sleeping in the passenger seat beside her. She was sure that Pepper missed Ace between visits, and Ace often expressed how much he missed his pup. Ace attended a school for dyslexic students in Houston and ever since Merit had enrolled him there, Ace had been thriving. It had been a solid choice, even though she missed him dearly during the semester, between visits.

In addition to mother-son time, Merit needed to escape from Austin for a while so she could process what had transpired with Patrick and lick her wounds. She didn't want to face any of her Austin friends at the moment and needed some time to decompress. So much had happened in the past few weeks and the worst of it had been Brad Lane's death and Patrick's arrest. She wasn't interested in being around to watch the news of the fall of Pot Luck. She also wanted to spend some time, in Houston, with her dearest friend of many years, Joy, and Joy's husband, Tucker. No matter how low she got, Joy was always able to lift her up.

When she turned onto I-10 in Columbus, Red's name showed up on Merit's caller ID. Red had called her a few times since Patrick's arrest, and Merit hadn't responded. That was one of the things she needed to mull over. How could her longtime friend drop a bomb like that and not give her a heads-up? Even if she had texted, she should have tried harder or left a message. It was unforgivable.

Her phone rang again, and seeing it was Ag, and assuming it was work, she clicked on the hands-free option.

"Hi, Ag."

"Hey, Merit."

"What's up?"

"I just wanted to see if you were okay."

She groaned. How had he known? Did Betty tell him? Betty wasn't the type to gossip, certainly not about Merit. Plus, she knew Merit would be furious with her if she revealed anything to Ag.

"I'm fine. I thought something might have happened with Thad or the case."

There was silence on the other end that spoke volumes. Merit wasn't in the mood to get into anything. She just wanted to forget it all.

"Yes. I do have an update. That's why I called." Ag fudged the truth a bit, but it was awkward between them.

"Okay. Shoot."

"Thad Lane is holding his own. I still have the hired security at the hospital in rotating shifts."

"Great. Be sure and bill me so I can pass that expense along to Lane. I cleared it with him right after Brad died. It's giving Gladys peace of mind to know someone is there at all times."

"Will do. Also, as you requested, I did some investigating

into the vandalism around the various counties outside of Austin."

"Will it keep until I get back? Or, can you put it in an email if it's not urgent? I just need a few more miles to decompress."

"Absolutely. I'll send you an update and you can look at it when you feel like it."

"Good work. I'm almost to Houston, Ag. Let me touch base with you in a few days. I'm about to grab Ace. Thanks for checking in, you know I appreciate it."

At the sound of Ace's name, Pepper perked up and started looking out the window.

"No problem, Merit. I'll talk to you when you get back. Enjoy your time off."

"Thank you." She clicked off the call. Her eyes welled up with tears and she cursed them. She hated crying, but she was just so confused about the whole situation.

The truth was that Merit was not going directly to Ace's school. She wanted to visit and have a heart-to-heart with her BFF. She planned to spend the night with Joy and Tucker and get up the next morning to pick up Ace and head to the beach. She didn't know why she was lying to Ag so much. She was hiding from him. Was it out of some type of shame? No, it was the need for privacy, especially from him. He was hanging too close lately, and she needed a break.

Merit circled the Galleria on Loop 610 and headed down 59 toward Joy and Tucker's home in the Sunset Terrace area just west of Rice University, her alma mater. She took a quick side trip through the campus, stopping in the circular driveway to look between the arches. She never failed to feel nostalgic at the sight of the beautiful campus with its majestic oak trees and

Revival-style architecture. It looked like something had been picked up out of historic England and dropped on three-hundred acres near the Art District and Medical Center near downtown Houston. What a privilege it had been to do her undergraduate work there.

Merit pulled into the driveway of her friend's home and opened the door for Pepper as Joy came out to greet her. Pepper jumped down, ran to the grass beside the driveway, relieved herself, and started exploring the landscaping.

Merit hugged her friend tightly. "You're a beautiful sight to see."

Joy stepped into Merit's embrace, feeling the weight of her friend's sorrow pressing against her own heart. She held Merit tightly, knowing that words alone couldn't heal the pain of a broken heart and betrayal.

"You're here," Joy murmured, her voice soft with empathy. "Come in, let's sit down. Tucker will be home soon. Let's have a chat before he gets here."

They moved through the beautiful entry to the lovely home and into the living room where Joy had a nice bottle of Margaux breathing on the coffee table. Two wine bowls awaited the luscious red liquid. Pepper and Joy's pup, Willie, a milky-white Westie, rooted around in the toy basket and occupied themselves on a play date, while the women talked.

Joy served them and Merit poured out her heart, tears mingling with each sip of wine as she recounted the pain of her recent breakup and the betrayal she felt from Patrick. He had lied to her when she asked him flat out what she had seen. And, even if he hadn't, lies of omission were just as lethal as lies of commission in Merit's eyes.

"What's worse is that everyone knows. I feel so stupid to have trusted him. I even had the armpit prickles and ignored them."

Joy listened, offering gentle words of comfort and understanding, her presence a steady anchor in the storm of Merit's emotions. She ended her words of kindness with a bit of humor. "He must have been pretty luscious for you to ignore the armpit prickles."

With that, Merit burst into laughter and released a bit of her pent-up feelings of anger and frustration at the situation. "He was pretty yummy."

Joy sipped her wine. "I doubt as many people know as you think. One news cycle and they'll be onto something else entirely."

Merit started to feel better and better from her friend's counsel and the wine, and just getting out of Dodge for a few days. Joy poured the last of the wine into their glasses. Good timing, as Tucker walked in the door soon after and opened another bottle.

The next morning, Merit said goodbye to Joy and Tucker over breakfast and drove to Ace's school. She had to go inside and check him out for the weekend, and she took advantage of the time until class was out to speak with the headmaster. He assured her that Ace was thriving and that he was getting tutorial help in any subjects that were challenging to him. At Merit's request, a landscaper watched Pepper outside in a small, fenced area.

Merit was glad that Joy had helped her pull herself together, because she didn't want Ace to see her upset or think that something was wrong. He didn't need to be worried about her. His top priority was school. Besides, she'd given Patrick enough energy for the time being.

When Ace appeared, still slim and blond, but a little taller than she remembered, they hugged for a little too long in Ace's estimation. They gathered his bag from his messy room, went outside and retrieved Pepper who wet herself with excitement, loaded up the BMW, and headed out for the weekend.

"How are you doing, Sweet Pea?"

"Same old, Mom. Nothing new."

"Oh really? I thought that you would have lots of things to fill me in on."

"No, everything has been going well. I officially have no complaints."

She laughed. "Well hallelujah. Are you looking forward to some time on the beach?"

"Yes, I can't wait. Let's make s'mores tonight."

"Deal. For now, Betty sent her famous lemon squares for the drive. They're in the tin on the back seat."

"Dope." Ace beamed at her, showing more happiness than he probably cared to express at seeing her and his beloved pup.

"Dope?" Are we playing the weed game again.

Ace laughed. "How about awesome?" He grabbed the lemon squares, put some music on from his iPhone, and the three rocked out all the way to the coast.

32

———————

After stopping for a bite to eat on the way, it wasn't long before Merit, Ace, and Pepper found themselves pulling up to the beach house in Port Aransas. As usual, Betty had arranged for the caretaker to stock the pantry, refrigerator, and wine chiller, and open the house to let in some fresh salt air. It was hot, but the ocean breeze felt good and both Merit and Ace took deep breaths and sighed a little. It was a start. The beach always had an incredible effect on Merit. It relaxed her the moment she drove onto the ferry, smelled the sea salt, and saw the dolphins jumping in the waves.

Ace went to his room to drop his backpack and change into beach shorts with Pepper following on his heels. Merit poured herself a glass of wine and went out to relax on the deck before she lit the firepit for the s'mores. The beach was beautiful this time of day. The magic hour. She could hear the waves lapping against the shore and see the setting sun reflected in the waves when Ace appeared and joined her.

It was in these moments that Merit truly appreciated the house. There were times that she never wanted to leave the

187

place, but of course at some point she would have to return to reality. For now, this was her respite. She grabbed some kindling beside the firepit and set it inside the brick ring. After it caught, Ace added cut logs and watched as they began to burn. They loved a good fire, and it was even more amazing at the beach.

Merit returned to the kitchen, poured another glass of wine, and collected the marshmallows, graham crackers, and chocolate. Ace found the long skewers in a kitchen drawer, and they roasted the white puffs into gooey balls of char. Merit watched as Ace's marshmallow hung precariously on the skewer, and they laughed when he caught it before it slipped off the graham cracker. She sipped at her wine as he took his first bite. It brought joy to her heart to see him happy. Pepper, too, seemed content as she tucked herself under Ace's chair for a nap.

"Mom, do you want one? I'll make it for you?"

"Yes, please."

Ace expertly prepared one for her, and they munched silently and listened to the gulls overhead. "You can't do much better than s'mores."

"Nope. Or the beach." Ace continued playing with the fire while she enjoyed her wine. It was the perfect first night at the coast.

"Mom?"

"Yes, Peach."

"Do you think Dad is looking down on us?"

She held her breath for a moment, surprised by his question. It had been a while since they talked about his father. It was hard to understand his suicide, regardless of the reason being Tony was so very ill.

"Yes, Ace, I do. I think Dad is going to be watching over you forever. He loved you very much. I hope you always remember that."

"I just really miss him."

"I know. I do too. Every day."

Merit thought of Brad and the Lanes. She had no idea what she would do if anything ever happened to Ace. He was her world and she hoped that the loss of his father would not permanently scar him. Change and pain were inevitable, but scarring might be avoided with the right support, which he had.

It felt to Merit that everything in the last week had happened in a whirlwind. She hadn't been able to fully process the fact that Patrick had been arrested. It seemed so unbelievable. He was so well respected in the Austin foodie industry, or so she thought. She couldn't believe he would get involved in something like drug distribution. Business couldn't have been that bad that he had to sell his integrity to make a buck. Maybe the fact was that she didn't know him well enough. His employees were helping him deal drugs in the restaurant, and she had been there when some of it happened. She had given Patrick a chance to tell her what was afoot and he lied. The thought of being with him the night before he was arrested made her face burn with humiliation.

Merit hadn't had the opportunity to confront him after his arrest, and she probably never would. Even if he wanted to offer an explanation or an apology, she could not take the chance of being near him. She was happy they never went public with their dating. It was enough that the employees of the restaurant knew. They would surely spread it through the foodie grapevine. Hopefully, any gossip that manifested would die down soon or be found untrustworthy. Her reputation in the legal community would take a hit if she was believed to have associated with a known criminal. She also hated that people might know she'd made a poor decision.

Patrick would likely be let out on bail, and she hoped that he wouldn't try to contact her. She had no intention of forgiving him, and she didn't want to hear any ridiculous excuses from him. His biggest punishment would be the loss of his precious restaurant. Pot Luck certainly wouldn't survive and, unfortunately, his investors would go down with him.

The next day was full of swimming and eating and playing with Ace and Pepper. Merit didn't have time to feel sorry for herself, and her mood began to lift even further. That night, Merit decided to take a walk on the beach after Ace and Pepper went to bed. Starry walks were her solace, a chance to get lost in her thoughts. The evening was still warm, with a breeze coming off the ocean. She wore shorts and a hoodie and walked barefoot, the sand still holding the heat from the day.

Her mind drifted to the Lane family and all they had suffered. Her issues were minuscule compared to the losses their family had endured. In a short amount of time, so much had happened since the fire on the Lanes' farm, a real tragedy. The twins had suffered at the hands of the heartless. Brad's death and his unbearable funeral were still heavy on her soul. Thad's life still hung in the balance.

Next, the news of the senator's murder had shaken the entire State of Texas. She still couldn't process it or internalize the horror Lindy must have endured at being strangled. No one should ever suffer that intense fear. Not the least of which, Lindy's death placed her clients in a vulnerable position. A new strategy was required to help the Lanes' business, but what?

And, Val's grandmother's case had taken a hard turn with

the report of the stranger who threatened her. How did it fit in the master plan of terror going on in the counties surrounding Austin? Was it part of a larger scheme, or just some greedy land grabber out to defraud the elderly?

She stopped on the beach, checked the mile marker posted in the dunes, and realized she had walked farther than planned. She turned back toward her beach house. It was getting late and she wanted to get some rest. She had processed all she could for the time being. The waves crashing against the shore healed her. It was a great end to her evening, ensuring a better night's sleep. She hoped.

On Sunday, Merit looked after some chores at the beach house with a sense of purpose she hadn't experienced in a while. As she moved through the familiar routine, a semblance of her former self began to resurface.

She and Ace took Pepper down to the shoreline for one last swim. The water was cool against their skin, a refreshing contrast to the warmth of the sun overhead. They laughed and splashed, savoring the fleeting moment of carefree joy. After their swim, they decided to fly the enormous kite they had discovered at Fly It Port A. It was a magnificent creation shaped like a shark. With a bit of effort and a lot of laughter, they managed to get it airborne while Pepper nipped at the long tail trailing off the end. They watched in awe as it soared gracefully against the backdrop of the clear blue sky. Ace started humming the theme song from *Jaws* and they both laughed as the sight of the shark kite, dancing in the breeze, brought a sense of whimsy and freedom.

As the day drew to a close, they began the meticulous process of closing up the beach house, securing it against any foul weather that might arise in their absence. The routine tasks felt almost ceremonial, a way of bidding farewell to a sanctuary that had offered them solace and respite. The act of tidying up and putting things in order brought Merit a quiet satisfaction and an organized mind.

The drive back to Ace's school in Houston was mostly quiet as they were both talked out. The rhythmic hum of the road beneath them, along with Ace's music choice, was a comforting backdrop as Merit mentally prepared herself for the challenges ahead.

By the time she dropped Ace at school, she felt like her old self. The time at the beach had been restorative, and she was ready to face the music about Patrick, Pot Luck, and Red. When she hit I-10 in Houston and headed toward Austin, she was ready to get back to defending her clients, especially the Lanes and Constance.

33

Upon her return to Austin, Merit found work piled high on her desk. She managed to bring it under control with Betty's assistance, sorted her email, then texted Clover and Red to confirm wine night. She had been friends with Red for many years, and it was time to clear the air about Red's reporting of the Pot Luck scandal and to ascertain her reasons for not letting Merit know what was coming. Merit's anger had mellowed over the long weekend at the coast with Ace, and she was ready to put the issue to rest.

Before she left for the day, Merit called Lane to ascertain the status of Thad's health.

"Hello, John. Any news?"

"Welcome back, Merit. Thanks for calling. I would have called you if there'd been any change. Betty checked in several times while you were out of town with your son."

At the reference to Ace, Merit swallowed hard. Her son was healthy and happy. One of the Lanes' sons was dead, the other fighting for his life.

"Of course. Betty told me. Just wanted to let you know I was thinking of you."

"Thanks. It's still touch and go. Cameron has been reading his favorite sci-fi books to him. He loves *The Martian* by Andy Weir. We don't know if he can hear her in his unconscious state, but it can't hurt. It makes Gladys feel better to see his sister trying to reach him."

"Of course, it helps. I'll talk to you soon, John. My best to Gladys."

As Merit locked up the office for the evening and started down the hallway toward the garage elevators, Kim Wan Thibodeaux appeared. Highly unusual for him. He rarely came by without an appointment. He was a Cajun litigator with a heavy accent that he didn't seem to lose no matter how long he lived in Texas. They were colleagues, and he was married to Clover, so Merit knew him well. Actually, she had known him longer than she had known Clover because their career paths had often crossed, years prior. Merit had relied on him frequently over the years for heavy litigation, some criminal law, and other things she didn't handle. The look on his face said that he didn't have good news.

"Hi, Kim Wan. Good to see you? Want to come in?"

"Hi, Merit. Yes, please. I saw your car was still in the garage. Hope you don't mind my dropping in."

"Of course not."

Merit walked back, bent down, and unlocked the glass door she had just locked. They entered the office, and Merit put her purse and briefcase on a chair in the reception area.

"What brings you by?"

"Are we the only ones here? This is a little sensitive."

"Yes. Everyone else left a while ago."

"Clover told me you were meeting for girls' night, and I

wanted to relay a message before you went out. It might make a difference in your evening."

"Sounds mysterious. Have a seat. Would you like something to drink?" The two sat on the sofa in the reception area.

Kim Wan loosened the knot in his tie. "No, thanks. This won't take long."

"Okay." Merit smoothed her skirt and sat up straight, waiting for a hit of information.

"You probably don't know that Patrick Herbert hired me to defend him in the drug case he's charged with."

Merit was taken aback. "Really? How did he come to hire you?"

"He remembered your talking about me and reached out with his one phone call when he was arrested."

"I see."

"He has authorized me to share certain information with you. Confidentially, of course."

"I hope you can help him, but I've distanced myself from the whole affair. I won't be seeing him. He lied to me and I don't trust him. You shouldn't either."

"I trust him about as far as I do any other criminal defendant that I represent, but I've verified some of what I have to tell you."

"Okay. Let's have it then."

Kim Wan took a deep breath, then began. "When Patrick first opened Pot Luck, he borrowed money from legitimate banking sources and his investors were aware of those loans. After the restaurant got rolling, he had the need for more cash to keep the doors open until he could establish a clientele and start making a profit."

Merit looked thoughtful. "He alluded to something like that in one of our conversations."

"The problem was, he couldn't borrow any additional legitimate funds as he was maxed out on his collateral with the first loans. He didn't want to alert the investors to the issues he was having, so he borrowed money from some dark sources."

Merit didn't interrupt, as the picture was coming into focus.

"When it came time to pay the interest, Patrick didn't have the money. Only then did he realize how dark the money was, as the lenders were connected to mobsters, drugs mostly. They forced him to liaison the drugs through the restaurant to cover the juice and keep him from defaulting on his loan. He thought it would give him time to get on top of the business, then he could repay the principal and be done with them."

"I see."

"When things didn't go as planned, he began moving even more drugs to cover part of the nut each month to the legitimate lenders, unbeknownst to them, of course. They assumed the restaurant had become profitable."

"Well, sounds like it had. Just not legally and not with all that debt to carry."

"Right. He kept sinking further and further into a money pit because the restaurant's income couldn't pay its employees, cover the legitimate debt and overhead, plus make the payments to the dark money lenders. To add extra cash to the till, he moved a small amount of marijuana through the waitstaff, skimming a bit of product off of each delivery from the drug traffickers. That's how he got caught. The petty crime led investigators to the bigger picture."

"So, he made poor choices and now he's suffering the consequences."

"Yes. Once these people got their hooks in him, he was pretty much doomed. He kept looking for a way out that never came until the police got wind of what was going on with the petty marijuana sales and shut the whole thing down. The raid happened on the fly. News sources were called at the last minute. The police made an example of him. Then, the legitimate bankers stepped in and put a lien on the restaurant for repayment before anyone else could stake a claim."

Merit thought for a moment. How many clients had she represented who suffered similar destruction due to bad decisions? Good people who took a wrong turn. Only she hadn't slept with them.

"What will happen to him?"

"He'll probably plead out and cooperate with authorities. Right now, we're working on getting him out on bail, but he doesn't have the funds to pay the bond."

The thought of him in jail tugged at Merit's heart strings.

"I understand and I do have some compassion for the spot he's in, but I can't do anything to help him."

"Of course not. He's not seeking your help. He just wanted you to know and asked me to tell you that he's sorry."

"Thank you for relaying the message. Please tell him you delivered it. I don't have anything to offer in return."

"Of course. I thought you might like to know that Red didn't have any advance notice. She was notified just like the rest of the press. Clover said you two were at odds about it."

"Thanks, Kim Wan. It does make a difference. I know your time is valuable, and I appreciate your coming by."

"Sorry it couldn't have been under better circumstances, cher."

Fresh from the information delivered by Kim Wan, Merit left to meet Red and Clover for wine night. It was time to set the record straight. They met at Eddie V's, across downtown from the now closed Pot Luck, sat in the bar at a table, and ordered a bottle of red blend called The Prisoner. A small combo played smooth jazz in the opposite corner of the room. Clover's security detail disappeared into the wall at the back of the bar, one man, one woman, both drinking water. Merit, Red, and Clover all looked like fashion plates, but their faces did not reflect self-confidence and high spirits.

Clover attempted to lighten the mood. "How was your trip to the coast?"

"Fine. It was good to see Ace. Weather was perfect."

Merit looked at Red and then Clover, who seemed to sense the tension between them. "Let's taste our wine, then I have some things to say."

All three remained silent as the wine was sampled by Clover and served by the waiter, then Merit looked at Red.

"I was upset when you didn't give me a heads-up about Patrick's arrest."

Red waited.

"I thought our friendship was bigger than a news story." Merit stopped talking and waited for a response.

Red took a sip of wine and seemed to measure her words. "It is, and I'm sorry, but we've never asked each other to divulge secrets or put our relationships ahead of our careers."

"I realize that, but a text or a call would have made so much difference in my handling the news."

"I did call, but by the time you got back to me, I was knee deep in the story and my producers were feeding me information faster than I could process it. We only had an hour or so lead time before the story broke. The police surprised everyone with the arrest. They called the press because they wanted it to be very public, make an example of them. All the stations were carrying it, so we had to as well."

"I understand. Kim Wan came by the office this evening and filled me in."

Clover nodded as if she already knew that her husband had shared the news.

Red waited.

Merit took a long drink of her wine, then swallowed hard. "I realize I'm blaming you and it's mostly my fault. I should have gotten to know Patrick better before I jumped into bed with him."

Red considered. "Maybe. But you would not have discovered the connections. It went too deep and too dark. And, I did spare you the embarrassment of including you in the story. My producers wanted to throw in a one-liner about you and I killed it."

"How did they know I was seeing him?"

Red shrugged. "It didn't come from me."

Clover said, "The police were probably observing him and saw the two of you on the kayak tour, and maybe in the restaurant."

Merit had the feeling that Clover knew more than she could say. It was a delicate balance that they all three had to maintain to keep their friendship intact with the demanding and highly visible jobs that each had. Holding each other accountable was not the way to preserve their friendship, and Merit knew it.

"I'm sorry, Red. I didn't see the full picture in my embarrassment. As Betty says, 'Lay down with dogs and you're going to get fleas.'"

Clover put her hand on Merit's shoulder. "Don't beat yourself up too much, no one could have seen it coming. Besides, you have a right to a private life."

Red nodded. "I'm sorry too, Merit. I should have left a message, but by the time I realized that, it was too late."

Merit smiled. "Maybe you can do better next time."

Red looked at Merit in disbelief. "Next time?"

Clover almost spit her wine out with laughter. Merit

laughed too, revealing that she was joking. Red laughed so hard she had to run to the ladies' room to pee.

As the warm night draped its veil over Austin, casting a tapestry of shadows across the busy streets, Merit and her two friends emerged from Eddie V's restaurant. Their laughter rang out like delicate chimes, their steps guided by a bond of newly cemented sisterhood that seemed to momentarily shield them from the harshness of the world.

From his vantage point across the street, hidden within the shadows, Prince stalked and brooded with a mixture of envy and resentment burning in his chest. Merit, and her companions, radiated an air of confidence that seemed to draw the attention of everyone around them. They moved with the poise of women accustomed to admiration, their conversation punctuated by bursts of laughter and animated gestures. The three stood at the valet stand, saying long goodbyes, while they waited for Clover's driver to collect her. When Clover was settled into her transportation at the valet parking pickup, the vehicle exited the curved drive back onto 5th Street.

Merit and Red, who both lived within walking distance, braved the heat and started down Trinity Street toward the city center. Prince's eyes fixated on Merit's graceful figure, adorned in designer clothes that whispered of wealth and success. He noted that the redhead wore sexier clothes than Merit, showing cleavage and a bit more leg. With a pang of bitterness, he contrasted the women's radiant auras with his own tattered appearance, a grim reminder of his marginal existence on the fringes of society, even at home in New Jersey. No matter how much money he made, or what he wore, he would always be on the outside looking in, and the anger that boiled in him as that realization spilled over each time he considered it.

As Merit and Red approached the street corner, Prince saw an opportunity to infiltrate their world, if only for a moment. With a grim determination, the stalker shed his invisibility and emerged from the shadows, wearing the guise of a homeless beggar. His clothes hung loosely from his skeleton, bearing the stains of what appeared to be countless nights spent on the unforgiving streets. His unkempt hair framed a face weathered by air-brushed paint, mimicking hardship. With a trembling gloved hand outstretched, he stumbled toward Merit and Red, his gaze cast down to protect his identity. The eyes didn't lie, and no matter how much expertise he developed in his disguises, he couldn't change his eyes.

"Please, spare some change," he muttered, his voice barely audible over the din of the city. "I haven't eaten in days."

Merit hesitated, her expression a mixture of pity and discomfort as she reached into her purse, her fingers fumbling for a few bucks to placate the beggar's request. But before she could offer her charity, Prince seized his opportunity. With a sudden burst of energy, he lunged forward, his hands grasping for Merit's purse with a desperation fueled by envy and resentment.

Startled, Merit recoiled and Red gasped in shock as she instinctively moved to protect her friend. In the chaos that ensued, the stalker's true intentions were laid bare, his facade of frailty and helplessness shattered by his brazen attempt to snatch Merit's belongings. Several people on the street observed the attempted mugging, and one brave young man ran over to help. Prince disengaged, his task accomplished, and skulked off into the nearby alley.

"Thank you so much," Merit said to the young man.

"Yes, thank you." Red echoed.

Merit and Red hurriedly retreated, their faces etched with a mixture of fear and disgust. The stalker watched them go from the shadows, grinning behind his disguise and enjoying the fact that he had disrupted their perfect evening full of joy and laughter. A twisted sense of satisfaction gnawed at his conscience. For a fleeting moment, he had succeeded in disturbing their world, exposing the fragility of their privilege in the face of his own desperation. And for that, he savored a fleeting sense of vindication, even as the emptiness of his existence loomed large in the darkness. He had wealth, but he never felt like it was enough or that he truly owned it, as did Merit Bridges. His quest was never ending, and true satisfaction unattainable, driving his rage.

When he returned to his vehicle and unmasked, he saw that Harrison had left several messages on his phone. He started the SUV and turned onto the street to follow Merit and Red on their walk.

Oh no, Harrison, you won't be interrupting my fun tonight.

When Prince drove his car around to catch up with Merit and Red, he saw them climbing into the back of a small car with an Uber sign on the dashboard.

Prince laughed at the precaution the women were taking due to his menacing.

You better run.

34

Red sat at her desk at KNEW 9, surrounded by other reporters in cubicles, all with their eyes fixed on computer screens. The morning sun cast long rays of light through the office window, the hum of voices on the phone and clicking of computer keys provided a constant, rhythmic background noise.

She was working on her latest blog for KNEW 9 Online but couldn't focus her mind. She had the strangest feeling that she knew the mugger who'd accosted Merit outside of Eddie V's and tried to steal her handbag. There was something about the homeless man, something familiar that she couldn't shake. She couldn't pull anything from her memory and was determined to work on the next story, but the unmade connection nagged at her subconscious all morning, like a word on the tip of her tongue.

She put that aside and worked on the story of the moment, which was one she'd been researching for several weeks. It was about the homeless camps that had sprung up under the Ben White Boulevard flyover. The City of Austin had repeatedly cleared the homeless campers and removed the tents and makeshift firepits, but they always reappeared weeks later. It was as if they were drawn by an invisible force to the same spots.

She had spent hours in the field, talking to the people who called the camps home. Their stories were a tapestry of hardship and resilience. One man, his face weathered by years of exposure, spoke of losing his job and, subsequently, his apartment. A woman, clutching a tattered blanket around her shoulders, recounted how she had fled an abusive relationship, finding solace and safety among the others in the camp. The stories echoed in Red's mind as she sat at her desk, typing furiously, determined to do justice to their experiences.

Red had also interviewed city officials, who expressed their frustration over the cyclical nature of the problem. They spoke of limited resources and the challenges of providing long-term solutions. Their polished statements contrasted sharply with the raw, unfiltered reality she had witnessed on the streets. The disparity between policy and practice gnawed at her, fueling her resolve to highlight the human aspect of the issue. The city's efforts, while well intentioned, seemed insufficient against the backdrop of systemic issues that perpetuated the cycle of homelessness. She added that information to the story.

As she pieced together the narrative, her thoughts wandered to the small gestures of community she had observed among the camp residents: the shared meals, the borrowed clothing, the makeshift tents that offered a semblance of privacy and dignity. Despite their dire circumstances, there was an undeniable sense of camaraderie and mutual support. She wanted her readers to see what she had seen and feel the urgency of the situation.

Her fingers flew over the keyboard, weaving together quotes, observations, and data. Hours passed, and the light outside her window shifted away from morning brightness to remind her it was time for lunch. She paused to stretch, glancing at the clock when her stomach began to growl. She finished the draft, sat back, and reviewed her work with a critical eye. The piece was powerful, poignant, and, she hoped, persuasive. With a deep breath, she saved the document. She wanted to read it one last time after she'd had a night to sleep on it, before she submitted it for publication.

She scrolled through the various photos and videos on her phone to ascertain whether she had missed anything she wanted to include, when she came upon the video she had shot of the preacher in front of the Capitol while she and Merit were out jogging. The scene in the video was vivid. The preacher, in his booming voice, with his impassioned speech about justice and morality, pressed his views on the crowd. Red remembered thinking at the time that he was quite the performer, commanding attention with every gesture and intonation. She scrutinized the footage and opened the video to its widest angle so she could better view the preacher man with his thick dreadlocks, pulled back under his hood. She zoomed in on his face, studying his features–the sharp cheekbones, the intense eyes, the way his mouth moved when he spoke. Was the preacher the same man who tried to steal Merit's purse? She wasn't sure, but she felt that it was. If only she'd snapped a picture of the mugger, then she could compare the two.

She caught a glimpse of a well-worn plaid shirt under the preacher man's rain cape in the video. Although the image wasn't clear enough to be conclusive, the clothing under the outerwear looked exactly the same as that of the mugger. Red's heart raced as she played the video again, this time paying close attention to the clothing, the mannerisms, and the way the man moved. The more she watched, the more convinced she became. It was the same man.

Red documented her suspicions in an email to Merit, trying to keep her tone measured despite the unease bubbling within her. She attached the video to the transmission, urging Merit to watch it and consider her theory: *Merit, I think our mugger might be the same guy as the preacher we saw in front of the Capitol. Check out the video attached and let me know if you see it too. There's something really off about this whole thing.*

Hitting send, Red leaned back in her chair, her mind sorting the possibilities. Who was this man? Why did he feel the need to preach in front of the Capitol? What did he want with Merit's purse? As she pondered these questions, a sense of dread crept over her. She had a feeling that unraveling this mystery would lead to something much bigger–and far more dangerous–than she had anticipated.

Merit and Ag met at Polvo's on South First Street for lunch the next day, at Merit's request. Merit looked chic, in a white blouse and navy-blue pencil skirt, but her face looked pinched with worry. After they were seated in the bustling room, Ag, dressed in his typical Aggie maroon shirt and jeans, went to the salsa bar and brought back roasted chipotle salsa and chips. The waiter arrived and they ordered mixed beef and chicken fajitas with corn tortillas, to share, and iced teas.

The hum of conversations and clinking cutlery filled the air, along with the amazing smells from the kitchen, but Merit's mind was set on a particular purpose. Merit asked Ag to move over and sit beside her, as opposed to across the four-top, pulled out her iPad, and showed Ag the email from Red.

"Take a look at this." She opened the video attachment of the preacher and played it twice.

After she let him have a moment to watch, she said,

"Remember that I told you someone tried to steal my purse when Red and I left the restaurant the other night? Red thinks we've run into this homeless man downtown on two separate occasions. Once at the Capitol, preaching the good news, then when he tried to mug us. What are the odds?"

Ag grew thoughtful. "The homeless do tend to stake out their territory downtown. You could have seen the same man twice."

Merit considered his observation. "True. But they were across downtown, one encounter was at the Capitol and the other on the east side at Eddie V's. It's just creepy."

Ag nodded. "Not that far apart and not that unusual, but I see Red's point. And look at the dreadlocks under the preacher's cap. Does that look like a Bob Marley type image to you?"

Merit gave a little gasp. "Oh my gosh, do you think it could be the guy Thad Lane described as being at the arson site?"

Their iced tea sweated pools of condensation around the bases of their glasses. The food came and was laid out in the middle of the table, but they ignored it.

"Could be. Any chance he left a fingerprint on your purse?"

"He wore dirty gloves. The yarn knitted kind. I remember because it was hotter than hell out and I wondered why he'd wear them."

"Another indication that he might be more deliberate than your average homeless guy."

"Or, he's a little nuts. Either way, I'm worried."

"If he's following you, maybe I can catch him in the act. Keep your routine for a few days but be vigilant. I can't stay with you at all times, but I'll check in intermittently. I'll see if I can spot him and figure out who he is and what he wants. Be careful, and watch your rearview mirror when you drive."

"No worries. I'm on pins and needles lately."

"Would you feel better if I put some security on you all the time?"

"No, it might scare him away, and I'd rather you catch him. I can take care of myself. You focus on identifying the stalker, if he is one."

"I'll give Chaplain a heads-up, too. Maybe he can blow up this image and shed some light on the preacher."

"Thanks, Ag." Merit felt better, took a sip of iced tea, and filled a tortilla with meat, peppers, and salsa, rolling it up into a cylinder, and popping the end into her mouth.

Ag smiled, an expression that softened his otherwise rugged features. "I've got your back. We'll get to the bottom of this. Text me immediately if you see him again."

"Will do. I'll give Red, Clover, and Betty a heads-up as well."

Ag rolled his tortilla filled with goodies, slathered on a heaping of salsa, and before he took a big bite, said, "Good idea."

Merit couldn't shake the feeling that this was something significant. Not only would she keep her phone handy, but she'd be on high alert as well.

35

Merit and Betty had been checking in at the hospital every few days. Gladys was always there during their in-person visits, although they were told by Thad's sister, Cameron, that Gladys did go home for showers and rest from time to time. The moment Gladys stepped back into the hospital, she resumed her place at Thad's side, as if she could will him back to health through sheer determination.

John Lane was keeping the home fires burning by day and visiting the hospital at night. Several times, when Merit had met with him, he looked as if he might either pass out from fatigue or explode in anger at his helplessness to save his family. He had dark circles under his eyes and seemed to have aged ten years in the last few weeks.

It was a relief to everyone when Thad began to show some improvement and pulled through the dangerous part of his recovery. His vital signs further stabilized, and he started to regain consciousness, although each episode was brief and fairly incoherent. The relief that washed over everyone was palpable, like a collective exhale after holding their breath for too long.

When the doctors were comfortable enough, Thad was moved from intensive care to a regular hospital room where Ag's men continued to guard him. He had yet to be awake long enough to give a statement and, therefore, had not identified Prince or the Bob Marley character as his assailant and Brad's murderer. The change of environment was a small but significant victory and it offered the family some much needed privacy. While Thad's parents prayed for him to fully regain consciousness, they dreaded the day he would be awake enough to ask about Brad. The twins had spent their entire lives together, and before, having shared a womb, and the Lanes knew the loss to Thad of his brother would be devastating.

After what felt like an eternity of tense waiting, Thad regained total consciousness. It proved to be a setback when the news of Brad was shared. Thad was sedated following the sharing of the news, and counseling was scheduled for every day that he was awake between medication. He cried each time he regained consciousness and remembered the news of his twin, as if he'd just heard it for the first time.

Even though Thad was no longer in critical condition, the danger hadn't entirely passed. Ag's contract security men, stoic and imposing, continued their vigil outside Thad's room, their presence a silent reminder of the threats that still lingered. Unbeknownst to Thad, a shadow lurked in the background, relentless and dangerous.

Prince had been to the hospital several times, his attempts to gain access to Thad thwarted by the tight security. Each failed attempt only fueled his determination. Prince was an opportunist with a sinister agenda, driven by the need to silence the only witness to his treachery. His assumption was that Thad could identify him, and he worked off of that theory. His dark eyes gleamed with malice as he devised new plans to bypass the guards and put Thad permanently out of commission.

Prince's motives were as twisted as they were desperate. He felt that Thad's testimony could unravel everything he had worked for, exposing his crimes and forcing him to leave town before he accomplished his goals. The hospital, with its labyrinthine corridors and constant flow of people, was both a fortress and a potential hunting ground. Prince was adept at navigating such environments, and he was willing to bide his time until the perfect opportunity presented itself.

Prince watched, waited, and schemed, knowing that one slip-up, one moment of lax security, was all he needed to strike. Ag's men, having learned their lesson with Brad, were on high alert at all times. Each day Thad grew stronger, but so did Prince's resolve. It was a race against wits and time, and the stakes couldn't have been higher.

36

At the office, Merit had a fire in her belly as she put Betty to work on contacting the committee members about the permits for the co-op. The approval deadline was drawing closer, and Merit had not had any updates from the committee for her clients about the status of their applications. The goal for the day was to set up appointments to lobby the other senators on the committee to ensure continued approval for the co-op's permits now that Senator Linden could no longer fight for them.

Hours passed, and Betty could not seem to get in contact with anyone on the committee who could help. She was beyond frustrated. Things weren't adding up and Merit was starting to think that something was going on behind the scenes that she wasn't aware of, and probably wouldn't like.

Betty came into the office and Merit looked up from a case she was researching in the *Texas Annotated Property Code*. "Give me some good news."

Betty shook her head and Merit groaned.

"You know, I met a young aide in Senator Linden's office

who was managing the flow of legislation through the voting process. His name was Stuart Lawton. Seemed like a decent guy. Please call over discreetly and see if you can track him down. He may still be working in Lindy's old office, or he may have gone to work for someone else."

"Will do."

Later that day, after Betty had called around looking for Stuart Lawton in vain, she went into Merit's office.

"I still don't have a bead on Lawton, but our other clients are wanting attention."

"Who?"

"Slag called. He wants you to join him at the Yellow Rose. He says that it's important."

"What about?"

"He said that he wants you to meet a new real estate client."

"Okay. I'm always up for a new client. I just wish it wasn't today. While I go over there, please keep trying to reach Lawton."

Betty rolled her eyes to the heavens. "Will do, but I feel as useless as tits on a boar hog."

Merit smiled at her. "You? Never useless, Betty. Hold down the fort while I go to see Slag."

Merit drove over to the Texas Rose, in far east Austin. It was Slag's gentlemen's club, which was a nice way of saying strip joint. The place had a reputation for beautiful women, all tattooed with a yellow rose, strong drinks, and great smash-burgers. She checked her rearview mirror frequently on the drive across town, but didn't see anyone with dreadlocks following her. She had Ag on speed dial just in case, and her Ruger in the console of her SUV.

Merit pulled into the strip center that Slag owned and drove the length of the parking lot past the dry cleaners, convenience store, and other tenants who Slag had leasing from him. She parked at the end of the lot where the Texas Rose was located and went in. Merit had known Slag for some time and had been his attorney in all matters involving real estate, leases, and finance. Slag was a good businessman but was also known to have great knowledge of the underbelly of what was going on in Austin. Merit often got information from him when she couldn't get it from anyone else, as he walked just inside the line. All of his business dealings were straight up at Merit's insistence.

Merit was intrigued when she was escorted to and sat on a barstool near the stripper poles which were currently occupied by two very limber young women. They were both topless, with G-strings on their bottoms that gyrated to Taylor Swift's "Look What You Made Me Do."

As it was still early, and the place was almost empty, the rose tattooed hostess also served as bartender for the moment and offered a drink.

"I'll have a Dr Pepper." Slag kept Dublin Dr Pepper on hand for his clients who didn't drink, wanted one with lunch, or were just addicted to the stuff. Slag joined her shortly and sat on the barstool to her right. His tattoos, very colorful, but no roses, were spotlighted by the lights above the bar.

"Hello, Merit."

"Slag, good to see you. You rang and I'm here. You're looking great." Merit noticed that Slag had added another round or two of filler and Botox to his face since she had last met with him. It had become so ordinary that she no longer questioned it.

"You're looking good, too. Very tan, and love that dress you're wearing. Tom Ford?"

"It is. I'm feeling well, thanks. Recently had a long weekend at the beach with Ace. Very good for the soul. Who is this real estate client you want me to meet?"

"It's not a real estate client. I just said that to get you down here."

"Okay. Betty relayed the message. What's going on?" Merit trusted him and knew he would not lie without good cause and a plan to educate her as soon as possible to correct any misrepresentation.

"Come with me." Slag refilled her glass from the Dr Pepper bottle sitting beside it and carried the beverage for her to a table in the back of the bar. A man was seated there, not appearing to notice the mostly naked women all around him, drinking something that looked like bourbon with one big cube of ice floating around. It was legislative aide Stuart Lawton.

"Stuart. We've been attempting to reach you all day. My office manager is trying to track you down as we speak."

Slag pulled out her chair and placed her drink on the table. "I apologize for the subterfuge, Merit. I'll leave you two to talk."

"Thanks, Slag." Merit sat down and placed her Louis Vuitton tote in the chair next to her.

Lawton took a sip of his drink and looked sheepish. "Yes, I know you were trying to get in touch, and I apologize for this way of meeting. I just had to be as discreet as possible. I needed to see you away from the Capitol and away from the phones as well. I'm not sure who might be listening."

"Slag is always a good liaison. How do you know him?"

"I'm a friend of Slag's from way back and know he's a client of yours. I asked him to put this meeting together."

"Okay. This must be serious. What is it that I can do for you?"

"I'm highly emotional and, to be honest, a little scared. I

apologize for tricking you into coming here but I have some information that might be of some interest to you."

"Okay, so why are we here?" she asked as she took another drink.

"I know who killed Senator Linden."

She spit her Dr Pepper across the table. That was the last thing she expected to hear from him.

"Don't say another word until I'm sure I can represent you."

"What do you mean? Slag tells me that you're the right person to help me."

"I'll help you, but I may not be able to represent you. Let's clear a few hurdles before you tell me anything specific."

Lawton looked bewildered. "Okay." He appeared nervous again.

"Let's start at the beginning."

"What difference does that make? I need a lawyer, and he says you're a good one. Lindy respected you as well."

Merit looked around the room to see if she could find Slag. She didn't see him anywhere. There was no one in the back of the bar but the two of them. She turned back to Stuart. "I don't want you to incriminate yourself. I came here today expecting to meet a new real estate client. If you have information about the murder of Senator Linden, that's a different story and a different type of representation."

Lawton seemed to consider his options. He took a drink and then looked up at her. "So, you're saying that if I tell you, then you might have to do something about it?"

"Right. But if you hire me then it's confidential between us, but I have not agreed to take your case, so let's speak in hypotheticals for a moment."

"All right."

"Let's say you do know who killed the senator. If you do, how would you have come by that information?"

He sighed deeply. He was sweating profusely now.

"I've worked at the Capitol for several years, first as a page, then as a legislative aide to Senator Linden. I knew everything about her office and her files. I knew what she was working on at all times and the enemies that oppose her work. I know who killed her."

"And why would you think that you need a lawyer? Why wouldn't you just go to the police?"

"Because I don't want to die like she did."

She studied him. "Okay. What could I do that you can't do if you didn't kill her, but don't tell me if you did. How would an attorney help you?"

"Merit, I'll make this really easy on you. I didn't kill her. I could never do something like that. But I think I know who did and I think that person should be brought to justice. I'm afraid that if I go public without some assurances, I'll be incriminated along with the actual wrongdoers." He paused for a moment and looked thoughtful. "Or worse."

"Okay. This is starting to make some sense. What would you expect me to do If I were to take you on as a client?"

"I would want you to protect me so I don't get lost in the quagmire. I would want you to bring in the FBI or an outside party who's bigger and more powerful than the Texas Senate."

She raised her eyebrows. She blurted a half laugh, half cough. "There are very few entities that are bigger than the Texas Senate."

"Exactly. It could be someone else who could expose the wrongdoers, if that would work. Maybe the press or another senator who isn't involved."

"Okay." Merit folded her hands on the table. "I'm getting the picture. I think that I can help you. And, if we need advice, I'll ask my colleague, Kim Wan Thibodeaux, to join in. He practices criminal law, I don't."

"Criminal law? I'm not a criminal."

"No? Then let's get the best chance to keep it that way. Let's formalize this attorney-client relationship and then you can tell me what you know."

"How do we do that?"

"Give me a dollar and tell me I'm hired. I'll have my office manager draw up something formal tomorrow."

Stuart opened his wallet and, not having any singles, handed her a five-dollar bill. "You're hired."

She took it and dropped it into her tote. "I'm ready. Tell me everything."

Lawton spilled the entire story.

"I want to get back to my office and work some things out. Do you have a safe place to stay until I get back with you?"

"I'm staying with Slag."

"Good. I'll contact you through him. Keep your head down."

"Don't worry."

37

Prince removed his gloves, not because his hands were warm, but because it reminded him of the tactile experiences he'd enjoyed before at the expense of others. He watched Merit, escorted by Security, get into her car in her office garage. He'd hoped she would walk home as she often did, but apparently sometimes, when she needed her car during the day, or had boxes to bring in, she drove to work. He'd learned this from obsessive observation, his eyes tracing her movements like a predator studying its prey. The fluorescent lights in the parking garage cast eerie shadows, amplifying the sinister aura that surrounded him. Today, he was dressed in his Jamaican gear that revealed his dreadlocks and rainbow-colored skull cap. His heart was dark, far from the peaceful soul of Bob Marley, the singer he emulated. He drove his new stolen back-up vehicle, a Toyota four-door sedan, to make sure his gray SUV stayed off the radar of any unseen security cameras or targets, if they happened to notice his stalking. His license plates were also stolen, to add even more security.

Prince had decided to follow Merit and see if he could get

another chance at her. The process of preparing for the hunt had already begun, and it was difficult for him to stop once he'd set things in motion. As Merit's taillights vanished around a corner, Prince's lips curled into a twisted smirk. He imagined the thrill of wrapping his fingers around her delicate throat, the rush of power as he squeezed the life out of her. The memory of previous conquests fueled his dark fantasies, each one adding to the insatiable hunger for power over her that gnawed at his soul.

His last satisfaction had come from strangling Senator Linden. Lindy, as she was called.

Thought she was really something, dripping in jewelry and fancy clothes.

Women were his specialty, especially rich and powerful ones. He'd never strangled a man. What would be the point of grasping a masculine neck or touching rough whiskered skin? No, he enjoyed the softness of women, the fairer sex. If he had to take out a man, he simply ended him. Knife, gun, tire iron, whatever was handy. Women, he savored.

Little did Prince or Merit know that Ag was parked outside the garage on the street waiting for her to leave for the day. He had been checking on her off and on since their conversation about Red's research, and most days followed her to her condo.

Merit pulled out of the garage and Ag fell in a few cars behind her. He watched as she drove directly home and pulled into the parking garage under her building. After the gate closed behind her, Ag peeled off and went to the hospital to check on his men and Thad.

Prince, unfortunately for Merit, knew the security at her condo as well as that of her office. He had scoped out the cameras, security guards making their rounds, and of course, Merit's parking spots. He had the code to get through the security gate, easily obtained from watching another resident type on the keypad when they'd forgotten their clicker. He waited until the gate closed to make sure she didn't spot him, applied the code, and followed her in when the gate lifted. He parked beside a concrete column where he knew the cameras could not see him and resumed his observation of Merit.

She went around to the hatch at the rear of her BMW, rummaged around for a while, and emerged with her briefcase and some type of cardboard box. It looked like an Amazon delivery she'd brought home from the office.

His mind was consumed by visions of Merit's fear-stricken face, her pleading eyes as she realized the true extent of the danger she was in. He relished the thought of her desperate struggles, the futile attempts to break free from his grasp. He knew she'd be a fighter, just like Lindy. The spell was broken when he heard the closing of her hatch and the click of the car doors locking.

With predatory grace, Prince left his vehicle and moved through the dimly lit garage, his footsteps quieted by the careful placement of his feet. The scent of motor oil and exhaust mingled with the palpable tension, creating an atmosphere thick with menace.

Just as Prince prepared to leave the shadows and advance to reach out and seize his unsuspecting victim, a noise echoed through the garage, startling him. He looked up to see four women, dressed to the nines, one pregnant, leaving the elevator and apparently heading out to a social event. They joked and laughed, celebration and happiness dripping from their body language.

Prince's dark heart lurched. *Too bad there's more than one. I've never taken out a pregnant woman before.*

Merit entered the elevator lobby and the security of the cameras therein. She had escaped, at least for now. Anger burned in Prince's chest, fueling his determination to hunt her down again, to make her pay for defying him and his goals. Tonight, fate had other plans.

With a low growl of frustration, Prince slipped deeper into the shadows, his footsteps, no longer stealthy, echoing ominously against the concrete walls, and his obsession with Merit burning brighter than ever. He knew that their paths would cross again, and when they did, he would not be so easily thwarted. The hunt was far from over; it had only just begun.

Foreplay.

38

At their earliest possible convenience, Merit set up a meeting in her office with Stuart Lawton and Ag. She needed to ask Lawton some additional questions about Senator Linden's death and make sure he was ready to be useful to the authorities when they questioned him. She wanted Ag to evaluate the story from Lawton and get his input.

"Stuart, this is my investigator, Ag Malone."

Ag addressed Stuart, "Nice to meet you." The two men shook hands and all three sat at the conference table where Betty had placed a carafe of coffee and a set of cups on a tray. Ag poured a steaming brew and settled back in his chair to listen.

Merit began by looking at Stuart. "Let's start where we left off at Slag's place. Tell Ag what you told me."

Stuart froze.

Ag searched the young man's face. "Merit told me that you believe you know who killed the senator. That's quite the admission, considering even the APD has no leads. If so, there would be a lot of people interested in that information."

Stuart found his voice. "To be honest, I don't know exactly who killed the senator, but I have a good idea. I don't have solid proof, but I can offer information as to who I think did it and why."

Ag waited patiently, then said, "Well, let's hear it."

Stuart froze again.

Ag looked to Merit, and she shrugged. She wasn't thrilled by the turn of events. When she had first met with Stuart, he made her think he really knew who did it. Now he was backpedaling into not knowing but having a really good idea. She couldn't tell if he was lying, or if he was somehow involved, or just terrified. She guessed it was the latter.

"Stuart, just talk to us like you did with me at Slag's place. No one's going to hold you accountable for the statements you make here today. We'll work on the official details later, if we decide to go to the authorities."

Ag's eyebrows arched at the word authorities, but he said nothing.

Stuart took a deep breath. "Okay. You know what's been going on in the Senate with so many people vying for the medical marijuana licenses. It's been crazy, and the chaos has increased in the last few weeks."

Merit said, "Ag knows of the arson and vandalism and has been working on that part of the case."

Stuart nodded. "There are a lot of people seeking the new licenses that will be issued after the vote on expansion coming up."

Ag leaned in. "You think this has to do with the medical marijuana licenses?"

"Yes. Just so you understand, Blake Harrison is the second main candidate on the permit list, behind Lane and the farmer's co-op. He has Senator Ersery on his side, but Lindy was head of the committee and had most of the power on her side. She was supporting the Lane group, which directly affected Harrison's chances of getting the additional permits."

Ag scratched his chin. "So, you think Blake Harrison is behind the murder? Is that what you're saying?"

"Of all those applying for the permits, Harrison has the most to gain by the senator's death."

"Didn't Senator Linden sit on multiple committees? Could there be another reason? Are these marijuana licenses valuable enough to kill for?"

"The senator was also working on water rights in the Ogallala Aquifer, but those issues had been ongoing for some time. There was no voting imminent. The medical marijuana licenses were pending and much more valuable."

"How valuable?"

Merit looked at Ag. "The estimated revenues off the existing permits over the next few years is well over eight billion dollars. Add the additional licenses, allowing increased production, and do the math."

Ag whistled.

Merit continued. "It's amazing how the use of marijuana in Texas started off as part of a hippie culture before it was taken over by big money and turned into a wealth-making machine for those who bought medical marijuana growth permits. There was a time when you would never have believed that big corporations would be legally making money off of marijuana users."

Ag looked thoughtful. "Interesting. That's a lot of money. That could certainly be a motive for murder if there was someone who didn't like the direction that the senator was going."

Stuart nodded. "The world of medical marijuana sure has changed. The likelihood of new permits being granted in the future, after this round, is slim to none. If the growers don't grab them now, it will be a long time before they get another chance."

"I thought you told Merit that you knew who killed Senator Linden. Now, it sounds like you have an educated guess."

"Well, I think I do but it's not like I saw it happen. But yes, I think it was Blake Harrison and his cronies."

Ag blinked. "I don't see Harrison being able to kill someone."

"Well, I don't think it was literally him. I'm assuming that he hired someone to do it or hired a team. You know, like thugs or an assassin."

Ag's gaze met Merit's and lingered there. She nodded slowly. It was farfetched. She knew that it was a hard pill to swallow but it also made complete sense, in a way, that it would be Harrison.

Merit turned to Lawton. "Why would he do that, Stuart? Lots of people compete against each other for licensure and permits, but they don't light their competitor's farms on fire and murder senators."

"Look I can't say with one hundred percent certainty that he was involved, but I know what decision Senator Linden was going for and how she was managing the process. I can't say there's a smoking gun, but Blake Harrison had the most to lose by her decisions and it was clear she was not backing him. He tried repeatedly to convince her otherwise. On his last visit, things got hot and he stormed out of her office, slamming doors and spewing threats."

Ag just seemed to stare into space for a moment before looking at Merit again. She could see the wheels turning in his brain, he was thinking exactly what she was thinking. That it all fit perfectly.

Stuart continued, "It took years to get this round of new permits set up for a vote, and Senator Ersery was dead set against opening up new permits. Ersery will lose this vote, as it's already baked in with or without Senator Linden, but he'll probably hold off the next round for years, if not decades. That's probable enough for him, as he'll have control of the committee."

Ag considered for a moment. "Could Ersery be culpable as well? I mean in her death?"

Lawton looked stricken. "It never occurred to me that he would condone a murder. I just don't see that in him. He's a power player. He'd go more with the politics and regulation to get his way."

"If it's all so regulated, why is Ersery so against expansion?"

Merit said, "Apart from his deeply held religious beliefs, the fewer the licenses, the more valuable each one is. The ones with the licenses now want to close the door to others who want licenses. Smaller pool of growers, more profit."

Merit and Ag exchanged a knowing glance, both remembering the research about the largest political donors to Ersery's campaign.

Lawton misread their exchanged look. "You believe me, don't you?"

Ag nodded. "Yes, Stuart. I believe you think that Harrison is guilty, but it's going to take some looking into to confirm the theory. What are you thinking, Merit?"

"I'm working with Stuart as his legal representative. We are considering speaking with the FBI."

"The FBI?" Ag was well aware of Merit's last go-round with the FBI. It had almost gotten her killed when she was redacting documents behind a Chinese Wall for a judge in a case involving domestic terrorism.

"Yes, Stuart didn't feel comfortable approaching the authorities with what he knew without representation."

"That's smart, Stuart." Then to Merit, "You don't want to go to Chaplain at first?"

"Maybe. If we find that LaGrange PD is involved, it might be a conflict for Chaplain."

"True, but I've never seen Chaplain run from a fight." Ag looked thoughtful. "Merit, what can I do to help?"

"While I research the right entry into the FBI, can you pick Chaplain's brain? Maybe throw this theory at him and see if he thinks it's plausible. Don't mention Stuart by name, yet. I don't plan to during my inquiries either."

"Will do, and if Harrison has someone on the payroll doing his dirty work, Chaplain might have a guess as to who it might be."

"Good thinking. Keep me posted."

"I always do." Ag turned to Lawton who again appeared terrified. "Are you concerned about your safety?"

"Of course, wouldn't you be?"

Merit looked at Ag. "Let's set up some security for Stuart until we decide about the FBI meeting."

Ag stood to leave. "Stuart, would you like to come with me?"

Stuart looked at Merit with frightened eyes. She nodded at him reassuringly. "I trust Ag with my life."

"I'd like to stay at Slag's place. Can you guard me there?"

"Yep." Ag was starting to wonder how many men he could find to cover everyone, but he knew he'd work it out. What Merit needed; Merit got.

Stuart got up and followed Ag out the door.

Ag strolled into Chaplain's office about half an hour before lunchtime and asked if he was available. Chaplain welcomed him in and offered a seat.

"I thought we might have some lunch if you're not too busy." Ag knew that Chaplain was always busy, but it was a nice gesture.

"I'm in the middle of this mess with all these protestors on campus."

"I understand. Maybe I should have set an appointment."

Chaplain reconsidered. "Gotta eat." Chaplain picked up his mobile and put his Glock in the holster on a harness wrapped around his back. They retrieved Ag's Glock from the weapons locker and headed out the door.

Ag and Chaplain walked down the sidewalk listening to the roar of cars going by on I-35, just a half block away, and found the very popular Asian cafe, Koriente.

They took a seat, glad they had beaten the lunch crowd, and both ordered vegetarian curry.

Ag laughed. "No meat here. Not exactly cop fare."

Chaplain patted his belly. "Rabbit food. My wife says I need to eat better. Today, I'm on the wagon. Tomorrow, who knows?"

Ag nodded. "I like this place. I don't need a nap after I eat here."

"Let's talk before the food arrives. I assume this isn't a social visit."

"A bit of business and pleasure. I'm buying. Expense account. It's on Merit Bridges. I want to talk to you about the Lane case."

"Figured." Chaplain took a drink of water then looked at the glass like it needed something, probably tea, lemon, and sugar.

"We might have a lead on who killed Senator Linden.

Maybe. No witness or anything like that, but we're starting to put two and two together, and have almost reached four."

Chaplain's eyebrows went up. "You've got my attention."

"We've come across someone who was working at the Capitol. The guy knew Lindy quite well, knew a lot about the cases she was working on, and thereby who could benefit from her murder."

Chaplain nodded. "Sounds like we should have gone for drinks, not lunch."

"Maybe. The guy thinks that he knows who killed the senator."

"Really? So, we're not just talking about John David Lane?"

"I think it's all connected, to be honest with you. The fire, the kids in the hospital, the vandalism, the senator's death, all of it. I think it might all be part of a master plan."

"Hmm."

"What do you know about Blake Harrison?"

Chaplain nodded. "So, that's where we're going with this. He's one step up from scum as far as I can tell. Plays the big man in a small town. Likes to throw his weight around LaGrange. DEA thinks he's selling pot for public consumption in addition to his medical marijuana crops, but they've checked his farm with drones and found nothing. So far, they haven't been able to get a search warrant. No probable cause."

Ag sipped his water. "He's acquired a lot of land lately. Acres and acres. He might have motive to have the senator removed from the picture."

"I can't say that the thought hadn't crossed my mind that he would benefit, but why does your source think that he killed her?"

"I'm getting to that. Do you think there's a chance that he has men working for him?"

"Yes, absolutely. I can't say fully on the record, but there have been rumors for years about Harrison being connected."

"So, he does fly below the radar?"

"As I said, we've suspected, but have never been able to prove it. Are you going to tell me what's going on?"

"It appears as if Harrison wasn't going to get approval from the senator for additional medical marijuana permits. He's spent a fortune, through a shell corporation, buying up land to use as cultivation sites for the expanded product. Also, he wants to keep prices high by controlling supplies in the market and limiting what's sold by others. Senator Linden was supporting Lane and a co-op of farmers in her district and that moved Harrison further down the list."

"Motive to kill? That's pretty intense."

"In our line of work, we've seen people kill for a whole lot less."

"True. Of course, we know it wouldn't be Blake Harrison burning down crops and choking a woman in a dark corridor."

"No, you're right. He would have kept his hands clean and had someone do it for him."

The food was served, both men dug in and finished their entire meal. Chaplain wiped the last of his sauce with a piece of garlic naan.

"Anything around the murder investigation to give us an idea of who he might be using for muscle?"

"No fingerprints that we can tie to the actual murder, but the Capitol is full of fingerprints. We have a little DNA from the senator's throat and face. It's not Harrison's, if you're wondering. So far, no hits, but if we can find something or someone to match it to, we might find our killer."

"Let me pass this information on to Merit and I'll circle back. We have her witness under protection for now."

Chaplain's eyebrows shot up. "Protection?"

"Yep. He's terrified that someone will try to kill him, too."

"I'll trust that this is not a senator or member of the House of Representatives and stay out of it, but if I'm mistaken, I'd like to know sooner than later."

"It's not. I assure you."

"Okay, then. Let me know what I can do to help when she's ready."

"Thanks, Chaplain."

"Don't thank me yet."

"Right."

39

When Thad's doctors allowed John and Gladys to take him home, everyone was elated. Ag and his men also appreciated the break, as security had been on high alert for so long that combat fatigue was setting in. Ag arranged an escort to the farm, made sure Thad was well protected by his parents and farm staff, then let Merit know that his duties pertaining to Thad were over.

The drive home was long and quiet. Thad, leaning back against the seat, watched the familiar landscape roll by through the window. The vast fields, the old oak tree that had stood sentinel for generations, and the distant silhouette of the barn stirred a sense of nostalgia within him. But these memories were tainted by the loss of his twin. The car slowed as it approached the driveway, and Thad's heart ached with the bittersweet realization that he was home, but nothing would ever be the same again.

When they finally pulled up to the farmhouse, John Lane was the first to step out, his eyes scanning the horizon as if expecting Brad to come running out to greet them. Gladys helped Thad out of the car, her strong arms supporting his unsteady steps. Thad's legs were weak from inactivity, but the fresh air filled his lungs with a revitalizing sense of homecoming. His father's hand, resting lightly on Thad's back, guided him toward the front porch.

Gladys had transformed the dining room into a makeshift hospital room, complete with a hospital bed and medical equipment. Despite the palpable grief that hung over them surrounding Brad's death, they were determined to create an environment conducive to Thad's recovery. The house was a sanctuary of familiar scents and sounds. Thad lowered himself into the hospital bed, feeling a wave of exhaustion wash over him. Gladys sat by Thad's side, her eyes filled with a mixture of relief and sorrow.

For hours, Thad lay in the hospital bed, staring at the ceiling and listening to the bullfrogs in the nearby tank. The weight of Brad's death pressed heavily on his chest, but he found solace in the thought that his twin's spirit still lingered in the places they had shared so many memories.

"We're glad you're home, Thad," his mother said quietly. "We'll get through this, together."

Thad nodded, his throat too tight to speak. He knew the road ahead would be long and difficult, but at least he was home, surrounded by the people who loved him most. As the evening wore on, neighbors dropped by to offer their support and left casseroles. Each visit, kept short by Gladys, was a reminder of the tight-knit community that had always been a part of the Lane family's life.

One of the first visitors was Sheriff Burke who requested a brief visit with Thad to ascertain what he remembered from the attack.

"Do you remember what you told the ambulance attendants on the night of the fire?" Burke was testing the water to make sure he didn't, through the power of suggestion, place thoughts in Thad's head.

"Yes. I told them the guy who burned the field and attacked us looked like Bob Marley."

"You mean he had similar features?"

"I mean he had dreadlocks, dark skin, and was wearing a rainbow skull cap and some type of Rastafarian T-shirt."

"That's a lot to remember when you're coming in and out of consciousness. Are you sure you didn't dream it all?"

"Yes, I'm sure. I'll never forget his face."

Sheriff Burke drove from Bastrop County to Blake Harrison's farm in Fayette County and parked in front of the wide front porch, complete with columns and porch swings on each end. Harrison sat in a wicker chair beside a small table that held a pitcher of iced tea and a couple of glasses. Sweat dripped down the pitcher and puddled on the table in the heat.

"Anybody see you come in here?"

"Nope, and what if they did? I have some excuses handy, if I'm caught out of my jurisdiction and anyone asks." Burke's uniform shirt stuck to his back with sweat.

Harrison poured a second glass of tea and Burke adjusted his duty belt so that he would fit in the chair opposite the table as he sat. He took a big drink of the tea and wiped his mouth with the back of his hand.

Harrison looked at him with no small amount of disgust. "All right. What's so important that you had to come all the way over here?"

"Thad Lane woke up in the hospital and came out with his story intact about the arsonist looking like Bob Marley. He now knows about his brother's death, and he's recovered enough to give a statement about what he remembers. Chaplain thinks that the story is accurate, despite the long session of unconsciousness and drugs they've been pumping into his veins, and I re-questioned him myself at the Lanes' farm. He wouldn't budge."

"Setback."

"APD plans to have Thad come in to work with a sketch artist when he feels up to it. They tried in the hospital, but that Merit Bridges lawyer cut them off when Gladys Lane started losing it. The twins' mother has been through enough to send someone off the deep end."

"That asshole Prince. He was only supposed to burn the field, and now this. The spotlight just won't go out on his shenanigans. I'm beginning to think he likes to keep things stirred up."

"Isn't that why you hired him?"

"I should have just had you do it."

"I told you, I'll provide information, but I'm not carrying out any activities in my own back yard. Every person in town can identify me."

"Yeah. Yeah. So you said." Burke was obviously doing only part of his bidding, but Harrison needed to keep Burke happy, as information was vital to his master plan.

"What else?"

"You know those keys that Ag Malone found at the arson site?"

"Yes, the ones you should have found and gotten rid of?"

Burke bristled, but let it slide. "Well, there's DNA on the keyring from blood. They're trying to match it now. Might be one of the twins' blood, might be Prince's."

"Shit. Prince again. He's more trouble than he's worth."

"Maybe it's time for him to go."

"Probably so."

"That's all I know for now. If APD comes up with anything else, I'll be in touch."

Harrison nodded. "I might want you out here for a little protection later."

"Protection is my specialty. Just say the word."

Little did both men know that they would never speak again.

After Burke left, Harrison relayed the information about Thad to Prince, by burner phone, his voice low and measured. He kept secret that Burke was the one who'd given him the information.

"The kid is sure that Bob Marley tried to kill him. You might need to get rid of those dreadlocks before you're seen in the area again," Harrison affirmed, pacing the length of the long porch.

Prince responded with a grunt, the sound barely audible to Harrison. He had no intention of cutting his hair and going back to Jersey and rap with a crewcut.

"Another thing." Harrison glanced toward the pasture, the barn, and the workers on farm equipment in the fields. "The keys you lost at the arson site might have some DNA on them. Apparently, you were bleeding. APD is running it now."

"My DNA is in no database anywhere on earth that can connect to me. I've made sure of it." His voice was filled with cold confidence. "Besides, the twins were bleeding too. Might be one of theirs."

"Well, regardless, you better get rid of that truck." Harrison pressed, his forehead beading with sweat.

"That truck was gone the night of the fire. Don't worry so much, Harrison. I know what I'm doing." The line went dead with a click, leaving Harrison alone with his racing thoughts. He shoved the phone into his pocket and took out his regular iPhone.

He dialed his farm supervisor. "Make sure the front gate is locked and keep an eye out. I'm a little concerned about some things going on around town."

"Will do, Boss."

Harrison used the boot jack at the door to remove his dirty boots, then went into the house in his stocking feet and poured a stiff bourbon. The last thing he needed was for Mrs. Harrison to come home and find a mess. He couldn't shake the feeling that things were spiraling into chaos, and he craved order around him. He needed to keep his head clear, but the stakes were higher than ever, and he felt that he'd lost control.

With a deep breath, he resolved to wrap up this part of the plan and send Prince packing. There was no turning back now, but he could mitigate his exposure as much as possible. His mind was already strategizing the next move.

40

Constance, Connie, and Val waited in Merit's conference room. Betty served coffee and got to know Constance a little better.

"Constance, do you still grow any crops on your land?"

"Only a small garden for our own use, mostly tomatoes and herbs."

"I have the same at my house, plus a few string beans. Any chickens?"

"Yes, fresh eggs for the whole family."

"Nice. Nothing like fresh eggs."

Merit entered the room. "Sorry for the delay. Couldn't get off the phone."

Val stood, then after Merit sat, took his seat again. "No worries. We were early. Betty took good care of us."

Connie looked at her son and beamed with pride at his good manners. There was a time when she'd had to dig deep to adjust to his lifestyle choices. Now, she often wondered why she'd made it so hard.

Betty stood and went to the door, her hostess duties complete. "I'll leave you to it."

Merit opened a file Betty had left at the head of the table and turned to Constance. "Are you ready to go over the trust documents?"

"With some regret, but yes."

Merit took several copies of a document from the file and passed a set to each in attendance.

"I think we can strike a balance between protecting your assets and maintaining your autonomy. Want to give it a try? Your call. You're my client. Nothing will be done without your say so."

Constance looked a bit more relaxed. "Okay. What do you have here?"

"First, as you'll see at the top, this document establishes the Stanhope Living Trust. All rights to occupy the land, and use it as you please, remain with you."

Constance examined the document, as did Connie and Val.

"Title to the land and the house along with ancillary rights, such as oil and gas and water rights, are conveyed into the trust. Connie and Val are co-trustees, and any action taken to dispose of or manage the land requires both their signatures. They cannot interfere with your personal use."

"So far, so good."

"As co-trustees, Connie and Val will collect the lease rentals from the company that's running cattle on your back pastures. They'll pay the electric and water bills, the taxes, and any other expenses out of that income. There should be plenty left over, and part of that will be placed in your bank account. The rest will remain in the trust account to cover anything unexpected."

"So, I'll get an allowance?"

Val patted her hand. "You could call it that, but it's just a matter of which account the money is in. Anything you need will be paid for by the trust. The money in your bank account is for you to spend any way you wish."

Connie nodded. "As for the bills, they will all be set up on autopay. It will just happen every month without anyone having to do anything but make sure enough money is in the account. The CPA you've had for all these years will give you a report each month."

Constance looked pleased. "It would be a relief to have everything automated. I'm tired of going down to the grocery store to pay the electric bill."

Constance nodded her understanding. "So, the money in my personal account will be like pin money?"

Connie nodded. "Exactly. A little pocket money to spend as you please."

Merit went through the remaining clauses of the document. With each explanation, Constance let out the breath she was holding, her confidence in Merit's expertise and trust in her family bolstering her resolve.

Merit flipped to the last page of the document and looked up. "Do you have any questions?"

All three shook their heads. Constance said, "No."

"If you're ready to sign, I'll call Betty back to notarize your signatures."

"Okay, I'm ready now."

Constance didn't look ready. Merit thought she looked like her grandmother had when the family had taken away her car keys and sold her car. Loss of independence and control over her life had not sat well with her either.

"Let's get it done."

Merit pushed the button on the intercom and asked Betty to come in with her notary kit. Betty had anticipated the request and appeared immediately.

Merit pointed to a spot on the last page of the trust document. "Constance, if you'll sign on this line on all three copies."

Constance nodded, her fingers curling around the pen as she added her signature. Val facilitated the document passing. With each stroke of ink, Constance fortified the bulwarks of her family's legacy, warding off the encroaching darkness of those who would take advantage of her as she aged.

Merit passed the documents to Connie and Val. "Now, if you two will sign where indicated."

Betty swore in all three signatories and had them acknowledge that the execution was of their own free will, then she executed her notary signatures and pressed a seal into the documents in the three duplicate originals.

"Thank you, Merit," Constance said, her voice tinged with gratitude as she met her attorney's gaze.

Merit smiled, a glimmer of pride dancing in her eyes. "It was my pleasure, Constance. Your family's legacy is in good hands."

When the final signatures graced the parchment, a sense of triumph spread over Constance's face. She had looked aging in the face and handled it with grace. It was the best she could do under the circumstances.

Connie and Val looked gratefully at Merit, and Val said, "Let's celebrate." Neither Constance's daughter nor grandson revealed the next step: someone to live in and care for her. One step at a time.

41

———————

In his garage, Prince placed on the stolen white boll weevil inspector's truck a magnetic sign he'd had printed at a nearby Speedy Signs shop. It said: Traveling Baptisms. Jesus Saves. The cross in the corner was surrounded by lines that meant to signify light beaming from the icon. He used the sign to cover the logo on the side of the truck of a round seal with the shape of Texas in the middle and the image of the nasty beetle crawling across the state. He used a wide piece of duct tape to cover the registration number painted on the truck's tailgate.

Prince drove to east Austin to finish equipping the back of the inspection truck, tricked out to baptize the young and unsuspecting, using a water trough. He drove the truck over to Thompson's Farm Supply and picked up a large silver metal water trough used for watering cattle.

Next, Prince filled the trough with stolen water from a hose at an old, closed Sinclair gas station on the outskirts of Bastrop, while hiding behind the decaying repair bays. He then drove through the countryside, the water sloshing with each turn.

He drove through downtown Bastrop, then onward into the county and turned onto the backroads toward his destination. It wasn't uncommon in the old days to see a moving baptismal driving the roads in the rural areas, but there hadn't been one around in some time. Prince had no intention of immersing anyone unless he had to do a quick dunk to maintain his cover.

For now, keeping eyes on the truck's new purpose and off of its original usage was his goal. He'd enjoyed the anonymity of the inspection truck for weeks, but Harrison had advised that it was starting to get noticed. Who told him that, Prince didn't know, but it was obvious that Harrison had spies in all the right places. Regardless, the bug truck was going to have to go and needed to be camouflaged for this last run.

He went onto the property of Miller's Farm in Bastrop County and pulled into the area with the cisterns and tractor storage. The property was a perfect spot for his plans because it only housed residents during harvest season, one of the many absentee-owner farms in the area. The bunkhouse was currently empty, and the live-in supervisor was conspicuously absent because his pickup truck was not parked at the door as it usually was. This he knew because he'd done recon on the farm, in the truck before the magnetic sign, and knew what to watch for.

Prince dumped two gallons of Crossbow, a pre-packaged mix of 2,4-D and triclopyr, into the baptism water, the acrid smell mixing with the morning dew, then stirred it with a fallen branch from a nearby oak tree. Using a portable pump, he transferred the tainted water into the holding tank for the morning's watering of the hemp plants in the adjacent field. The plants would soak up the toxic water, when the timer went on to automatically irrigate, ensuring the crop's destruction.

With the water tainted and his job complete, Prince left the property and drove out onto the county road. He pulled under a large tree on the roadside, parked, and removed the trough from the bed. He left it beside a fenced-in pasture full of cows who looked confused when they couldn't get through the fence as they tried to approach the empty trough for a drink. Prince left the area, tossing the depleted poison jugs and pump into a different field from the roadside.

Prince hated to lose the vehicle, as he'd easily driven onto many farms using the truck sans magnetic signage as cover. Farmers were required under legal mandate to maintain an easement for access of boll weevil inspectors onto their property. The inspectors did not wear uniforms, carry clipboards, or even carry a badge. There was an ID that they were issued, but it wasn't displayed, and the truck was enough. Everyone recognized the vehicle. No farmer had ever asked to see his identification or even stopped to speak with him, they were so accustomed to the official visitor to their property.

Just last week, he'd done recon on a farm in far north Bastrop County by installing traps around the farm's cotton fields, adjacent to the hemp fields. Little did the farmers know Prince had no interest in cotton. He was accessing the cotton only to spy on their hemp crops.

He'd watched the inspector in the Rio Grande Valley and an online video to learn how to hammer the eight-inch cone-shaped trap into the ground by using a stake holder so he wouldn't damage his fingers. Of course, he didn't log the traps into the GPS system on the iPad containing the app for such purposes. He also didn't bother to replace the deadly insecticide strip or the fragrant pheromone strip that lured the boll weevils into the trap.

Farmers supported the program because proof of testing lowered their crop insurance rates and allowed them to place a special stamp on their cotton bales at market. Prince had been hiding in plain sight the whole time, actually welcomed by those he was terrorizing.

Prince, having been warned by Harrison that the boll weevil inspection truck was getting too hot to keep, devised a plan to get rid of it at Austin-Bergstrom International Airport. He couldn't very well go to the crusher with a truck in good condition and belonging to a quasi-state agency. How would he explain that?

Upon arrival at the airport, he parked the truck in long-term parking outside the departure area, meticulously wiped down the steering wheel and dash to remove any fingerprints, knowing it would be weeks before Security realized it was abandoned.

Prince, carrying a small bag, strode into the airport with a practiced air of calm, blending in with the bustling travelers. He located a men's room, pulled off his preacher baptism outerwear, and deposited the clothing in a trash receptacle. He pulled on an Austin Ice Bats cap with the signature bared fangs logo and requested an Uber on his phone. He noted the pickup spot just outside of the airport departure area and used the address of a coffee shop a few blocks from his temp housing as his destination.

As the app showed his ride approaching, he exited the terminal, scanning the area for any signs of suspicion, more out of habit than real threat of danger. The Uber pulled up, a green sedan with a driver who looked like he was too young to have a license. Prince slid into the back seat, the door closing with a solid thunk, and gave the driver a nod.

"How are you today?" the driver asked, glancing at him through the rearview mirror.

"Just drive," Prince replied, settling into the seat. The car pulled away from the curb, merging into the stream of traffic, and Prince allowed himself a moment to relax, the adventure of the morning behind him. Before they reached the airport exit, he was already planning the next step in his treacherous mission. By the time the poisoned watering system kicked on, and the damage done, he'd be back in his comfy crash pad working on the next dastardly step on his path of treachery or taking a nap. He hadn't decided yet.

42

———

Kim Wan and Patrick met with DEA agents in Kim Wan's office and hashed out a plan for Patrick's release and entry into witness protection. It was the price Patrick had to pay for allowing his restaurant to serve as a front for the illicit activities of some very dangerous people. He had to get out, and the only way to do that was to turn against those who had once been his dark money bankers.

Kim Wan warned. "If you want to remain quiet and go to jail, the DEA cannot protect you there."

Patrick winced. "I know. I'll never make it inside."

Patrick's financiers had a reputation for taking out anyone who could finger them, and Patrick did not want to be in that group. His decision had not come lightly. The final straw had been the death of a young dishwasher, who had orchestrated deliveries, and, therefore, had seen more than anyone else at Pot Luck. Patrick took it as the warning it was meant to be, but it had the reverse effect. He did not shut up, as the mobsters had planned, but had told Kim Wan to take the deal. Both

251

knew he was a man on the brink of destruction if he didn't find a way out.

Patrick would have to come back at some point in the future to testify, but until then, he would start over somewhere with a big foodie scene and count his blessings that being a chef could not be traced that easily by the mobsters who might seek him out. People had to eat everywhere.

Of course, awards and publicity would have to be avoided. He would work behind the scenes and give up the notoriety that he had so enjoyed in Austin. Patrick would later testify against the drug ring, providing detailed accounts and evidence that could bring them down. In return, he would be given a new identity and relocated far from Austin.

"I understand," Patrick had replied when given his choices, his voice shaky. If he chose not to assist the Feds, he'd be moved from the safe house while out on bail and left to fend for himself. "I just can't live like this anymore."

Kim Wan had worked tirelessly, negotiating with the federal authorities to secure the deal. It had taken time, filled with clandestine meetings and coded phone calls, but finally, the arrangement was in place. The night of his departure, Kim Wan sensed in Patrick a mixture of fear and relief. Two of the DEA agents working the case arrived to collect him at the safe house.

"Are you set to go?"

Patrick grabbed a small duffel bag and swallowed the lump in his throat. "Yeah, I'm ready." He turned to Kim Wan for the last time. "Please tell Merit that I'm really sorry and that I'll miss her more than she knows."

Kim Wan did not commit to relaying the sentiment. He wasn't Patrick's messenger, he was his lawyer, and Merit didn't need to hear it. He'd decide later, if the opportunity presented itself, whether to share the information. In the meantime, he'd spare his friend's feelings with silence.

As they prepared to leave, Kim Wan said, "You've made the right choice. This is your chance to start over. Don't blow it."

253

43

———————

The large, oak-paneled hearing room was filled with the murmur of hushed conversations going on behind Merit and her client. A small group of interested parties filled the gallery. This was not big news, it was part of the grind that makes the law work behind the scenes.

Merit was considered by the Regulatory Board to be a seasoned attorney and had a reputation for tenacity and fair dealing. She stood and straightened her navy blazer as she prepared to address the panel. Beside her sat Lane, whose weathered and weary face was stoic. Years of experience with red tape had taught him patience.

The chairperson, an austere woman named Martha Greene, banged her gavel, calling the room to order. "We are here to review the application for a medical marijuana grower's license under the Texas Farm Bill submitted by Mr. John David Lane, et al. Attorney Bridges, you may proceed."

In the back of the room, a door opened quietly, and Blake Harrison, sans Stetson, slipped into the chambers. He settled his bulk into the back row on the aisle and watched the hearing unfold.

Merit leaned into the small microphone on the table, smoothed a few stray strands of her blond hair, and smiled at the panel. "Thank you, Chairperson Greene. Members of the board, I am here today to represent John Lane and the Bastrop County Grower's Co-Op. My clients are dedication to sustainable farming practices and community support making them an exemplary candidate for this license."

"Welcome back, Ms. Bridges. Please give me a moment to go over the file."

Merit wondered why Greene wasn't already briefed on the case, but of course, couldn't show her impatience. After all, the board did have hundreds of applicants to consider over the next few days.

Ms. Greene adjusted her glasses, peering down at the paperwork. "Mr. Lane, can you please state for the record why you believe you should be granted this license?"

John shifted in his seat before leaning forward. "I've been farming in Texas for over twenty years, and my family for over one hundred years. We have always believed in using methods that respect the land and provide healthy, natural products to our purchasers. This license would allow us to expand our capacity to grow medical marijuana, which is crucial for many patients who rely on it for relief from chronic pain and other conditions."

Merit piggy-backed on Lane's comments. "In addition, conventional wisdom says that environmental regulations hurt businesses' bottom lines, but my clients are showing that it doesn't have to be that way. Indeed, cultivating, manufacturing, packaging and selling cannabis in an environmentally sustainable manner can reap multiple benefits that bolster the bottom line. They are setting an example."

One of the board members, a middle-aged man with a stern expression, interjected, "We're aware of the profitability and the benefits of medical marijuana. I don't think you've answered the question."

Lane looked at Merit and she took the microphone again. "My client is a humble man and finds it difficult to blow his own horn, but I can attest that he has gone above and beyond in many areas that place his farming techniques on the leading edge. For one thing, he's exceeded Texas environmental regulations regarding electrical usage, water usage, waste disposal, and other business operations that companies of any kind must abide by."

Lane took up the baton. "For example, in advance of being asked to do so, we installed solar panels, enhanced HVAC systems, and energy efficient LED lights."

Another board member piped up. "Although that's admirable, an additional issue here is concerns about the security measures on your farm. How do you intend to address those issues given the nature of the crop you plan to grow?"

John cleared his throat. "I understand your concerns. For one thing, we've added 24/7 surveillance cameras to all of our greenhouses, drying sheds, and entrances to our farmlands." He paused to think.

Merit stepped in. "Mr. Lane has implemented several other security measures in addition to surveillance cameras, including reinforced fencing, and secure storage facilities. Documentation is in your materials."

"Noted. Let's turn to the matter of compliance with the pesticide regulations. Can you speak to that, Mr. Lane?"

Lane cleared his throat. "We use entirely organic pesticides, which are not only safer for our crops but also for the environment and the people who consume our produce. We also conduct regular soil health assessments. Any contaminated greenhouses and pastures have been treated and taken out of rotation for planting until they test organic grade again."

Merit made another point. "Before you bring it up, the field with the mite infestation on neighboring land was handled before it effected Mr. Lane's crops. Also, the male plants that were introduced into the area have been wiped out by each individual land owner."

A younger board member with a kind face leaned forward. "Mr. Lane, could you share any specific examples of how your farm has positively impacted your community?"

John smiled, a glimmer of pride in his eyes. "We donate a portion of our produce to the local food bank every month. We also host educational tours for students to teach them about sustainable farming and responsible marijuana use as a medical product."

Merit started to add something but decided not to guild the lily, as she felt that they had made their point.

Ms. Greene conferred briefly with her colleagues before addressing the room again. "Mr. Lane, Ms. Bridges, we appreciate your thoroughness. The board will take your application under advisement and will notify you of our decision."

Merit and Lane both stood, walked forward, and shook hands with each board member in turn. Harrison rose quietly and eased out the same door he'd entered.

As they exited the hearing room, John turned to Merit, relief evident on his face. "Do you think we did enough?"

Merit gave him a reassuring smile. "I think we did more than enough, John, but politics are always the wild card. Now we wait."

44

M erit and Ag entered Chaplain's office, this time with an appointment. They hoped that Chaplain had discovered some new information about Blake Harrison and his team of thugs.

After going through the entry ritual and settling into guest chairs before Chaplain's desk, Chaplain opened a file on his computer and cleared his throat.

"So, I think you two have cracked the vandalism case. My investigation confirms what you've discovered about Blake Harrison and his corporate set up. I've also discovered that Sheriff Burke has been assisting him."

Ag's eyebrows went up. "Whew! Bruce Burke? That's a surprise."

"Yep. We picked him up leaving Harrison's farm. He tried to weasel out of it at first, then copped to giving information but doing nothing with regard to the vandalism or violence. We've turned Burke, and he's given us some additional information."

Merit wanted to clarify. "So, he's confirmed that Harrison is behind the dirty tricks and the murder?"

"That's not the half of it. Burke thinks that Harrison has been using a fixer operating under the name of Raiden Prince, among other false monikers. No Raiden Prince exists that we can find, but that would be par for the course if someone didn't want to have their identity discovered."

Merit asked Chaplain, "So, do you think this Raiden Prince would be the type of person to commit arson and murder?"

"Burke seems to think so. Harrison was not supposed to share information about the guy, but he needed Burke to keep an eye on him."

"Blake Harrison ordered the murder?"

"Maybe. Seems the murder of the senator was way beyond what Harrison ordered this Prince guy to do, according to Burke."

Merit looked angry. "It's still his responsibility. He put all this in motion."

"True."

Ag pointed to the computer on Chaplain's desk. "Anything else in there that you can share?"

"We did find DNA on the keys discovered at the arson site. It matches the DNA found on Senator Linden's throat. It's definitely the same perp, probably Prince. If we can find a suspect to match it to, we'll have him."

Ag whistled. "Holy shit."

Chaplain looked lost in thought. "So much heartache. All from greed. You might want to tell the Lane family to watch out. Either could be a target. You need to be careful, too. Doesn't seem Prince has any compunction about going after his perceived enemies."

Ag nodded. "Will do. Any lead on where he might be?"

"Not yet, and if Prince gets wind we're onto him, he could go underground. I hope he doesn't. I'd like to catch him before he moves on to another town and another target. We haven't arrested Harrison, but we're watching his farm in the hopes to snag Prince first. No one knows we have Burke except APD, and now you two."

"Smart move."

"Be on the lookout as you move around the Lanes."

"I'll keep an eye out. I also don't want anything else to happen to the Lanes, they've been through so much."

"Agreed. Please keep your guard up. I'll let you know if I find out anything else."

Ag nodded. "In the meantime, do I have your permission to advise John Lane about your findings?"

"Yes, just ask him to keep it quiet until we see if we can catch this guy before he disappears."

Merit and Ag got up to leave and shook Chaplain's hand. "Will do. Thanks, Chaplain."

Merit and Ag returned to her office to strategize. Betty served up tea and coffee and Merit gave her a summary of Chaplain's most recent update.

Betty looked pensive. "What are you two going to do while Chaplain is still putting the puzzle together?"

Merit nodded. "Things are moving fast now. It shouldn't be long before he connects the dots and hopefully grabs this Prince guy."

"In the meantime, I don't want anyone else to get hurt." Ag was looking into Merit's eyes now.

Betty looked worried. "How are you going to prevent that? There's nothing worse than a trapped animal."

Merit looked away. "I think we should go see Lane right away."

Ag agreed. "Okay, let's drive out there now."

Betty asked, "You two are packing, aren't you?"

Ag turned to the side and showed his Glock in the holster. "Hope we don't need it, but I'm ready."

"Merit?" Betty knew that Merit usually had her Ruger in the console of her car.

"I'll grab mine on our way out."

"Good. Remember what happened last time." It was actually more than one 'last time' and Betty remembered them all.

Merit hugged her. "I remember."

"I'll lock up. Call me if you need me."

As Merit and Ag hustled out the door, Betty muttered under her breath, "Get a room, already!"

45

Prince woke to the shrill ring of his phone, the sound slicing through the heavy silence of his bedroom. He rolled over in bed and growled when he glanced at the screen. It was Harrison. With a huff of irritation, Prince answered the call.

"What is it?"

"I'm getting wind that something might be coming down." Harrison's voice crackled through the line. "I haven't been able to reach Sheriff Burke, and his office doesn't know where he is. It can't be a coincidence, and I don't know if he'll tell them about you if he's caught. I think it's time you get out of town."

"How the hell would Burke know about me?"

"Because I told him. I know it's against your code, but I needed to keep an eye on you. You went too far and now the heat is coming our way. APD is all over this and the Lanes' lawyer, Merit Bridges, and her investigator have been doing some digging."

"I know who she is. Do you want me to get rid of her?"

"Hell, no. Are you deaf? I want you to get the hell out of town before someone grabs you."

"No one's going to grab me. I've been doing this for a long time. If you insist, I'll make my way out of town tonight, but I want the final payment before I go. Cash, as usual."

"Okay, come and pick it up. Don't come to my house, I think it's being watched. Meet me at the greenhouse on the new property in Bastrop County, the one off of Dandelion Lane. After that, leave directly from there. I don't want to hear from you again unless I make contact."

"I'll see you there. Have my money ready to go."

Prince clicked off the call and clenched his jaw, his fist tightening around the phone. He hated the way that Harrison talked to him. It also infuriated him that Harrison had broken the rules and revealed his presence to Burke. It made him want to pay Harrison a visit before he left Austin. Two could play that game.

He threw the phone on the bed and started wiping down the room and packing what he didn't want to leave behind, which wasn't much. He did place most of his disguises, wigs, and makeup into a large black trash bag. Now was the time to destroy all the evidence. He wouldn't be needing them anymore on this job, anyway. He dressed in his dreadlocks and colorful clothing of the Bob Marley outfit for his final visit with Harrison.

When he was finished cleaning up, he looked around at his handiwork and made sure he hadn't missed anything. Now, he just needed to get to the greenhouse, get paid, teach Harrison a lesson, and then disappear as he always did. These Podunk Texans would never think to look in New Jersey for anyone. He'd be a ghost before nightfall, as usual.

✳

Prince arrived at the greenhouse at Harrison's new property in Bastrop County on Dandelion Lane. It was just before sunset, the golden light casting long, eerie shadows across the sprawling fields. His gray SUV was packed and fully gassed up, every detail meticulously planned for the journey ahead. He had swapped out the license plates earlier in the day, a precautionary measure to ensure he remained untraceable. He planned to abandon the vehicle as soon as he reached New Jersey. Nestled in the cup holder was a large Yeti tumbler filled with steaming hot coffee, its rich aroma filling the air. His playlist was ready, old-school rap queued up to provide the perfect soundtrack for his escape. This road trip was not just a necessity; it was a calculated move, a critical part of his plan. Yes, he could fly, but this way, there would be little or no trace of his exit. He'd take no toll roads and go through no tunnels. He'd done this many times before, sometimes by boat, sometimes by train, but always with a meticulous plan of escape in mind.

Before he got out of the SUV, Prince looked around the perimeter of Harrison's land to make sure no one was watching, then turned into the long driveway. The trip up to the greenhouse seemed like he was arriving at a ghost ranch. There were no vehicles, farm hands, or sign of Harrison. When Prince arrived and entered the greenhouse, Harrison was waiting toward the back of the steamy structure. The atmosphere was thick with the musky smell of weed and an impending sense of finality. Harrison's greeting was cold, his expression was stern, and his eyes dark.

"Hey, Harrison. Where's your buddy Sheriff Burke?"

"Still haven't located him. You didn't kill him, too, did you?" Harrison was only half joking, as he put nothing past Prince at this point.

"I wish. You shouldn't have told him about me."

"You shouldn't have gone off the reservation."

Prince laughed, a cold heartless sound coming from his throat. "You didn't hire a Boy Scout."

In return, Harrison's voice became low and measured as he pointed toward a small black duffel bag sitting conspicuously on a potting table. The zipper was partially open, revealing several neat stacks of cash inside. The sight of the money was both reassuring and exciting to Prince, a tangible reminder of the last of their business dealings.

"There's your final payment. Take it and leave."

Prince looked inside the bag. "Is it all here?" His tone was devoid of any warmth.

Sarcasm dripped from Harrison's mouth. "What do you think? Like I said, don't contact me unless I call you. I think you've left enough breadcrumbs around here, so I suggest you leave immediately before someone puts two and two together."

If they haven't already, Harrison thought. His eyes narrowed slightly as he spoke, his mind racing with a mix of frustration and regret. He had brought in Prince on a strong recommendation, believing him to be a professional, someone who could handle the job with precision and discretion. Instead, Prince had turned out to be a loose cannon, his unpredictable actions leaving a trail of evidence that might lead straight back to Harrison. Now, the burden of cleaning up the mess fell squarely on Sheriff Burke's shoulders, if he could find him, and Harrison knew the cost of such loyalty would be steep.

Prince picked up the duffel bag, the weight of the money a stark reminder of the transaction's gravity. He glanced at Harrison, who stood unwavering, his eyes hard and unyielding. This was a delicate dance of power and survival, and both understood the stakes.

With a final nod to Harrison, Prince turned and walked through the greenhouse between the tables of plants and workstations, the duffel bag clutched tightly in his hand. As Prince made his way toward his SUV, Harrison made his way through the greenhouse, out the back, and down a narrow path to where his truck was parked on an electric easement leading to the main road. He didn't need any prying eyes on him today.

46

———

Merit and Ag headed to the Lanes' farm in Bastrop County in Ag's blue F-150. They needed to let Lane know that APD was suspicious of Harrison and looking for Prince, and that the family should be careful until they could catch the hired thug. When they arrived, the farm was bathed in afternoon light that was starting to turn into a beautiful sunset.

Ag knocked on the screen door, and they were welcomed inside, but it was apparent that Gladys was not leaving Thad's side in the dining room turned hospital annex. Thad was sleeping at the moment, but his skin looked almost normal, still a little pale. He was obviously gaining weight and didn't look so frail. Cameron sat nearby, always with one eye on her brother.

Lane steered Merit and Ag back toward the front door. "I assume you guys have some information about my permits," he said as his eyes flickered to his wife. "Why don't we take this on the porch with a drink."

Gladys looked relieved not to be drawn away from her

nursing tasks but seemed to remember her manners at the last minute. "Would you like a beer or tea?"

"Tea," they said together for Gladys' benefit more than their thirst. She sent Cameron for the refreshments and remained inside with Thad while the three settled in the rockers on the front porch. Cameron only appeared briefly to deliver the cold drinks then returned inside.

Lane looked at Merit. "I don't think you came all this way to talk about permits, so what's happened?"

Merit cleared her throat. "We think we know who is responsible for the fire and what happened to your twins."

Lane pursed his lips. "Who was it?"

"It appears it was Blake Harrison who hired someone to do the dirty work."

"Harrison did this?" Lane's face was glowing red.

"It looks like Harrison was not only the one behind the fire, but also the senator's death. He was trying to stop your licenses from being approved."

Lane hung his head. "He would do this to my kids over money?"

Merit shrugged. "We don't know the details, of course. We're not sure how much he knew about what happened to the twins or Lindy, or if his fixer and hitman was improvising. Regardless, he set things in motion and he's responsible."

"Fixer? Hitman? Who is he?"

"Chaplain says he goes by the name Raiden Prince. We're not sure how easy it will be to find him. Apparently, he's a gun for hire. Chaplain is trying to get a lead on his home base, but so far, he's only traced him to another job in Phoenix."

"How did APD find out about all this?"

Merit said, "I'm sorry to say it was Sheriff Bruce Burke who was facilitating some of the dirty work."

Ag nodded. "Mostly information, but he knew what was going on."

Lane looked as if he might spit. "Have arrests been made? Harrison? Burke?"

"Not yet, but the authorities have pieced together the story behind the treachery, so we hope it will all happen quickly. Chaplain's men are watching Harrison's farm in LaGrange in hopes that Prince will show up there. They plan to take Harrison in for questioning if they can't get Prince soon by using Harrison for bait."

"That bastard. Harrison and I have never been on good terms. He's a nasty fellow himself, plays dirty, but this time, he went too far. My boy. Brad." His voice hitched with emotion. His eyes welled up with tears.

"He killed my boy, Merit."

"I know," she whispered.

"And Thad, we still don't know if he'll have a normal life. You don't go around murdering young men over this crap. My business was not worth Brad's life, Thad's health. I would have handed him the keys to my door in a second, if I could have spared their pain."

Merit and Ag exchanged glances. Everything that he said was true. They were trying to help him as best as they could but, in the end, nothing they could do would ever make up for what was taken from him.

"And to kill a senator for God's sake. This is madness. How could someone stoop to such a level?"

John was just ranting now and neither of them would have been able to stop him, even if they wanted to, which they didn't. He had every right to be upset.

Merit touched his arm. "I'm so sorry, John, for everything."

"Merit, I appreciate what you've done for me and my family. I appreciate your coming all the way down here to tell me yourself. I'm glad that the authorities are involved because if I were to get my hands on anyone, they wouldn't see the light of day again."

Ag and Merit both rose from their chairs and thanked him for the drinks. There was still much work to be done and it was getting late.

"We'll be in touch as soon as we know anything further."

Lane just sat looking out across the pasture, a fixed expression on his face as the sun got lower in the summer sky.

Lane sat on the porch for a long time, after Merit and Ag left, staring at the pasture and thinking about Harrison. He finally determined to avenge Brad's death and give Harrison some payback. He told Gladys he was running an errand, and that wasn't a lie. His plan was to burn Harrison's new farm to the ground. His errand was revenge.

Gladys yelled at Lane from the porch. "John, no. I know what you're doing. Come back inside. Let the police handle it."

Lane paused. He could hear the desperation in her voice, the fear. But, he also heard the echo of Brad's laughter, a sound he would never hear again. The memories of his son, his bright future snatched away, propelled him forward. He started the truck and sped from the sound of Gladys' pleading.

Lane drove down to the barn, loaded his pickup with two cans of gas, then headed out to Dandelion Lane where Harrison's new property was located. He had begged his neighbor not to sell to Harrison, but to no avail. He planned to burn it down, just as Harrison had burned down his farm. Lane was just sorry he couldn't burn down Harrison's home and farm in LaGrange, but he knew the police were watching it. The new property would have to do.

Now, Harrison could have the land, but all would be burned to the ground. Harrison could feel the sting of finding his hard work reduced to a pile of ashes. It wouldn't make up for Brad's death, but it would be something.

As he drove, the road stretched out before him like a dark ribbon, winding through the quiet countryside. The familiar sights of the farm and neighboring fields blurred past, but Lane's mind was elsewhere. He thought about the day he found his twin sons near death by the charred remains of the hemp field, the acrid and exotic smell of smoke still haunting him. Now he knew that Harrison was responsible for it all.

Lane's knuckles whitened as he gripped the steering wheel tighter, his breath coming in sharp, angry bursts. He wouldn't let Harrison get away with it. Not this time. Lane was tired of feeling impotent and helpless. This, he could do. For Brad.

Merit and Ag had left Lane sitting on the porch at his farmhouse and started the drive back to Austin in Ag's truck.

Merit was ashen. "That was an awful experience," she whispered. It hurt her physically to see the pain that Lane was in. She hated what had happened to him, but there was nothing she could do to change it. She could only hope to help bring the culprits to justice.

She looked at Ag in the driver's seat. "Let's get back to Austin and see if Chaplain has an update. Maybe the bait has caught a prince."

"Yes. That we can do." Neither had much more to say about the news of Harrison and his henchman.

"I need to get gas. Let's pull in at the next station."

"Okay." Merit spotted a Valero up ahead on the corner of

the county road and highway leading back to Austin and pointed to it. "There's one."

Ag pulled in, queued up his credit card, inserted the nozzle in the tank, and started the pump.

Merit jumped out of the cab and walked toward the store. "I'll grab some Cheetos and Dr Pepper. Want anything else?"

"Nope. That'll do."

47

When Prince left Harrison's greenhouse and opened the door of his SUV, instead of leaving, he threw the bag of cash onto the back seat, then went to the hatch where he retrieved a full red gas can. He walked back into the greenhouse and began to drench the interior. He splashed gas onto everything, including the marijuana plants, potting tables, grow lights, bags of potting soil, and thick plastic walls. He threw the can over to the side, backed up to the greenhouse door, and pulled out his Zippo lighter.

Just as he thumbed the wheel, he felt someone come up behind him.

"Hrmph." The Zippo flamed and the gas caught fire.

Lane's truck rumbled over the gravel, the cans of gas clanking ominously in the back. He could see the outline of Harrison's new property in the distance, the greenhouse a silhouette against the darkening sky.

He pulled up to the gate and cut the engine. The silence was deafening, broken only by the soft rustling of the wind through the trees. Without hesitation, he climbed out of the truck and grabbed the cans. The smell of gasoline filled his nostrils, sharp and acrid. He made his way to the greenhouse, but someone was in there, backing out the door. Lane dropped the cans on the ground and walked over to see who it was, hoping it was Harrison. There stood the Bob Marley look-alike, complete with the dreadlocks that Thad had described. Lane moved quickly, his heart pounding in his chest.

As the man he now knew to be Raiden Prince threw a gas can aside, and backed out the door, Lane could see the Zippo lighter in his hand. In the moment that the lighter sparked to life, Lane shoved Prince forward, causing the flame to fall into the poured gasoline. The fire spread quickly, engulfing the greenhouse and licking at the edges of the marijuana plants.

The flame from the Zippo had caused the gasoline to explode upward, catching Prince in the flames, causing him to fall. He stood and turned to run out, but Lane held the door to the greenhouse shut, trapping Prince inside. Prince turned and flung himself into the plastic sheeting, trying to make a hole, but it was too late. The flames devoured his clothes, ran up into his dreadlocks, burning them to ash, and melted the skin off his face. He fell to the ground in a blazing heap of stinking flesh.

As Lane watched him die through the milky plastic, he felt little. He knew this wouldn't bring Brad back, but it was something. A small measure of justice in a world that had taken so much from him.

The flames inside found their way to a chemical target and exploded again, shattering the greenhouse into a million pieces. Lane fell back onto the ground and crabbed his way away from the flames as they reached skyward. He protected his face with his arm from the heat, as he watched, his task accomplished.

As the flames danced and crackled, casting long shadows, Lane grabbed his still-full gas cans and turned back to his truck. The heat was intense, the air thick with smoke. He placed the cans in the truck bed, walked around, and climbed into the driver's seat, his mind numb, his heart heavy. He glanced back one last time at the burning property, knowing the target of his revenge was dead inside.

It was then that Lane saw someone moving in the trees. It was a large man pulling a long water hose. Recognizing Harrison, he grabbed his revolver from the glove box and jumped from the truck.

48

When Merit returned to the truck with a bag full of junk food, Ag was standing by her door and opened it for her. She thanked him and looked over his shoulder.

"What's that?"

Ag turned to see what she was indicating. Smoke was billowing into the sky on one of the country lanes. Which one, they couldn't see from their vantage point.

"Looks like someone let a grass fire get out of hand. Maybe burning a field?"

Merit grimaced. "Oh, no. We're not that far from the Lanes' farm. Not again."

Ag shook his head. "No, I think it's farther away."

At that moment a pickup truck with Lane Farms signage and logo on the side sped by, leaving a cloud of caliche as the driver cut the corner too tight and went partially into the ditch.

Merit recognized the driver. "That's Thad Lane."

Ag agreed. "What's he doing driving? Hop in. Let's follow him."

Merit climbed into the cab, threw the snacks into the club

cab, and fastened her seat belt. Ag went around to the driver's side, jumped in, and fired up the truck. He spun out of the driveway, throwing gravel, and headed in the same direction as Thad.

As they tried to keep up with Thad's reckless driving, Merit's phone rang. The ID indicated that it was the Lanes' home. She clicked on the call. "Hello?"

"Merit, it's Gladys. John left here in a fit and Thad went after him. Cameron and I aren't sure where they went, but it doesn't look good. John is out of his mind, and Thad is still heavily medicated."

"We haven't seen John, but Thad just drove by like a bat out of hell. We're following him now. We'll catch up with him and call you back."

"Please. Please."

49

Merit and Ag followed Thad down several country roads, the truck bouncing on uneven gravel, and found themselves on Dandelion Lane.

"Up ahead is where Harrison bought his latest property. The one with the greenhouse that I told you about."

"Oh no. Why would Thad be going there? And, where is John?"

"I think we know why, and he probably followed his dad out here."

"I'll call the fire department."

"Please call Chaplain, too. Put him on speaker."

Merit first rang the fire department, reported the fire, then called APD. "Ag Malone calling for Detective Chaplain. It's urgent."

When Chaplain came on the line, Ag spoke toward the speaker, "I'm afraid John Lane is taking matters into his own hands. Send someone to the Harrison property on Dandelion Lane asap."

"Good grief. On it."

As they rounded a bend, they lost sight of Thad in a gray cloud. The acrid smell of smoke hit them, and Ag slammed on the brakes. They both stared in horror at the scene before them. Harrison's greenhouse, a once-impressive structure of wood, plastic, and steel, was now a flaming pile of rubble. Flames licked hungrily at the remaining tinder, and thick black smoke billowed out. Thad's truck was parked nearby with the driver's door open. He was nowhere in sight. Another Lane farm truck was parked near the tree line. John Lane was not inside.

"Oh no." Merit threw open her door and jumped out. Ag was right behind her as both sprinted past Thad's truck toward the burning remains. The heat was intense. They got as close as they could, covering their mouths with their arms, and looked for Thad.

A figure emerged from the smoke behind the flaming greenhouse, stumbling and coughing. It was Harrison, his face streaked with soot and panic. He clutched a hose, spraying a feeble stream of water at the inferno, but it was a losing battle.

"Harrison!" Ag yelled. "Get away from there! It's too dangerous!"

Harrison didn't seem to hear him. He moved closer to the flames, desperation in his every movement. Then, another figure stepped out from the tree line. It was John Lane. His expression was one of cold determination and, in his hand, he held a revolver.

"Stop right there, Harrison," Lane commanded, his voice carrying over the crackle of the fire.

The big man froze, the hose dropping from his hands. He turned slowly to face Lane, his eyes wide with confusion and fear.

Lane raised the revolver. "Don't move."

Merit and Ag exchanged a horrified glance. Harrison took a

hesitant step back, but Lane advanced, his grip on the weapon steady.

"This ends now," Lane said, his voice cold and final.

"John, don't!" Merit shouted, stepping forward with her hands raised. "Think about what you're doing. This isn't the answer."

Ag joined in, his voice urgent. "There's still time to make this right. Put the gun down, Lane. We can explain everything to the police."

Merit turned to Harrison. "Where's Prince?"

Harrison looked confused but didn't admit that Prince had left.

Instead, Lane turned to Merit. "He's dead. In the greenhouse."

Merit's mouth flew open.

"Harrison must die, too. For Brad. For Thad and Cameron. For Gladys."

"No, John. Please."

John moved toward Harrison, the revolver outstretched.

Merit moved forward too. "Please listen to me." Ag began to skirt the edge of the property behind Lane, formulating a plan as he went.

For a moment, it seemed like Lane could not hear. His eyes flicked between Harrison and the burning greenhouse, his finger tightening on the trigger. But then, a new voice broke through the tension.

"Dad, stop!" Thad yelled, emerging like an apparition from the smoke on the other side of the greenhouse. "Don't do it!"

Lane hesitated, his resolve wavering as he looked at his son. The fire roared on, a devastating backdrop to the emotional standoff.

"Brad?" Lane's voice cracked, the anger and determination in his eyes softening.

"Please, Dad. It's me, Thad," the twin pleaded, stepping closer. "This isn't the way. We can't get Brad back. Let the police handle it."

Merit took a step toward Lane. "He's right, John. There is justice to be had, but not like this. APD is on the way. Let them handle it."

With Lane's attention diverted, Harrison recognized his chance. He lunged toward Lane and grabbed for the gun. Ag flew into the melee and tried to get hold of Harrison's arm. In the scuffle, the gun discharged, and Harrison fell back and onto the ground with a thud. "Pfuth."

Ag fell back as well, leaving Lane holding the smoking gun. Lane leveled it at Harrison again who was writhing in the dirt, moaning in pain, and bleeding from his shoulder.

Thad rushed up to his father and pulled on his arm. "No, Dad. No."

As the sound of sirens grew louder in the distance, Lane slowly lowered the weapon. Merit and Thad deflated with relief. Thad put his arms around his father while Ag took the revolver from Lane's hand.

Ag tucked the gun in the back of his waistband and went over to check on Harrison who was writhing in pain and yelling, "He shot me. You saw it."

After a quick check, Ag said, "Oh, shut up, you'll live. You're lucky you didn't get worse."

Merit looked surprised at Ag, then smiled ever so slightly. The tension in the air eased, but the situation was far from over.

50

Within moments, police cars screeched to a halt and officers from Austin and Bastrop swarmed the area, guns drawn.

"Hands up, everybody!" one of the officers shouted.

Everyone complied, until things were sorted out, when Chaplain arrived and took charge. He pointed to Lane and Harrison. Lane was whispering with Merit. Harrison was sitting on a downed log, under a tree, holding up one arm, the other bleeding and limp on his lap. "Take these two into custody. Get that one some medical attention." Two officers moved in quickly, cuffing Lane in back and Harrison in front because of his injuries. Relief mixed with lingering tension was felt by all as the two were placed in separate police cars.

Chaplain pointed to Merit and Ag who watched as the scene unfolded. "Those two are clear."

Thad sat on a rock nearby with his head in his hands. He was shaky from the exertion and shock of seeing his father almost kill someone. Little did he know what had happened with Prince in the greenhouse.

Merit walked over to Chaplain. "I appreciate all you've done, but you know Lane's my client. You can't question him without legal representation."

Chaplain stared at her. "You're kidding me, right, Merit?"

"No, I'm not. I have to protect him, and Thad. You can do what you want with that Harrison piece of shit."

Ag walked over and talked to Chaplain. "You know she has to do it."

Merit looked at Chaplain with hopeful eyes. "May I speak to John briefly?"

Chaplain looked at Lane in the back of the cruiser, walked over and opened the back door, and motioned for Merit to get in with him. She slid into the seat. "Five minutes." Chaplain closed the door behind her.

"Look, John, I know that you might be in shock right now, but you need to keep your wits about you. Say nothing until I can brief Kim Wan Thibodeaux and we can visit you in the holding cell. Not a word to anyone, including your family. Understood?"

John looked down at his feet. "They killed my son, Merit."

"I know, but you must remain totally silent. Please trust me on this."

"Silence. Silence. Silence." He said it like a mantra. He appeared to be out of his mind.

Merit was not totally confident in her client's ability to help himself, but exited the car and stood back, looking at Lane through the window glass. About ten minutes later, an officer got in and drove him away toward Austin, on Chaplain's orders.

Merit walked over to Ag, whose eyelashes were like little scoops holding ashes. Merit's blond ponytail was gray. They were both covered in soot, their clothes a disaster.

Ag's laughter broke the tension. "You've never looked lovelier."

Merit laughed too. "Well, you look like shit."

Ag laughed louder.

Merit took a deep breath. "I need to get to my phone."

51

The next day, Merit's phone rang; she pulled it out of her pocket and saw it was Ag. She clicked on the call. "Hello, Ag, what's up?"

"Merit, how are you today?"

"Tired, but aside from that, I'll survive."

He chuckled on the other end. "I do have some good news for you, depending on your perspective."

"Great, lay it on me."

"Chaplain just called me and said that the remains of the body in the greenhouse have been run through the DNA database. The DNA is not on file anywhere, except in connection with Lindy's murder and the murders in Phoenix."

"Then how do they know it's him?"

"They've been searching all night with facial recognition software from Constance's drawing and Red's video. They finally matched him. He's apparently a hip-hop artist out of New Jersey."

"Jersey? You're kidding me."

"Nope, and get this. Both Thad and Constance have

confirmed the ID from the facial recognition image. Constance dodged a bullet that night he was at her house."

"Oh my gosh! I guess Prince believed he would never be caught. I hope that John is going to get out of this mess."

"Me too. Have you heard anything?"

"Not yet, I'll keep you posted. Thanks, Ag, I appreciate it, and I appreciate you."

"Any time."

She clicked off the call and went to her office. She was exhausted, the whole ordeal had taken its toll on her. It had been a hell of a week, and she was glad that it was finally over. Not only that, but Raiden Prince wouldn't be able to hurt anyone else. He had died in the same type of fire that he had set on the Lanes' farm. His treachery had come full circle. In the end, Prince got exactly what he deserved, and Harrison would hopefully spend the rest of his life in prison.

Karma's a bitch.

In her office, Merit and Betty watched Red Thallon report for KNEW 9 about the chaos that had ensued the night before. Merit had given Red a sound bite, that morning, on camera, and the network ran it over and over between updates on the case from APD.

"Justice has been served," Merit said into the camera like Wonder Woman.

Betty shrugged. "Damn straight, and any publicity is good publicity."

The Bastrop Sheriff's Office was basically out of the loop with Burke in jail, but Chaplain was doing a fine job piecing things together. Ag filled in a few blanks for him, as well. All was reported by Red as it unfolded.

Merit was still waiting to hear about John Lane's fate. She had gone with Kim Wan to see him early that morning, and she knew he was in good hands. It turned out he was in very good hands because Kim Wan had him out on bail by late afternoon.

When Lane arrived at Merit's office on his way home from jail, Betty escorted him in, and he sat down in the chair across from Merit's desk. He seemed to have a little light back in his eyes. He waited quietly, as if waiting to see what she had to say.

"How are you doing, John?"

"Never been better. Slept in jail like a baby."

She hadn't seen him this content since before Brad's death and the original arson by Prince. She wasn't sure what he was about to say, but she had a pretty good guess.

"How did you leave it with Kim Wan?"

"I didn't see him after the bail hearing. I thought you'd fill me in."

"So far, the prosecutor in Bastrop County says there's no way to know if Harrison or Prince set the fire that killed Prince. They know your gas cans were still full and sitting in the back of your truck."

"I didn't set the fire."

"I'm glad to hear that."

"The DA has enough on Harrison to convict him, and he has no appetite for going after you. He won't prosecute you because he can't win. Harrison pointed to Prince, as the arsonist, and they don't have a lot of choice but to believe him. Whether it was Harrison or Prince that set the fire, they have no real evidence one way or another. Since Prince was the bad guy in all this, they figure it's more likely he did it. Though I doubt they are going to charge anyone with the fire, there's just not enough evidence. No one knows what happened out there but you, Harrison, and Prince. After the initial statement,

Harrison lawyered up, and Prince is dead. Want to shed some light on things?"

"Just between us?"

"Yes. Just you and me."

"Prince spread the gas in the greenhouse. He was lighting it up when I arrived. I told APD that it was already burning when I drove up. That's why I didn't need the gas cans. I intended to burn it, but it was already burning."

"So, Prince accidentally set himself on fire?"

"Not exactly. He might have had a little help."

"Did you really set the fire?"

"No, Prince started the fire. I just made sure he stayed in the greenhouse."

"Oh, John."

"He killed my boy, and I've avenged him. Prince did all of his dirty work without a care in the world about my family. He deserved everything that happened to him. I don't regret a thing. I just wish that Thad hadn't come up. I would have killed Harrison, too."

"I don't believe that."

"Believe it, Merit. This has changed me. Harrison better not get off or I'll go after him again."

"He won't get off. They have him dead to rights on hiring Prince. Bruce Burke and Stuart Lawton have provided enough information to keep Harrison in jail for a long time. If that isn't enough, they also have the bag of money with Harrison's fingerprints that Prince left in his SUV."

"Burke can share a cell with Harrison, that bastard."

"Burke's made a deal, but he'll still get jail time. Not much. He provided information but didn't actually take any violent action. It's still conspiracy, but hard to prove with only Harrison's word. He's a co-conspirator and the testimony would have to be corroborated. He isn't talking anyway."

"He's still a dishonest bastard."

"He is, indeed. I understand the folks over in LaGrange PD are cleaning house. Nothing specific, just too much good ol' boy going on."

"Good. I'm tired. I just want to get home to Gladys."

Merit nodded. "I understand. Everything is going to be okay. Just follow Kim Wan's lead."

A few weeks later, Merit, Betty, and Ag attended another barbecue at the Lanes' farm. This time, it was smaller, just friends and family. No fundraising or politicians to make speeches. Everyone wore shorts and jeans and the lightest shirts they owned to ward off the heat. The farm hands grilled huge ribeye steaks, butchered from the farm's cattle. They buried foil-wrapped potatoes in the coals and grilled fresh corn in the husks. Gladys made all the rest of the sides. She was back to baking cast iron skillet cornbread and whipping up huge vats of coleslaw. Jumbo-size watermelons were brought out of icy chests and sliced into wedges. No caterers this time, much to Merit's relief.

Merit left Ag and Betty to schmooze and went to find John and Gladys. She gave Gladys a hug on the front porch. "You must be thrilled to have Thad up and around."

"It's been good. He seems almost back to normal. He gets a little winded sometimes, but aside from that it's like he took a nap and just woke up. The doctors say that by the time school starts, he'll be back to Friday night lights."

"That's wonderful, Gladys."

When it was time for dinner, Lane called the group to silence, said a prayer, and had a moment of bittersweet silence to remember Brad. When the moment ended, they all said in chorus, "Amen."

The beer was cold, and the chow was amazing. Toward the end of the meal, John came over to Merit. He gave her a huge smile. "Get enough to eat."

Merit rubbed her tummy. "Too much."

"Let's get another beer."

The two walked over to a pony keg with red cups stacked beside it. John drew two drafts with plenty of foam and handed one to Merit.

Merit accepted the cup. "What's next on the horizon?"

"We're headed out to MJBizCon in Las Vegas in a few months."

"Vegas, baby. Sounds great."

Lane smiled. "Now, about my licenses."

Merit laughed. "I'm surprised you waited this long to ask."

"Gladys likes it when I use my manners. Food first, then business."

"Smart woman. From what I hear, everything has been approved by the review committee at this stage. With Harrison and his cohorts out of the way, you moved right up the list. Also, Ersery could hardly work against you and not show bias in light of the contributions he received. He moved as far away from Harrison's group as possible. You are officially re-opened for business under the new licenses."

"Thanks, Merit. Now there's no reason that I can't expand the planting and start to dig my way out of the hole."

"No reason at all."

As the evening wore on, the sky turned a deep indigo, speckled with stars. Fireflies dotted the landscape, their tiny lights flickering in the darkness. The sound of crickets and distant frogs created a symphony that harmonized with the laughter and chatter of friends.

Merit felt a sense of peace wash over her. The case that had consumed so much of their lives was finally behind them. Thad's recovery was nothing short of miraculous, and the farm, once under threat, was now ready to thrive again. She looked at the faces around her–friends who had become like family–and felt a deep sense of gratitude.

Lane, standing beside her, took a deep breath and looked out over the fields. "We've been through a lot, haven't we?" She couldn't help but think that she was standing beside a murderer and felt surprisingly okay with it.

Merit nodded. "More than I ever imagined. But we made it." Merit smiled, feeling the warmth of the evening, the friendship, and the promise of better days ahead. It was a new beginning and John seemed ready to embrace it. Merit decided that any guilt he felt was between him and his God.

Betty and Ag found their way over and all four raised a glass.

Merit said, "To the future."

"To the future."

THE END

For a sneak peek at **Dead by Proxy**, the first book in Manning Wolfe's new Proxy Legal Thriller Series, click here or continue.

Sign up for Manning Wolfe's FREE newsletter and get a FREE book. Claim your copy:
www.manningwolfe.com/giveaway

LEAVE A REVIEW!

Thank you for reading **Killer Weed**. Please leave a review to help future readers find their way to this series.
Click here, or go to Amazon and Goodreads. Thank you.

MANNING WOLFE

DEAD BY PROXY

1

———————

Byron Douglas never forgot his last jury trial in New York City, not because he won, but because it forced him to become dead by proxy.

It started in the grand wood-walled and portrait-adorned federal courtroom, with Byron's client, Killian Tyrone, on trial for murder and RICO charges. The Feds were sure that Tyrone had violated several sections of the act in conjunction with the murder of one Morgan Allen White in his own home.

Voir dire went well, Byron was always good before a jury, especially when the members of the box had not yet gotten to know his client. That would change. Killian Tyrone was not a likable fellow, and the charming, well versed, and talented Byron could only go so far before the jury could see through to the rat-bastard he was representing and surmise the truth. Guilty of something, if not the crime at hand. And, surely lying.

In defending Tyrone, Byron knew he had to be especially charming and likable, not hard for the six-foot three-inch, lean barrister with sparkling blue eyes, thick dark hair, and engaging smile. He moved gracefully from one candidate to the next during the preliminary examination of the jury.

"Do you believe that you can be a fair, impartial, and objective juror in this case?" The answer was always yes and, as doubtful as it was for every person in the jury pool to be totally objective, Byron looked as if he believed and trusted the word of each one. "Thank you."

Byron knew that most criminal attorneys assume their clients are not innocent and it's their job to get them off and obtain a not guilty verdict. Byron didn't see it exactly that way. He assumed that the client was probably guilty, but he put himself in the shoes of the jury and said to his inner judge, "Prove it." Byron believed 'innocent until proven guilty' was one of the founding tenets of criminal trial law and one that he embraced fully. If he could provide any explanation or alternative for his client to be innocent, he fought like hell for that position.

Byron's view of being a trial lawyer harkened back to the days and ways of fictional Atticus Finch, real life Ruth Bader Ginsberg, and historical Oliver Wendell Holmes. He had been a disciple of justice ever since his mentor in law school had inspired him with the culture of the judicial system. Byron saw the law as did legal historian, F.W. Maitland. He often quoted him, "The law is a seamless web." Byron loved the intricacies of the history, tradition, and patriotism attached to the legal process and the way it crisscrossed into every area of the world.

Byron was not jaded or trapped into being an attorney as many he knew were, and he was not in it for the money, although that part was nice. And, he was not naive, as he was aware of severe injustices in the criminal justice system and felt improvement was needed. Byron continued to be on the playing field because he was one of the last true believers. The system was the best available right now, and he actually trusted the outcome, most of the time.

Having deceased parents, one semi-estranged sibling in California, and no current plans to marry, Byron embraced the law as his mistress and his life. He simply loved it all. As most careers went, loving it meant he was devoted to it and good at it. He never glossed over a precedent or twisted a legal argument beyond its parameters. He was thrilled every time he set foot in a courtroom to do battle for his client, guilty or innocent.

Across the aisle, the prosecutor, Sebastian Roberts, relished this chance to incarcerate another criminal. Roberts moved his short spark-plug-of-a-body, decorated with a vest and bright paisley bow tie, around the courtroom as he laid out the federal government's view of the case. He looked at Byron and his client, then back to the twelve chosen members of the jury.

"Ladies and gentlemen, I promise that I will prove in this trial that Killian Tyrone not only murdered Morgan Allen White, he did so as a part of a RICO conspiracy, involving gang-ster activity as defined in 18 USC Section 1961. While the Irish mob and crime boss, Tua Dannon, are not on trial here, Killian Tyrone's connection to them and his work at their behest is an integral part of this case. And, while our case is circumstantial, as we have no witness who actually saw Mr. Tyrone pull the trigger, we will show, beyond a reasonable doubt, that there is no other logical conclusion, featuring the facts, other than his guilt. Simply put, we, the prosecution, allege that Tyrone killed Mr. White, that he did so at the behest of Tua Dannon, head of the Irish mob, and we'll prove it."

Byron organized his thoughts, felt excitement tingle through his fingers and toes, and stood up at the defense table. In defending Killian Tyrone, Byron's opening argument went something like this: "Your Honor and members of the jury. Today, I'd like to introduce you to my client, Killian Tyrone, the accused in this case. Now, I know what the prosecutor said about what he did, and that is probably swirling around in your brain right now, but I'd like for you to take a step back and listen to both sides of the story before you make a decision about my client's behavior, guilt, or innocence. You also heard his inference about defense attorneys, that would be me." He smiled and the jury laughed. "I'll leave it to you to decide, but I have no intention of tricking you or trying to hide the ball."

Byron pointed at his co-counsel, Michael, a shorter, younger version of himself, but with brown eyes. "My colleague, Michael Everett, and I will present Mr. Tyrone's side of the case and, when we're finished, I'm certain that you will find him not guilty."

Byron smiled at the jury and took pride in the fact that when he won, he won fair and square, and he instilled these principles in his protégé, Michael. Byron encouraged Michael not to be blinded by the legal system, nor be immune to the tricks of the trade. Byron used the tools expertly, but he wanted to win with an equal playing field, or not at all, and the law allowed for plenty of ways to win. To Byron, what was the point if cheating was involved? That only proved he was the best cheater, not the best lawyer.

Byron moved past the bench to stand directly in front of the jury box. "Judge Linton has instructed that each of you keep an open mind until all the evidence is presented, and during voir dire I asked you to do the same. I'm asking you again now. Listen fully and then decide."

The jury seemed to pay close attention to what Byron was saying, but their eyes were on Tyrone who was sweating under his dress shirt.

As Byron returned to the defense table, he winked at Michael, who smiled. The two litigators, who weren't far apart in age, had clicked when they were introduced on Michael's first day at the firm and had grown closer as they worked together, sometimes finishing each other's sentences and often coming up with the same legal strategy independent of each other. The two men had planned their courtroom strategy in defending their client, so both knew what was coming.

Byron stood behind Tyrone and put his hand on the man's broad shoulder. "My client did not grow up with advantages and may have the demeanor of someone you might not befriend. Hell, he's not my friend, either, but I have not walked in his shoes and neither have you. Here in New York, he encountered some unsavory characters when he was just a lad. You may have heard or read about the origins of the Irish mob in Hell's Kitchen, and you may think that the same mob is still alive and active today, but all that is the stuff of movies and novels. I won't deny that there remain criminal networks around the world, but the modern-day mob is nothing like that of the stories you've read and heard. The mob today consists of businessmen in suits and ties, going to work in offices, and flying around the world on airplanes. My client is far down the pecking order of this organization in today's times, and he has no power or control over what they do. Nor is he controlled by their decision making."

Juror number three fidgeted in his seat. Byron made a mental note to have Michael look at the juror's history and try to discern why he was so uncomfortable.

Byron took a few steps closer to the jury box. "My client deserves a fair trial with a full understanding by you, the jury, of how things work in his world and what he could and could not do to promote criminal enterprise under RICO. The elements that must be proved by the prosecutor are specific. I think you'll see at the end of this trial that the burden of proof has not been met, and you'll find my client, Killian Tyrone, not guilty of any RICO activity. He's just a muck who happens to know some guys. Whether they're in the mob or not is none of his business, or ours here today.

"Next, as the prosecutor said, with regard to the second element of the charges, the murder of the deceased, this is a circumstantial case. There is no smoking gun, no witness who saw my client shoot the deceased, no CCTV footage placing him at the deceased's home."

A female member in the gallery yelled out, "His name is Morgan Allen White, not the deceased."

Just as the judge raised his gavel, Byron turned and looked at the grieving widow of Mr. White. Then, he turned back to the jury. "She's correct. Mr. White deserves our respect, and his family deserves our sympathy, but that cannot affect the verdict in this case. We must give Killian Tyrone the full benefit of the doubt. I plan to show you that he is not a murderer. He is not a mobster. He is an unlikable, and unfortunate, man who got caught in the wrong place at the wrong time, and the police grabbed him up on suspicion of association, without searching for the actual killer. Mr. White deserves better than lazy police. He, and his widow, deserve to know the truth."

During the lunch break, Byron and Michael braved the cold, took a short walk from the courthouse toward the World Trade Center Memorial, and found a seat at the Stage Door Delicatessen, an iconic lunch spot decorated with New York memorabilia and crammed with rows of wooden tables. They ordered up a pastrami on rye for Byron and a corned beef on sourdough for Michael – both with spicy mustard. They read each other's minds, each expressing the desire for a beer, but refrained because of the trial, and ordered sodas.

While they waited, they took a look at the big-screen TVs

hanging on the walls at each end of the room where ESPN was showing the latest March Madness scores.

"Looks like your Longhorns beat Gonzaga."

"Hey, sure does." Byron put up his fingers in the form of a horned steer. "Hook 'Em."

"You can take the boy out of Texas, but you can't take Texas out of the boy."

Byron laughed. "Actually, you can. Since my mother's gone, I have no reason to go there ever again."

Michael looked sympathetic.

The men had three things in common besides the law. First, both came from humble beginnings. Byron's mother worked as a maid in a hotel in Houston and brought home whatever was left in the rooms to stretch the budget and make ends meet. Byron had not seen a full roll of toilet paper in his home until he went to college. He often ate whatever packaged goods were abandoned by hotel guests, although he wasn't aware of that until he turned about eleven or twelve. For his mother's sake, as he grew older, he pretended that he didn't know, even to the day she died. Michael's mother was a domestic servant in Buffalo, New York, cooking for, cleaning up after, and taking care of other people's homes and children, until she developed Alzheimer's and had to have constant care.

Secondly, and maybe most importantly, both had absent fathers. To repay their mothers for their many sacrifices, both Byron and Michael had supported them in their later years, buying homes and providing living allowances until Byron's mother died in Houston, and Michael's went into a nursing home in the Bronx, where she still resided. Although Michael visited regularly, most days she didn't know who he was.

Last of all, they shared the love of pimento cheese, a leftover from the south for Byron and a recent discovery by Michael at the insistence of his mentor. To the disgust of Byron's girlfriend and Michael's wife, they lunched frequently on southern pâté, the orange and red mayonnaise concoction, wherever they could find it.

When the food arrived, Byron tucked a napkin into his collar, took a big bite of the fatty pastrami, and talked with his mouth half full. "Did you notice Roberts almost spilled the beans about White's three-year-old son being in the house?"

"Yep. That would have been a mistrial for sure. Judge Linton was very clear that the information about the son was to be excluded."

"I don't think he wants a mistrial any more than we do. Besides, there's no way to know if the kid saw something or slept through the whole thing. A three-year-old can't testify."

"Lucky for Tyrone, is my guess."

Byron snapped off the end of his pickle between his front teeth and crunched on it. "Right. How do you think the opening went?"

"The jury clearly likes you, hates Tyrone, and is giving the prosecution the benefit of the doubt. Juror number three is just a natural fidgeter, I think. I couldn't find anything unusual about his history. They understandably feel sorry for Mrs. White."

Byron chewed thoughtfully.

"Oh, and they love me."

Both men chuckled.

"Yeah. I agree. I'm going to have to make old Prosecutor Roberts look like he's being dishonest."

Michael took a long pull on his soda straw. "Right, or at least manipulative, without looking manipulative yourself."

Byron grunted and chewed, then put down his sandwich and rubbed his chin. "I need to discredit their first witness right out of the gate."

"How are you going to do that?"

2

After lunch, once Judge Linton settled himself into his robe on the bench, Prosecutor Roberts, and his minions, put on their case.

"Call your first witness, Mr. Roberts."

"Thank you, Your Honor. Today, we will show through Federal Bureau of Investigation agents the pervasive nature of the Irish mob in New York and its control over Killian Tyrone."

Byron stood. "Your Honor, Mr. Roberts already had his opening statement. Now, he's testifying. Do we have a witness coming?"

"Pontification and repetition are not welcome here, Mr. Roberts. I said call your first witness."

Roberts stuttered, then moved on. "The prosecution calls FBI Special Agent Frank Purvis." As the main witness for the prosecution, Agent Purvis's task was to provide an overview of the federal case, lay out for the jury each point that the prosecution would make via the witnesses who would follow, and connect the dots between those witnesses.

The prosecutor adjusted his lucky blue bow tie and

addressed the witness. "Sir, please state your full name and occupation."

The agent pushed up the microphone before him and cleared his throat. "Frank Purvis, special agent in charge of the FBI case against Killian Tyrone and other co-conspirators, known and unknown."

"Thank you. Now, Agent Purvis, can you tell us first about the murder of Mr. Morgan White and the evidence against Mr. Tyrone that makes you certain of his guilt?"

"Yes, the defendant had motive, means, and opportunity. First of all, Mr. Tyrone was seen in the vicinity of Mr. White's home on the day of the murder. He has prior convictions involving the same brand and caliber firearm that was used in the murder of Mr. White. Lastly, Mr. Tyrone was associated with higher-ups in the Dannon mob with motivation to remove Mr. White before he could work with my agency, as a confidential informant."

Byron stood. "Objection, Your Honor, no predicate laid as to Mr. White's plans for FBI cooperation."

"I'll rephrase. Agent Purvis, had your agency approached Mr. White to ascertain his interest in helping the FBI?"

"Yes, we had ascertained, by visual observation, that Mr. White was a dispatcher at the Dannon warehouse, sending trucks to and from delivery destinations. The legitimate deliveries masked the illegitimate ones. We needed Mr. White, among other things, to clarify which were which so that we could obtain search warrants and open the trucks that carried contraband."

"Was he open to discussing the case?"

"We spoke with him twice and were hopeful that he could be persuaded to assist us further."

Tyrone gently nudged Byron with his knee under the table.

He wrote a note on the yellow tablet before him: *Why aren't you objecting?*

Byron gave him a look that said: *Settle down. I'm the lawyer here.*

The prosecutor looked down at his notes. "Now, Agent Purvis, can you next tell us the elements of a Racketeer Influenced and Corrupt Organizations Act case and why Killian Tyrone's actions fit within that statute?"

"Yes, I can. The power of RICO lies in its conspiracy provision. The statute permits a defendant to be convicted and separately punished, as in this case, for the underlying crimes of the gang associated with a pattern of racketeering activity. It also forces convicted felons, such as Mr. Tyrone, to stay away from any organized crime gang, which he has not."

"Now, Agent Purvis, what have you concluded from your investigation with regard to Mr. Tyrone's affiliation with organized crime and how it led to the murder of Morgan White?"

"Mr. Tyrone is clearly a mobster and dangerous. He takes orders from higher-ups in the Dannon Irish crime cartel, and he carried out one such order in the murder of Morgan White."

Tyrone bristled from the top of his bald head, down his full six feet, to the bottom of his size twelve shoes. Byron stood and put his hand on his client's arm in order to restrain him as obsequiously as possible. "Objection, Your Honor. Opinion is not fact. Where's the proof?"

Byron sat and his client seemed satisfied with his attorney's vigorous attempt on his behalf. After Judge Linton adjourned for a break, Tyrone seemed calmer and under control of his emotions, but Byron could hear the tick of a time bomb in his client's chest.

When it was the defense's turn to question Agent Purvis, Byron stood and looked to his co-counsel, Michael, who handed Byron a file folder. He moved around the defense table, opened the file for effect, because he knew exactly what was there, then rolled his clear blue eyes up at the witness.

"Agent Purvis, what called your attention to my client on the date of the incident?"

Mrs. White squirmed in her seat at the use of the word incident but did not speak out this time.

Agent Purvis squirmed a little as well. "We did not identify him on the date of the murder. We found him through the investigative process."

"So, you looked for the killer and found my client. You didn't find him onsite with a gun in his hand, or handcuffed by responding police officers?"

Agent Purvis frowned. "No, we found him through good old-fashioned investigative work."

"How so?"

"As I testified on direct, we canvassed the neighborhood and discovered an eyewitness, Mr. John Didar. He reported seeing a man entering Morgan White's home prior to the murder."

"Was Mr. Didar crossing the yard? Sitting on the doorstep?"

"No, he was on the street walking his dog."

"And he reported seeing a man, at night, in the dark, at the back door of the house?"

"Yes, there was outdoor lighting in the area."

"Let's talk specifically about the lighting at the back of Morgan White's home. There was no onsite lighting turned on at the time, only street lighting one-half block from the back of the house. Is that correct?"

"Yes, but ..."

"That's sufficient, Agent Purvis. Now, there was no emergency lighting, motion sensor lighting, or even a back door light on at the time of the incident. Was there?"

"No, but ..."

"So, how did Mr. Didar identify my client?"

"Mr. Didar worked with a sketch artist, and we compared the drawing to mugshots and descriptions of known murderers, some known associates of Tua Dannon, and the cartel. We narrowed the pool of suspects and Mr. Didar pointed to your client."

"How many men in the mugshots were Irish, with Irish features, with my client's height and weight?"

"As many as we could find. They were all similar in coloring and facial features."

"Once Mr. Didar identified my client's photograph, did you indicate to him who he had identified?"

"I didn't, but I may have heard one of the police officers make comments about your client's rap sheet."

"Did you consider that to have made an impression on Mr. Didar and his possible witness testimony?"

"Not really. Besides, we had Mr. Didar come in for a line-up identification with your client in the group of possible suspects. You were there." His sarcasm wasn't lost on the jury.

"Yes, I was, and we're getting to that. First, the line-up was at the local precinct, but the police did not conduct the line-up, did they?"

Purvis obviously didn't like the line of questioning and became defensive. "The police facilitated the line-up, but it was conducted by me and other FBI agents."

"Why would the FBI be called in prior to the line-up identification of the suspect?"

"We were invited by the local police after the photo identification had given rise to the line-up."

"Even prior to knowing if there were any federal charges to

be made, you and your FBI buddies were invited to come on down to the local police station and interview a witness who matched up a drawing to a photo, then conduct a line-up?"

Purvis was obviously pissed. "Yes."

"Is that standard?"

"Sometimes. We had Mr. White under surveillance."

Byron looked at Purvis. "So, you were watching the house and you didn't see who murdered him?"

Purvis looked embarrassed. "No, somehow the killer slipped past our agents and entered the property. It must have been a professional."

"A professional? Any evidence of that?"

"None, except that he slipped by two agents."

"Are your agents professionals?"

"Yes, but they missed the perpetrator."

"Right. They could not see someone enter the back door of Mr. White's home, but an eyewitness could see him? Do I have that right?"

Purvis didn't answer.

Judge Linton looked at Agent Purvis. "The witness will answer."

"Withdraw the question, Your Honor." Byron walked back to the defense table and Michael handed him another file folder. Tyrone looked pleased. Byron shot him the evil eye and Tyrone put his game face back on.

Byron walked back to the witness box and paused for effect. "Agent Purvis, isn't it true that you were looking for a member of the Dannon cartel because of Mr. White's association with them, that you assumed the murder was ordered by Tua Dannon, and you focused only on faces that you deemed to be known associates of the cartel?"

"No, we looked first to mugshots of known criminals who might be in the area, then we looked to the cartel associates."

"Now, Agent Purvis, that's just not true, is it? The FBI was on the scene before the local police, you asked to be invited to conduct the line-up, and you had a book of photographs of possible suspects. That book of photos contained only alleged cartel members."

Prosecutor Roberts stood again. "Your Honor, he's testifying again."

"Ask a question, Mr. Douglas."

"Yes, Your Honor." Byron turned from the judge back to Agent Purvis. "Now, isn't it true that you actually made the identification fit your preconceived notion of who was responsible for the murder?"

"No."

"No? So, you were first on the scene, invited yourself into the investigation, conducted the line-up, and accused my client all without any preconceived idea that the Dannon cartel might be involved?"

"True."

"Did you look into any of the delivery patrons of the warehouse where Mr. White worked?"

"No."

"Did you look into any grievances that others may have had against Mr. White?"

"No, we didn't need to. We had an eyewitness who identified your client."

Byron looked at the jury as if to say: *You don't believe that, do you?*

"Agent Purvis, how reliable is witness identification in murder investigations?"

"It can be very accurate."

"Isn't it true that the Innocence Project has shown that misidentification is the leading factor in wrongful convictions?"

"I have no idea."

"Isn't that part of your job, to know what can and cannot be trusted in your line of work?"

"Legitimate sources are consulted and researched."

"The Innocence Project is not a legitimate source?"

"A biased source."

"Would you be surprised to learn that the Justice Department provides the background information used to compile statistics by the Innocence Project?"

"I wouldn't know."

"Okay. Agent Purvis, hasn't it been proven that in a standard line-up, the line-up administrator typically knows who the suspect is and often provides unintentional cues to the eyewitness about which person to pick?"

"That did not happen here."

"Isn't it true that eyewitnesses often assume that the perpetrator is one of those presented in the line-up and this often leads to the selection of a person despite doubts as to whether the suspect is in the line at all?"

"Mr. Didar said he was sure."

"Isn't it also true that the non-suspect fillers in the line-up often don't match the photograph by the sketch artist as closely as the suspect?"

"There cannot be exact matches, or all of them would have to be twins. By your standards, we wouldn't have line-ups at all."

"Maybe we shouldn't."

Prosecutor Roberts was on his feet. "Your Honor!"

"Watch the comments."

"Yes, Your Honor. Now, Mr. Purvis, did you confirm to the eyewitness that he had selected the correct suspect in the line-up?"

"Yes, but only after the identification."

"Don't you think that would increase his confidence that

he'd selected the right person and influence his testimony in this trial?"

"You'd have to ask him. He seemed pretty confident to me."

"My point exactly."

The prosecutor stood again.

The judge held up his hand prior to the objection. "I won't warn you again, Mr. Douglas."

"Yes, sir." Byron walked back to the defense table, smiled, and retrieved another file from Michael.

"Now, Mr. Purvis, let's turn again to the reliability of eyewitness testimony. Are you aware that over seventy percent of all convictions overturned due to DNA testing were prosecuted due to eyewitness testimony, making it very suspect?"

"Those statistics are biased and dated."

"Biased how? The number of convictions that are overturned has been calculated, the number attributable to conviction via eyewitness testimony has been calculated. The math has been done and it's seventy percent. What does outdated have to do with it?"

Purvis didn't answer. The judge started to speak.

"I'll rephrase, Your Honor." Then to the witness, "Don't cases, over the years, often cast doubt on the trustworthiness of witnesses to properly identify suspects?"

"That's ridiculous. Makes no sense."

"Actually, it does. What makes no sense is zeroing in on a small pool of suspects, influencing the eyewitness, and bringing these charges with no further corroborating information. The real evidence in this case is so scant it hardly exists does it, Agent Purvis?"

"What doesn't exist is your client's innocence. We have a witness, he identified Tyrone fair and square, and the jury can clearly see what you're doing."

Byron looked at the jury. "You overreached, didn't you, Agent Purvis?"

Purvis's face turned purple, and he began to sputter.

Before he could answer, Byron turned to the judge. "Withdraw the question, Your Honor. No further questions."

Agent Purvis left the witness stand in a huff, which was not lost on the jury. Byron had humiliated him on the stand, but Agent Purvis's testimony still carried weight as he was a veteran member of the FBI. Byron looked at the jury, but he couldn't read all of them, even with his best poker skills. A few kind expressions made him think he might be creating at least a scintilla of reasonable doubt.

The prosecution continued to put on its case, scoring points now and then. Tyrone appeared increasingly agitated as he sat next to Byron at the defense table. On more than one occasion, Byron asked for a break, proffering the need for a bathroom, in order to calm his client and admonish him about his body language and facial expression. "We get to go next, just remember that."

That seemed to appease Tyrone for a while, but as the prosecution's portion of the trial progressed further, Byron observed Tyrone's mood sully again when the prosecution called a list of witnesses from relatives of the deceased to jailhouse snitches. All testified for the government, and all pointed the finger at Tyrone, as a soldier of the Dannon Irish mob, and the murderer of Morgan White.

3

———————

The next day, when the prosecution finally rested and it was Byron's turn to present his case, he called as his first witness, Loki Murphy. Tyrone had not given his alibi witness's name to the FBI at the time of his arrest, but by the time of his first conference with Byron, at the county jail, he had identified Loki as his drinking partner for the evening.

Byron smiled at Loki who smiled at Tyrone. "Thank you for being here today. Would you please state your full name and city of residence?"

"Loki Murphy. I live in Queens." Loki seemed to stretch to look taller in the witness chair, but he didn't have the height or swagger to pull it off. What he did have, and what made him a good witness, was a nice smile and a friendly disposition.

"Thank you, Mr. Murphy. Where do you work?"

"I work construction jobs around the five boroughs. I'm a pretty good carpenter, and contractors call me when they need cabinets, bookshelves, crown moldings, that type of thing."

"Got it. Good with your hands." Byron smiled again. "Have a family?"

"I have my mom in Queens. I live in her basement and help out with the taxes and maintenance on the house."

"Good son." Byron punctuated the testimony. "Does Mr. Tyrone work with you?"

"No, he's a dock worker. He loads and unloads stuff off ships."

"So, your relationship with Tyrone is just friends?"

"Right."

"Now, could you please tell us where you were on the night in question?"

"I was in Queens at O'Grady's Pub."

"What time?"

"From about eight thirty at night until they closed at two."

"Who was with you on that night?"

Loki pointed to the accused. "Killian Tyrone."

"The entire time?"

"Well, we didn't go to the john together, but all but a couple of minutes, yeah. Dell O'Connor, a buddy from the neighborhood, was with us."

"None of you left the bar at any time?"

"No. Not until we shut it down."

"Now, the prosecution has established, through the medical examiner, that time of death was within a few minutes of midnight. Are you sure you were with Mr. Tyrone at that time?"

"I'm sure. We threw some darts, drank some stout, hit on some pretty girls, got rejected, and left just before they locked up the doors at two." Loki laughed at his own joke. "There were lots of people there who saw us."

"Thank you." Byron let the clarity of the timeline sink in for the jury, then said, "Pass the witness, Your Honor."

Prosecutor Roberts stood and walked toward the witness box. "Mr. Murphy, are you employed by the Dannon Irish cartel?"

Loki lost his smile. "No. I work contract construction."

"So you said, but aren't most of those jobs part of the cartel business? Buildings or houses owned by the mob?"

"No way. I work hard for a good wage and keep my nose clean."

"You said you were hitting on some girls the night of the incident and that lots of people saw you. Do you know the names of any of the other people who saw you in the bar?"

"No, girls don't give their names or numbers if they don't want to take you home."

A few in the courtroom laughed.

The prosecutor kept a straight face. "Are you aware that investigators could not find a single witness who remembers seeing either you or Mr. Tyrone after ten o'clock?"

"Well, it was crowded and they were probably all drunk by then. Did you ask the bartender?"

"I'll ask the questions, but since you mention it. Yes, we did. He was a witness on direct. He remembers both of you earlier, but only you later in the evening."

"Well, he had lots of customers to serve, and we were in the back playing darts later."

"So you said."

Loke smiled. "Yes, I did."

"Did Dell O'Connor stay with you and Mr. Tyrone until the end of the evening?"

"Most of it." This was Murphy's first seemingly evasive answer.

"Do you know where Mr. O'Connor is now?"

"Nope."

"Is there a reason he's not testifying today for Mr. Tyrone?"

"I have no idea."

"And you can't think of a single reason that he wouldn't come forward and tell the court about your night out?"

Byron was on his feet. "Objection, Your Honor. Asked and answered."

Byron and the prosecutor had battled it out in chambers before the trial about the unavailability of Dell O'Connor. The prosecutor had asserted foul play in the witness's absence, and Byron asserted that there was nothing to connect Tyrone to the disappearance. Byron had won, and the judge had ruled any testimony about the absence of Dell O'Connor was to be excluded and the jury could think what they would. Now, the prosecutor was trying to bring in the absence of O'Connor through the back door with Murphy's testimony.

The judge wasn't having it. "Mr. Roberts, you're standing on shaky ground. Move on."

The prosecutor returned to the attorney table. "Release the witness, Your Honor."

Murphy smiled at Tyrone as he exited the witness stand.

A day later, Byron met with Michael for a sit rep in their office conference room. It was late and the support staff was gone for the day. It was eerily quiet with no one bustling about.

The firm was a midsize, midtown, metal-and-glass office, with respect in the legal community that provided a steady stream of referrals. Byron had joined it because he could work hard, get high-level cases, and make all the money he could ever want. He had all the support he needed and little interference once he'd proven he could take care of his clients without supervision. Michael had been assigned to him when he could no longer juggle the load on his own.

Over the last day and a half, Byron had put on the remainder of their case, consisting mostly of character witnesses and an expert on faulty eyewitness identification.

Both Byron and Michael thought they had presented a fairly good case with what little they had to work with. Tyrone's alibi witness, Loki Murphy, was his strongest defense. Loki could not be linked to the cartel by the prosecution, and he had no criminal record, so his testimony was somewhat believable. Also, Loki owned a small carpentry business in Queens, so was not the type to lie and put his life and livelihood at risk. But, did his testimony provide reasonable doubt that Tyrone had not gotten the order from his mob bosses and murdered Morgan White, as most of the prosecution witnesses had testified? Did the jury think that Murphy would lie for his friend? Trying to show Tyrone detached from the cartel had been challenging, but the prosecution had done no better proving that he was attached.

Byron stretched his arms up toward the harsh ceiling lights to release his tense neck muscles and looked at Michael. "I feel it's down to whether the jury believed the prosecution witnesses or the defense witnesses."

Michael agreed. "I observed several jurors nodding positively during your questions on direct and during cross-examination. It looked promising. I think Tyrone has half a chance at an acquittal if we're lucky."

"I agree. It's a roll of the dice, but we have a shot. I think we're finished for the night. Let's get out of here. I'm beat."

They parted in the parking garage, Michael driving home to Brooklyn, and Byron exiting to the street to catch an Uber to the gym. Neither realized they were being watched and followed.

Byron had long used exercise, especially swimming laps, to restore his equilibrium, to think before or after court, and at any other stressful time in his life. GYM, as it was simply labeled on a black and white sign, looked a lot smaller from the front than it was. In typical New York style, the double glass doors, facing 43rd Street, presented a small store front that opened to a much larger space behind. Byron went through the reception area to a room of exercise machines and free weights in a configuration aligned with upper or lower body work. At the back were twin doors to locker rooms labeled MEN and WOMEN.

Byron went through the masculine door, changed into his favorite blue Speedo, and went out the back of the locker room to the club's sparkling blue-green heated lap pool. He could smell the chlorine and feel the dampness. The rectangle was marked off with floating yellow plastic buoys that divided the water into swim lanes. He chose an empty lane, number three, dropped into the cool water, pulled on his goggles, and began to swim the length of the pool. He crisscrossed with two other patrons, a man in lane one and a woman in lane six. His progress was slow at first, then picked up speed as his breath fit with the rhythm of his strokes, while the other two swimmers finished and left.

When Byron had the pool to himself, he let his thoughts run free and the case started to work itself out in his mind. He saw the issues on both sides, the strengths and weaknesses of his position and major points of his closing argument clearly. When he'd strategized all the counterpoints that the prosecution might make, his mind let go and he went into what he called the zone. His muscles relaxed, his breathing became effortless, and his stroke automatic. When he finished the last lap, he climbed up the chrome ladder on shaky legs, out of the blue-green water.

He grabbed a towel from a rack in the corner and dried himself off, satisfied that he'd processed all the angles. *Swim-*

ming never fails me. Little did he know swimming was, and was not, going to save him.

Byron and Michael arranged a quick visit with their client in the attorney-client meeting room at the courthouse before the weekend break. Byron gritted his teeth and waited for the guard to open the door. Byron had grown weary of Tyrone's constant complaining and questioning of his expertise. Tyrone was sitting at the usual metal table, waiting for them, smiling and upbeat. The lawyers sat down and summarized the case to date and the fifty-fifty, or better, shot they thought Tyrone had to win.

Tyrone smiled even larger. "So, you think we've got this?"

Byron grimaced. "No. As I've said from day one, there are no guarantees. Maybe your chances are more like sixty-forty. We're not out of the woods yet, but I think there's reasonable doubt. Murphy did a good job with the alibi testimony and the prosecutor didn't shake him. Your character witnesses were positive, and they didn't falter in their praise of your recent good deeds."

Tyrone smirked. "Good old Loki Murphy. Out for a night on the town. Can't be in two places at one time, can I?"

"Exactly. The rest depends on the other witness's testimony seeing you near the back door of White's house and all the rest."

"But, as you told me, eyewitnesses are known to make mistakes. Aren't they?"

"Yes. It's all down to who the jury trusts more. Which witness seems more credible. Not just whether they are lying, but whether they are secure in their memory of the night's events."

Tyrone grinned. "So, you think we've got it in the bag."

Michael looked incredulous.

Byron was frustrated. "No way. I said we have a shot, but there's no telling who the jury will believe more or what they're thinking. We were lucky the judge excluded the evidence of Dell O'Connor's disappearance. It would be difficult to explain how the person who was allegedly with you and Loki during the murder suddenly vanished from the face of the earth."

Tyrone averted his eyes. "Right. Well, Dell could be sunning on a beach in County Cork for all we know."

Byron rolled his eyes. "True, he could be in Ireland, but we don't need to worry about that, thanks to Judge Linton's ruling, and he was correct. The evidence was not relevant and too prejudicial and there's no proof that you had anything to do with his leaving town."

"Good, so when do I get to testify?"

Byron scoffed. "You don't. I'm getting ready to rest our case and proceed to closing arguments."

"What is the jury going to think if I don't tell them I'm innocent? Besides, I can look them in the eye and tell them I was at O'Grady's Pub across town, just like Loki said I was."

"Maybe, but what if you get the time wrong or the dates mixed up? What if you connect the dots for them to prove the racketeering charges by your association with Tua Dannon? Can you be sure to remember every place you were on every day of the last few years? Can you swear you were never seen with cartel members?"

"I won't get mixed up and I'm good with people. The jury will believe me. I insist on defending myself. I'm innocent."

Byron scratched his chin and looked as though he'd swallowed his tongue. He could not knowingly put a liar on the stand and, although he had no direct knowledge of Tyrone's guilt or innocence, just looking at his face made Byron believe he was not telling the truth.

"I can't in good judgment let you take the stand. And, you really don't want to. It's a faulty idea all around."

Tyrone's face grew red. "You can't stop me. I know it's my choice under the law."

"That's true, but you'll be going against advice of counsel, and I strongly urge you to sleep on it. We've gotten you this far and we don't want to blow our lead. It's a bad call." Michael nodded in agreement, and both lawyers left the holding area less happy than they had been going in.

As he signed out at the guard's desk, Michael asked, "Do you think he'll insist on testifying?"

Byron took the pen from Michael and wrote his name on the sign-out sheet. "Not if he knows what's good for him."

Byron sent Michael home as he had a lovely wife, Nina, and baby girl, Sophie, Byron's goddaughter, to care for. Truthfully, Byron preferred to create his closing argument without input, at least on the first draft. He intended to rest his case after the weekend, after he'd had a chance to swim again and sleep on it. He'd send the draft to Michael for a quick review. That was the best he could do for Killian Tyrone, guilty or innocent.

Continue reading **DEAD BY PROXY !**

www.manningwolfe.com

BOOKS BY MANNING WOLFE

MERIT BRIDGES LEGAL THRILLERS

Dollar Signs

Music Notes

Green Fees

Chinese Wall

Killer Weed

Texas Toast (Short Story)

PROXY LEGAL THRILLER SERIES

Dead by Proxy

Hunted by Proxy

BULLET BOOKS SPEED READS

#1 Killer Set: Drop the Mic

#2 Iron 13

#3 Bloody Bead

#4 The Hot Seat

#5 Stabbed

#6 Man in the Client Chair

#7 Only a Pawn in Their Game

#8 Dangerous Practice

#9 Two Bodies One Grave

#10 Last Call

#11 The Last Straw

MANNING WOLFE, an award-winning author and attorney, writes cinematic-style, smart, fast-paced thrillers and crime fiction. Manning was recently featured on Oxygen TV's: Accident, Suicide, or Murder, and has spoken at major book festivals around the world.

* Manning's Merit Bridges Legal Thrillers features Austin attorney Merit Bridges, including Dollar Signs, Music Notes, Green Fees, and Chinese Wall.
* Manning's new Proxy Legal Thrillers Series features Houston attorney Quinton Bell, including Dead By Proxy, Hunted By Proxy, and Alive By Proxy.
* Manning is co-author of Killer Set: Drop the Mic, and twelve additional Bullet Books Speed Reads.

As a graduate of Rice University and the University of Texas School of Law, Manning's experience has given her a voyeur's peek into some shady characters' lives and a front-row seat to watch the good people who stand against them.

www.manningwolfe.com

Visit the author's website:
www.manningwolfe.com

Follow Manning Wolfe on Social Media:
www.facebook.com/manning.wolfe
www.twitter.com/ManningWolfe
www.instagram.com/manningwolfe/

Sign up for Manning Wolfe's FREE newsletter and get a FREE book.
www.manningwolfe.com/giveaway